Cambridge 1962.
At the dawn of the decade of the cultural
revolution.
What the Wheatcrofts don't have isn't worth
having...
And they have everything to lose.

Prelude
March 1931

'Nobody gets justice. People only get good luck or bad luck.'
Orson Welles

Snowdonia. Dark clouds skate across an ice-blue moon. The driver of the slate grey Bugatti 46 Faux Cabriolet is slumped awkwardly across the steering wheel. Blood is caked on the back of his head, across his shirt collar and the shoulders of his jacket. The car is free-wheeling down a steep hill slowly gathering speed as it hurtles towards the stone wall at its base.

A second man, running behind the car with a petrol can in his hand, watches as the Bugatti rams into the stone wall. The rear end of the car looks as if it will flip over, but it doesn't. It rears up with a scream of tearing metal and falls back to the ground with a crash that echoes through the valley. The man flinches but continues his downhill run. When he reaches the wrecked vehicle he glances briefly at the driver then empties the contents of the can over the Bugatti. He lights a match, drops it into the driver's lap, steps back, then runs rapidly away back up the hill.

Chapter One
The House

Early August 1962. Adams Road, Cambridge.

The sun dances through the trees and bounces in waves off the lily pond, rippling across the gabled walls of the big house, echoing the sparkling atmosphere within. Two small dogs, Bella-Blue, a Cavalier King Charles Spaniel, and Tiger-Lily, a Jack Russell, run in circles round the garden chasing each others' tails.

Freddy Wheatcroft has just been appointed Dean of St. Andrew's College. He shines as he sits at the head of the table, surrounded by his family and closest colleague. He has just turned 50. He is a tall, handsome man, lean but muscular. His thick black hair frames a high forehead above a slightly aquiline nose. There's an innate air of arrogance in his bearing.

His wife, Mary, sits at the opposite end of the vast oak table. She is a year older than Freddy and even though she has borne their three children she has a trim figure and a youthful face. She's beautiful and elegant yet she radiates a child-like innocence. She shivers as a cloud passes across the sun and the light in the dining room is momentarily dimmed.

Their twin sons, Mark and Dominic, have benefited from their father's success and position in society. They have both won places at Cambridge University in the college of their choice, not fully aware of just how effectively their father's standing has played its part in their acceptance at St. Andrews. Mark is going to read Physics and Dominic will be taking English Literature.

Dobbo Finding, their cheery, plump housekeeper and cook, is finalising the starters in the kitchen. She gestures impatiently to Jack, the gardener and chauffeur, that he should start serving the first course. Jack is devoted to his employer in particular and to the family in general. His loyalty knows no bounds. He loves his job as does Dobbo. Jack is particularly attached to and in awe of Freddy, who is singularly unaware of this and treats Jack like a serf and with heartless contempt.

The phone rings and Dobbo springs across the room with surprising agility. She picks up the receiver. 'Cambridge 55795. Good evening. Can I help you?' Dobbo listens, puzzled. She holds the phone away from her and shakes it. She waves at Jack to hurry him up and puts the phone back to her ear, waiting. She can hear organ music in the background.

'Hello. Anyone there?' She hisses her annoyance and replaces the phone on its cradle.

Freddy and Mary's daughter, Lauren, is standing by a deep bay window which opens onto the garden. She looks out across the lawn then up into the sky as the cloud clears the sun and the light falls on her, illuminating her honey-coloured hair. She shares her mother's good looks and charm and something of her father's confident bearing. Paul Bowler-Thompson, the college's obese and balding Senior Tutor, watches her intently. Lauren can feel his eyes on her. She turns to him and smiles. He smiles back and winks at her, which she finds unpleasant and somewhat lecherous.

Jack pushes open the door to the dining-room with his hip and walks to the table. He puts a fine china plate of smoked salmon with iced cucumber in front of Lady Mel Osborne, Mary's sister. She nods her thanks. He goes next to stand behind Paul, waiting while he drinks noisily from his glass. He leans back and Jack puts a plate on the table in front of him. He nods his thanks to him as Jack moves towards Mary. She glances across at Lauren as she takes a plate from him.

'Do come and sit down Lauren.' Mary does her best to keep the impatience out of her voice. She smiles sweetly, falsely.

Lauren ignores her. Dominic gets up from the table and moves over to his sister. He puts his arm round her and leads her to the table. Jack waits until she sits down then puts her food in front of her. Freddy smiles at her and glances across at Paul, who is still watching Lauren. She looks down at her plate without enthusiasm. Her eyes flick up, meeting Paul's gaze. He smiles again and she looks away and across to Freddy. Jack leaves the room. A breeze ruffles the leaves on the grand old oak tree that dominates the garden, sending patterns of light and shade dancing across the dining room floor.

The phone rings again in the kitchen as Jack backs out of the room with four more plates on his arm. Dobbo picks up the receiver. 'Good evening.' She waits. Once again there is silence on the line. 'Goodbye.' She slams the phone back on its cradle and moves over to the big Aga stove to work on the main course.

Conversation in the dining room builds to a steady hum as the party start to eat. Jack goes round the table offering to top up the wine glasses. Mary declines his offer as does Lauren. Freddy allows him to fill his glass. He is drinking heavily. Freddy is worried by Dominic, but he takes comfort from his favourite son, Mark. He lost his own brother James when he was just 20 in a horrific car crash. James had taken their father's Bugatti without his permission and, mistaking the tightness of a turn on a steep and narrow country road he had driven it straight into a dry stone wall. The car caught fire and the petrol tank exploded. James' body was incinerated and left unrecognizable. The family never recovered from the loss and Freddy was left confused and scarred. They all were. The memory of James is always with Freddy, lurking like a deep, dark chasm at the edges of his mind.

'Why isn't Grandma living here?' Lauren's voice cuts sharply through the conversation.

'She...has to...stay in hospital, dear', Mary replies with an awkward shift of her shoulders. She is clearly uncomfortable with the direction the conversation seems to be going.

'Still!'

'Yes, Lauren. Still.' Freddy snaps back at her, hoping to close that particular issue as quickly as he can.

'Why do they keep her there?' Lauren is not going to let it go.

'They have to.' Mary barks.

Later that night while the family and their guests are sitting on the terrace with coffee and brandy Freddy goes to the kitchen to thank Dobbo for her efforts. He ignores Jack. As he's leaving he is struck by a thought and turns back towards her.

'By the way who was it that called?'

'Both times I answered the phone, Sir, there was no one there.'

'Strange.'

'It was, Sir.'

'Nothing?'

'I could just hear some of that organ music you like so much playing in the background.'

'The Bach - Prelude & Fugue No.2 in C minor.'

'Well, I wouldn't know what it's called, Sir. But I recognized it. Many's the time I've heard it coming from your study.'

'Thank you, Dobbo. Good night.'

'Good night, Sir."

Freddy makes his way slowly through the house to join the party on the terrace. He pauses in the dining room. He looks distracted and agitated. Lauren appears from out of the shadows, startling him.

'Are you alright, Daddy?'

'Ah...Lauren...I didn't see you there.'

'Just taking a break.'

'Aren't you enjoying yourself?'

'I was, but what about you? You look...a bit down, Daddy.'

'I'm OK. Just thinking.

'About what?'

'Oh, I don't know. This and that.'

They stand in silence facing each other. Freddy makes an effort to say something, but seems unable to speak.

'What is it, Daddy?'

Freddy pulls back his shoulders and says, 'Why did you ask about Grandma out of the blue like that?'

'It wasn't out of the blue. I think about her a lot.'

'Do you?'

'Yes, I do.

'Why's that, Lauren?

'I worry about her. We are - were - very close.'

'I know you were close. But why d'you worry about her?'

'I can't bear to think about her imprisoned in that awful hospital.'

'She's not a prisoner. Well, not exactly…and it's not that awful.'

'It is, Daddy. You know it is. She can't leave there. They won't let her. But you and Mummy could insist on it.'

'What good would that do? She can't look after herself.'

'But you could.'

'Could what?'

'Look after her. Bring her here to live with us.'

Freddy looks cornered. 'Impossible, Lauren.'

'Why?'

'She's impossible. Impossible to live with. She'd drive us all mad too.'

'I could look after her.'

'No, you couldn't. You have your own life to live. You couldn't be with her night and day…devoting your life to caring for her.'

'I could!' Lauren stamps her foot.

'No. Enough of this.' Freddy turns his back on her and leaves the room to join the party on the terrace. Lauren watches him go. She is fuming.

Chapter Two
The Hospital
If all is not lost, where is it?

Two months later Lauren walks up the long, tree-lined drive, which runs through an immaculately kept park, towards the formidable grey Victorian building. Marchman House Hospital. She's nervous. She's come to this place in secret, aware of how much her visit would upset her parents. The weather's fine but her heart is heavy. As the drive opens onto a forecourt she stops. She's shaking and turns to walk away. But she takes only two steps before she pauses and, taking a deep breath, swings round and strides purposefully up the steps to the main entrance. The door is heavy. The brass doorknob is highly polished, reflecting the sun, making her squint. She holds it, turns it with surprising firmness and slowly pushes the door open. She steps into a high-ceilinged, wood-paneled reception area. A portly middle-aged man looks up from his paper and slowly eyes her up and down. His scrutiny unsettles her. Again she wants to turn away, leave, run, but something compels her to press on.

'Can I help you, Miss?'

'Yes. I have an appointment with Dr Bohm at

11 o-clock.' She glances at her watch.

'Name?'

'Lauren Wheatcroft. I...'

'Yes?'

'Nothing.'

The receptionist slides a heavy ledger across his desk and opens it ponderously. He slides his finger down a page, pausing. Finding her name, he looks up at Lauren. 'Take a seat, please.'

He gestures irritably towards a well-worn leather seat, running the length of the wall. The seat is empty. Lauren turns her back on him and sits down. She stares at the wall.

'I'll inform his secretary that you're here.' He picks up a phone and dials.

Lauren glances back at him. 'Thanks'. She sits down, twisting her hands together.

'Good morning, Miss Vranch. There's a young lady here called...' He glances at the ledger. 'Lauren Wheatcroft...to see Dr Bohm at 11.'

'Thank you. I'll tell her.' He glances across to Lauren. 'His secretary will be down to collect you in a few minutes.' He goes back to his paper.

Lauren stares down at the parquet floor. She makes an effort to pull her hands apart and relax. The receptionist glances up at her. There is a sound of heels clacking on the broad wooden staircase leading down to reception. Lauren looks up. A tall, thin woman comes slowly down the stairs. She is imposing in a tailored navy blue suit. She stops for a moment, looking down at Lauren, who attempts a smile without success. She continues down the stairs and across the reception to Lauren.

'Good morning, Miss Wheatcroft.'

'Good morning,' Lauren replies. Her voice is hoarse. She stands. She is shaking. The woman appears not to notice.

'Follow me, please.' She turns her back on Lauren and heads back up the stairs. Lauren trails meekly in her wake. At the top of the stairs the woman turns right, glancing back at Lauren. The long corridor is dimly lit. Gloomy. Six doors down on the left the woman stops, opens the door for Lauren and stands back to let her in. Lauren takes a deep breath and enters hesitantly. The woman gestures to a chair by the window. Lauren walks to the chair but doesn't sit down immediately. She stands at the window looking out over the park. The sun is still shining. The woman goes through to an inner room, closing the door behind her. Lauren sits. After a few minutes the woman returns.

'Dr Bohm will see you now.' Again she stands back from the door, allowing Lauren to enter. The room is surprisingly bright. Dr Bohm is much younger than Lauren had expected. He is slim and well-dressed, dapper in a grey three-piece suit. He has a light blue bow-tie, which Lauren finds somewhat overdone and unsettling.

'Please sit down Miss Wheatcroft.' He gestures to the chair across his desk. Lauren sits.

'How are you?'

'Um...OK...nervous.'

'Nervous?'

'Yes...yes. I've never been to a place like this before. I haven't seen my grandmother for... I...don't know what to expect.'

'I can understand that. It's certainly not easy.'

Lauren doesn't respond. She looks from Bohm to the window, waiting.

'I can tell you that Grace Middleton isn't well.'

'In what sense?'

'What d'you mean?'

'I mean, Dr Bohm, what's wrong with her?'

'She's mentally ill.'

'Yes, yes. I appreciate that. But what do you call her illness? D'you have a name for it.'

'Yes, we do.'

'And it is?'

'I am puzzled, Miss Wheatcroft. Haven't your parents told you?'

'They don't speak about her. Don't want to talk about her. I don't understand...'

'It's not unusual. Mental illness is a difficult issue to deal with for any family. It's hard to understand and there is frequently considerable stigma attached to the issue. It's often, as they say, swept under the carpet.'

'I want to try and deal with it.'

'Why?'

'She's my grandmother and she was very kind to me when I was a little girl and before...she fell ill. What is wrong with her? What d'you call her..illness?'

'We call it Manic-Depression. Episodes of extreme euphoria and delusions of grandeur followed by a period of deep, dark depression. Your grandmother is severely affected.'

'How d'you mean?'

'Well, some people have periods of sanity between episodes and can be completely normal for months on end before the illness strikes again. Your grandmother's cycles are continuous. She never has any respite.'

'What's caused it?'

'We don't know. We don't understand the condition. It may be hereditary. It may be set off by some trauma. It may just...happen.'

'Is there no cure?'

'No. Not that we know of...yet.'

'So how do you treat her?'

'All we have are tranquilisers. She does see a psychiatrist. And then there's electro-convulsive therapy.'

'Jesus!...have you?

'No. I'm personally not in favour of that treatment. Some of my colleagues are though, but Grace is my patient and I will not allow it.'

'Good.'

Lauren looks down at her feet, struggling to hold back her tears. She presses her palms to her eyes. She chokes back her sobs and looks up to Bohm. 'I want to see her.'

'You can. I can't deny you that, but I won't let you go alone. I insist that I go with you.'

Chapter Three
Grace Middleton

*We exist midway between the extremely large and the
extremely small -
between the universe at one end and the Planck
Length at the other.*

Lauren follows Bohm up two flights of stairs
painted in a pale, institutional green. There is no
carpet. She can hear laughter, some moaning and
the occasional scream. She falters, gripping the
banister rail. He turns back to her.

'Are you sure you want to go on?'

'What will she...be...like?'

'She is manic at this time. Delusional. She...she
believes she is the Virgin Mary and that she has
given birth to Christ. She may not recognize
you....d'you want to go on?'

Lauren gathers her strength. 'Yes. I must. I've
come this far.'

'All right. But please understand that she's on
a secure wing and that we have to go through
two sets of locked doors before we can get to her
room. OK?'

'Yes.'

They reach the top of the stairs and Bohm leads
Lauren to a heavy steel door. He presses a
buzzer twice and they wait.

21

'Does anyone come to visit her?'

'Only your mother.'

'How often?'

'Well, I would say usually a couple of times a year.'

'Is that all?'

'Yes. To be frank with you she hasn't been here for many months?'

Lauren thinks about this, taking it in. 'And no one else?'

'No.'

'Never?'

'Never.'

The door swings open and a male nurse nods to Bohm, letting them through, closing the door behind them. Lauren cringes as it bangs shut. They walk down another corridor. There are close-set bars over the windows, which are dusty and smudged with grime. They reach a second door. As Bohm's hand goes to press a buzzer, Lauren asks, 'Why is she behind these doors, these barred windows?'

Bohm considers the question for a few seconds then turns to her. 'When she's manic she is driven to escape. She believes she has to tell the world about the second coming. She did get out once and caused trouble in the local town. She has tried to get away on several other occasions so we were forced to take steps to keep her under lock and key.'

'It's so sad. So very sad...and shocking.'

'I know it is, my dear. But I must just make this point before we go in here. There've been some remarkably talented and creative manic-depressives over the centuries. When we look at diaries, letters, biographies whatever, reading between the lines, it's clear to us that Charles Dickens, Van Gogh - even Teddy Roosevelt - were all sufferers. And that's just a few. It's a long list. There are many highly successful manic-depressives in important jobs today.'

'Really?'

'Yes, I can assure you. I know it for a fact.' He presses the buzzer. They wait.

'Look, I'm not trying to give you false hope. I fear your grandmother will never contribute anything...anymore.'

Once more the door is opened for them and they pass through. Bohm and the male nurse lead Lauren to a door. Under a small viewing window there is a typed card in a brass holder. Grace Middleton. The nurse unlocks the door and opens it to let them through. He closes the door behind him.

They are greeted by a strange and, for Lauren, disturbing - even frightening - sight. Grace is standing on her head. Her hair is short. She is naked except for the lime green nightdress that falls in folds around her head and shoulders. Her face, hands and lower arms are red from the strain of being upside down. Her whole body trembles with the effort.

'Hello, Grace. You have a visitor.' There is no response. 'It's your grand-daughter, Lauren.' There is still no response. Bohm goes to the door, opens it and asks the nurse to come in and help him. They walk over to Grace, gently lowering her into their arms. They carry her to the bed and lay her down. Grace shrieks - a long, piercing wail. Lauren trembles from head to foot and leans back against the wall. Her knees are weak and she feels faint. There's no chair for her to sit on. Bohm goes to her and puts his arm around her. She clings to his shoulder, sobbing. The nurse leaves the room.

Grace sits up and stares around her. She looks at Lauren for a moment, but says nothing. She looks at Bohm and laughs - a dry crackling cackle. 'Look at him!' Her voice is a whine, a high-pitched birdlike screech. 'He's back.'

Bohm smiles at her. 'D'you know who this is Grace?'

'I know who it is. 'Course I do.'

'Who is it, Grace?

'It's that bloody menstruating Mary Magdalene. Jesus cast out seven devils from *her*. What does she want?'

'It's not Mary Magdalene. It's me, Grandma. It's Lauren.' She attempts to move towards Grace, but Bohm holds her back. Lauren tries to pull away, but he doesn't release her. She tries to shake free, but he holds her firmly, pinning her arms. He hisses in her ear. 'She's dangerous. You mustn't go near her. She may try and hurt you. She *will* try and hurt you.'

Lauren breaks. She shakes, her body wracked with wrenching sobs. 'I can't bear this. Take me away - now, please...please.'

Bohm leads her to the door, waving his hand towards the small window. The nurse charges into the room, moving straight to the bed as Grace pulls herself upright and makes to lunge after them.

Outside in the corridor Bohm takes her to a chair and helps her sit. 'I'm sorry, Lauren. I tried to warn you.'

'I had no idea...how bad...'

'How could you? If you've not seen...experienced anything like this before.'

Lauren's journey home is painful. Although she manages to find a seat, the train from London to Cambridge is packed. She has no book or newspaper to read. To hide herself away she pretends to sleep. When she finally arrives home she runs quickly through the house without meeting anyone and goes straight to her bedroom. The dogs follow her into the room. Lauren throws herself on the bed, covering her head with pillows and sobs. The dogs jump on the bed beside her. They nuzzle up to her, aware of her distress.

An hour or so later there is a knock on her door. 'Are you there, darling?'

She doesn't respond.

'Can I come in?'

'Yes, Mummy.' Lauren lifts her head from the pillows and turns towards the door as it opens.

Mary steps into the room. She stops abruptly when she sees the anguish etched on her daughter's face. She moves to the bed and sits down gently next to Lauren. She strokes the damp hair away from Lauren's eye and forehead. 'What is it, Lauren? What's happened?' She's very concerned.

Lauren tries to speak but nothing comes out. She turns away from her mother and stares towards the window.

'Please tell me, darling. I…I'm sure it would help.'

Lauren turns back to her mother. 'I'm not so sure it would.'

'It usually does. A trouble shared…'

Lauren takes a deep, shivering breath. 'I went to see Grandma.'

'What!'

'I went to the hospital.'

'Why?'

'I needed to see her. You never talk about her.'

'We…'

'I've been having dreams...thinking about her a lot.'

'But she's...'

'When did you last visit her Mummy?'

Mary looks uncomfortable and turns away from Lauren.

'When, Mummy?'

'Not for quite a while.'

'How long?'

'Eight months or so. Maybe more.'

'That's terrible. She's your mother.'

'Was.'

'Is.'

'She's not who she was anymore, Lauren.'

'I saw that. But she's still your mother. That will never change. You can't just turn your back on her.'

'I haven't...not exactly.'

'What d'you mean?'

'We talk to her doctor.'

'Bohm?'

'Yes him. He's a good man.'

'Yes, he is.' Lauren starts to cry again and speaks stumblingly through her sobs. 'He was very kind to me. He tried to prepare me...warn me. But nothing could possibly...what I saw...heard.'

'She's very ill, darling.'

'I know. I know that. But why - how did it happen?

Mary takes Lauren in her arms and hugs her. 'No one knows. No one can explain it. It just came out of the blue.'

'It must have been terrible for you...and Daddy.'

'It was. We'd just been married. Mummy didn't like him and didn't want me to marry him.'

Lauren gasps. 'My God! There's so much I don't know about...your lives.'

This time Mary looks away. Guilt is painted on her face. She can't hide it. 'I let her down, Lauren.'

'Marrying Daddy?'

'No. Not that. Afterwards, when she started to become strange and difficult. Not sleeping, bothering people all the time. She talked endlessly. Wild theories, seeing signs everywhere - in car number plates, in the price of groceries, in the clouds. Everything had meaning to her, but they were meanings we couldn't understand or make sense of. We didn't know what to do. She refused to see a doctor - even her GP. We had no...experience of...mental illness. We thought she was having a breakdown and that it would pass, but it just went on and on and on.'

'Why d'you think it happened...started, Mummy?'

'I don't think she ever recovered from Grandpa's death.'

'His suicide.'

'All right. His suicide.'

'Not surprising really.'

'No, darling, not surprising.'

'How old was I then?'

'Ten…no, eleven.'

Mary breaks. The tears run down her cheeks smearing her mascara and softening Lauren's heart. She takes her mother's hands in hers. Rain falls on the bedroom window, pouring down the glass in rivulets, slowly turning into a torrent like the waves of the sea. The room darkens reflecting and seeming to share in the mood of the two women.

'After about six months of this…extreme behaviour she fell into a depression. It was a terrible thing to see, but strangely it was better than the mania. More manageable. It was then that we took her to see a psychiatrist. She didn't resist. She was too low. All her strength had left her. It was a long consultation. I told the psychiatrist everything I could and he quickly came to a conclusion. It was, he said, a classic case of manic-depression. Of that he had no doubts. He'd seen it before.'

Mary stands, walks to the window and watches the rain run down the glass. Her shoulders are slumped. She wipes her eyes with a handkerchief and turns back to Lauren. 'We would've done anything to make her well again, paid anything, gone anywhere but there was nothing to be done. The psychiatrist insisted she be hospitalised for her own good and for ours too. I couldn't resist and they took her away to that...that terrible place you visited today.'

Mary comes back to the bed and helps Lauren to her feet. They hold each other.

'We must go down now and see Daddy. It's nearly time for dinner and we should tell him where you've been.'

'Must we?' The colour drains from Lauren's face. She looks smaller, shrunken in the dimming light.

'Yes. He should know. I can't keep it from him. He won't like it, but...'

Lauren follows Mary to the top of the broad oak staircase. The highly polished wood is alive, with reflections of the rain-soaked windows, shimmering with a sad optimism. Lauren pauses. Mary turns back to her, takes her hand and leads her down. As they reach the ground floor she calls out, 'She's here, Freddy.'

'In the study. Just finishing a report, but come in.'

The study is lit only with the fading evening light. The walls are lined with glass-doored bookshelves. The books are neatly arranged more by size than by subject - something Lauren had observed in one of her rare visits to this room. It was an unspoken rule in the household that it was out of bounds to the children. Mary wasn't a frequent visitor either.

As they enter Freddy looks up from his work. He doesn't smile. 'Your brothers started college today. You weren't here to see them off. Why?'

'I forgot, Daddy.'

'You forgot, did you?'

'Yes.'

'It's not good enough, Lauren. They were very disappointed. Big day for them - both of them. You let them down.'

Lauren squirms. She lets her hair fall across her face. Mary is still holding her hand. She fears the worst. Freddy stands and comes round to the front of his desk. He walks over to Lauren.

'Where were you Lauren?

'I...'

'Yes?'

Lauren pulls back her shoulders and looks her father in the eye. 'I went to see Grandma.'

'You did *what*?'

'Went to see Grandma.'

Freddy rocks back on his heels. He half raises his hand as if to hit her. Mary steps forward and he thinks better of it. He swings round abruptly and walks to the window. It's still raining though the sky looks a brighter shade of grey.

'How did you know where to find her?' Freddy barks, his voice shaking.

Mary glances at Lauren. She too is waiting for an answer.

31

Lauren finds an inner well of strength and answers to her father's back. 'I saw a letter once in the morning post when I was sorting it. I was waiting for a letter myself. I saw it was from a hospital and I remembered the name. I went there on the off chance that Grandma was still there and...she was.'

'Bohm let you see her! I'll report this - have him fired. He has no right.' Freddy's voice has risen to a shriek.

A picture of an incident flashes in Lauren's mind from her childhood when she and the twins had been knocking pears off a tree and stabbing them with sticks. Freddy had been furious. He had been nurturing the fruit. The pears were rare and difficult to cultivate. He and Jack had given great attention to their well-being. Without a second thought the children had cut through the protective netting over the tree and had made a camp inside. Freddy would have beaten them all if Mary hadn't come into the garden and stopped him, dragging him away and into the house. It had been days - nearly a week - before he would speak to any of them again.

Mary goes towards him and stops by the desk. 'He didn't do anything wrong, Freddy. It's not illegal to visit a relative. He couldn't refuse her.'

'He should have known. He should've realized it would do no good - that it would only upset her.'

'It did upset her. You're right. But isn't it best that she knows why her Grandma is there.'

Freddy's shoulders sag. He is deflated, defeated. 'Michael's suicide was bad enough. So hard for all of us. And then this...madness. It's more than I can take.'

'Michael was my father, Freddy, and Grace is my mother.' She puts her arm round Freddy. Lauren slips out of the room silently, closing the door behind her.

Chapter Four
The Twins

The twins' personalities are as different as their looks. Although they're both slim and well-built Mark is dark-skinned, his hair straight and shiny black. Dominic is fair with light brown wavy hair. He has Mary's complexion. Mark is a clone of his father. He is academic and devoted to science. Dominic is a reader, a dreamer and a poet. He's passionate about literature and music. Modern jazz is what he likes. The more avant-garde and free-form the better he likes it. Ornette Coleman and Albert Ayler are his musical heroes. He reads Arthur Rimbaud, Samuel Beckett, Jack Kerouac, Somerset Maugham, Hermann Hesse and William Burroughs. All of which this completely lost on Mark, who doesn't listen to music or read fiction. Art to him is frivolous - even meaningless. Dominic is also drawn to mysticism and eastern philosophy. He dreams of travelling to India to visit ashrams and to learn something of the spiritual path direct from the teachers. He's been influenced by Maugham's *The Razor's Edge*. He and Mark play with the famous Albert Einstein quote: 'Science without religion is lame.' That's Dominic's pitch, to which Mark always comes back with 'Religion without science is blind.' They complete the circle. Mark is a devout atheist like his father. Mary is more open to discussing the meaning of life. She's a Christian, though not a regular church-goer. She would like to go more than to just the family's regular attendance at Christmas midnight mass. This would irritate Freddy so she lets it go. She was born into a Christian household and grew up with the faith, which she accepted without question. She doesn't doubt.

The twins are both cheerful and full of hope on their first day at college. Once the formalities are completed they go for lunch at The Eagle, a long-established and popular pub in the centre of the city. The food is good and the prices reasonable, within the budgets of most undergraduates.

They carry their pints and their food to a table in the cobbled courtyard. The pub has an ageless feel to it, its time-worn character remaining intact. It's claimed there had been an inn on the site since the 14th century. It appeals to Dominic's artistic nature. The poetry of the place is invisible to Mark and out of reach. As far as Mark is concerned its greatest claim to fame is that it was there that James Watson and Francis Crick first announced to the world they'd discovered what they called 'the secret of life' in April 1953.

This phrase 'the secret of life' means something else entirely to Dominic. For him science can only explain how things work, not why they work as they do. Dominic has a deep belief that the universe exists by design and not by chance. He's not convinced that life could appear from matter as a result of random events. But, as much as science explains everything for Mark, it explains nothing for Dominic. He's convinced that there is deep meaning and purpose behind all the struggles, pain and joy of life. He wonders too sometimes why there is a universe at all. He struggles with the paradox of the two sides of life - the joy and the pain. He sees that life can be at the same time marvelous, miraculous, mysterious, miserable, mindful and mindless. He's tormented as he swings between awe and wonder, pain and suffering. He's aware that people are hardly ever honest about themselves and how they really feel. Like his friends, family and colleagues he puts on a brave face. How could he do otherwise? He realizes that we couldn't function as a group if we always told the truth about our feelings. Like so many of the poets, musicians and artists he admires and respects he's gripped by doubts and confusions, sure of nothing.

'Dad slipped a note through my door early this morning.'

Dominic looks put out. 'Why does he always

contact you first?'

Mark shrugs. 'Dunno. He just does.'

'OK. So what'd it say?'

'That Lauren had been to see Grandma in the nut…hospital.'

'Jesus!

'Yeah. And he's angry about it. Not just because she wasn't there to see us off. Grandma's out of bounds are far as he's concerned.'

'Yes, well, I know that.'

Mark starts to eat. Dominic studies him then asks, 'Is she OK? Did Dad say anything?

'No. He was angry. That's all.'

'I must call her.' Dominic starts to get up.

'Eat your lunch first, Dom. We'll call her after…on the way back to college.'

Dominic and Mark are walking across the Market Square. Gowned undergraduates weave in and out of the pedestrians on their bicycles. The stalls are busy with shoppers, the vendors calling out the bargains of the day. It's starting to cloud over and Mark puts up the collar of his jacket.

'Have you got any change?'

Mark rattles his pockets and brings out a handful of coins. Dominic takes a few and goes into a call box.

'Shan't be a mo'. He turns his back on his brother.

Mark nods and sits on the fountain's edge to

wait.

Dominic puts several coins into the machine. He dials and waits. The phone is picked up at the other end. He presses button 'A' and the coins clatter into the belly of the machine. 'Hello, Dobbo. It's me, Dominic.'

'How are you, Sir?'

'Thank you. I'm fine and so's Mark. We're getting ourselves sorted out in college. Are you OK?'

'Thank you, Sir. Well enough.'

'Can I speak to Lauren, please?'

'I think she's in.'

Dominic can hear Dobbo calling up the stairs. He waits. His fingers tap impatiently on the coin box. Mark glances over at him and then at the sky. He points up, making raining gestures with his hands. Distant lightning flashes flatly across the sky, followed by a low roll of thunder.

'Hello, Sis. It's Dom. Wanted to see how you are. I hear you went to see Grandma and caught some heavy flak from Dad.'

'I did,..yes.'

'And how was Grandma?'

'It was terrible Dom. Truly terrible. She's in…in a bad way. That's really all I can say.'

'What d'you mean? Is there nothing more…?'

'She's just ill. Out of her mind…completely. Didn't recognize me. She's in another world.'

'Another world?'

'Yes...a world of her own. Completely out of touch with what we call reality...our world.'

'Can they help her there?'

'It doesn't seem so, Dom. They just keep her locked up...safe, I suppose.'

'Look, Lauren. I'll come round tonight after supper. We could go for a walk - just you and me and the dogs.'

'That would be nice. I'd like to be able to talk to someone and get out of the house. Daddy just glares at me and Mummy looks helpless.'

'Right, Sis. I'll see you later. 'Bout six.'

Dominic comes out of the phone and walks over to join Mark.

'I guess you spoke to her.'

'Yes, I did.'

'She OK?'

'Bit shaken. I'm going to meet her later.'

Chapter Five
Grantchester Meadows

'In the lazy water meadow
I lay me down
All around me golden sunflakes
Covering the ground
Basking in the sunshine
Of a bygone afternoon
Bringing sounds of yesterday
Into my city room.'
Grantchester Meadows
Roger Waters.

Lauren and Dominic are walking though the meadows along the riverbank. Bella-Blue and Tiger-Tiger-Lily run and roll in the long grass. The water flows lazily over waving water weeds. Two swans glide by. Several ducks bob and weave along the bank. Willows hang their branches into the stream like green waterfalls, their leaves flickering in the warm, light breeze. It's early evening and the sky has cleared.

'Her doctor was as helpful as he could be. He warned me it'd be difficult. He didn't really want me to see her. I know why now. I mean, Dom, I've never been up close to a mad person before. Well, I've seen them on the street, but just crossed over and kept away. They've scared me.

And Grandma was truly frightening.'

'How d'you mean?'

'She was ugly. She was aggressive. I said on the phone she didn't recognize me, but I didn't tell you she thought I was Mary Magdalene.'

'Who?'

'Mary Magdalene. One of Jesus Christ's followers.'

'Oh, yeah. I remember. He cleansed her of seven demons…something like that.'

'Yes, something like that.'

Dominic puts his arm round Lauren. 'Poor you.'

'Poor Grandma.'

They walk on in silence, lost in thought.

Dominic stops and steps back from Lauren. 'It seems to me that we've been kept away from her because Mum and Dad are somehow ashamed.'

'I'd say that Daddy is and Mummy can't stand up to him.'

Dominic laughs. 'You can say that again. None of us can. Let's face it, he dominates us all.'

Lauren nods her agreement. She has nothing to add.

A young man on an old upright bicycle wheels towards them on a nearby path. He swerves to left and right, but straightens up when he catches sight of Lauren. He waves and calls out, 'Hi there.'

Lauren waves back. 'Hi.'

'Elvis is king!' he shouts out as he passes them.

41

Lauren laughs.

Dominic watches him go by then turns to Lauren. 'Who's that?'

'Richard.'

'Richard who?'

'Just Richard. He's an artist – a painter, I mean.'

'Boyfriend of yours?'

'No. He often hangs out in El Patio. Met him there.'

Dominic turns to watch the cyclist as he weaves across the meadows towards Cambridge. Deep grey storm clouds are building again over the city. The willows along the riverbank stand out starkly in the remaining patches of bright sunlight. Their leaves glint and sparkle against the blackening sky. Dominic gasps, 'Look at that.'

'Lauren turns in the direction he's looking. 'Oh, boy. That's…!'

'Isn't it just?' He smiles. 'Beauty is truth.'

They stand in silence as the cloudbank moves inexorably towards them.

Dominic glances at his watch. 'The Red Lion will be open. D'you fancy a drink?'

'Yeah, Let's go.'

He calls out, 'Come on, dogs.'

They walk away from the river up towards the top of the meadows.

Dominic kicks a pebble into the long grass. 'So why d'you think Dad's ashamed?'

Lauren thinks about this. 'People are often

ashamed to admit that they're ill - I mean physically - you know. And Dad is maybe ashamed to be attached to mental illness in some way.'

'Yeah, I guess you might be right.'

'I am right about it. My school friend Dorothy's mother had cancer. It was killing her but she denied to everyone that she was ill. Maybe she was ashamed.' 'What's there to be ashamed about?'

'The fact that they're not as perfect as they want everyone to believe they are. I read about it too in one of Daddy's newspapers.'

'Which he obviously didn't.'

'Or, if he did, the message didn't sink in.'

'You could say.'

They walk on in silence up to the kissing-gate at the top of the meadows. Bella-Blue and Tiger-Lily bound after them.

'There's a particular stigma attached to mental illness too, Dom. Somehow it's almost more shaming, more humiliating than something physical.'

'Why?'

'I can't tell you. Don't know enough about it. But I can tell you that I'm not ashamed of Grandma. What I saw at that hospital was terrible - frightening - but I wasn't ashamed. I never felt that. Not at all.'

'Well, I'm glad to hear that. I guess Dad has a

very high opinion of himself and he wants everyone to share that view. I think he wants people to believe that everything about him and his family is perfect. Other peoples' opinions of him are very important.'

'It's a burden that.'

'We're all a bit like that though, don't you think? Wanting to keep up appearances - worried about what other people think of us.'

'I suppose so.'

They reach the pub and go in with the dogs in tow as the rain starts to fall.

'That was good timing, Dom.' They laugh and sit at a table by a window.

'What would you like, Lauren?'

'Gin and tonic, please.'

Dominic catches a waiter's eyes and he walks over to them.

'Gin and tonic and a pint of bitter, please.'

'Ice and lemon, Miss?'

'Please.'

They wait in silence for their drinks, once more absorbed in their own thoughts. When they arrive Dominic pays. Rain is falling hard.

'Dr Bohm told me that only Mummy visits her and very rarely at that. It's so sad.' Lauren turns to the window. She's tearful. Dominic watches her then gently takes her arm.

'Don't take it on yourself, Sis. She's not your responsibility.'

'I know that but…I love her and seeing her like that was unbearable. It really was.'

'Is there nothing they can do for her?'

'Apparently not. There's no effective medicine and psychotherapy doesn't work - or so Bohm told me. He also said that he's against using electric-shock. But I got the feeling he does believe in it.'

'Oh, my God! Well, I mean, it sounds awful - desperate - though I admit I know nothing about it.'

'Me neither. But I don't like the sound of it.'

'Did he say what her illness is called?'

'Yes. He calls it manic-depression.'

Meaning?'

'Meaning she swings from mania, to depression to mania again. She goes from extreme highs to extreme lows. Up and down, up and down.'

'So what'll happen to her?

'Bohm says she must stay where she is - mostly for her own safety.'

'Will she *never* get out of there?'

'Guess no one knows the answer to that, Dom. From what I could tell the illness - or whatever you call it - remains a mystery.'

'And they don't know what causes it?'

'Bohm said it might be caused by something traumatic that happened to her or it might be hereditary.'

'Jesus! If it's hereditary one of us might get it.'

'If that's the case then I guess that's true. It might hit any one of us.'

Dominic finishes his beer. 'I think one of us should ask Mum if there is a history of manic-depression in her family.'

'Both of us should.'

'OK, Lauren. Let's do it now.' He glances out of the window. 'Looks like the rain's stopped. You ready to leave?'

'I don't look forward to this, but I'm as ready as I'll ever be. Yes, let's go.'

The dogs follow them out of the pub and they head back down the lane and out across the meadows towards the gleaming spires of the city.

Chapter Six
Learning the Hard Way

Marilyn Monroe was found dead in the bedroom of her Brentwood home on 5th October, 1962. She was 36 years old. Jack Clemmons, the first Los Angeles Police Department officer to arrive at the death scene believed that she was murdered. No murder charges were ever filed.

The path that leads up from the fen past the Leys School and onto Fen Causeway is still wet from the rain and shines in the fading light. Dominic takes Lauren's hand as they cross the road and walk up towards the Mill Pond. By the time they reach Adams Road it's almost dark and the street lights are coming on.

Dominic pauses at the top of the road. 'Have you read *The Razor's Edge* by Somerset Maugham?'

'No. I haven't read anything by him. Why?'

'It's probably his most successful book. It's certainly his most ambitious in my opinion. I've just finished it and it's made a big impression on me?'

Why's that?'

'It's the story of an American guy called Larry Darrell, who drops out of the mainstream after terrible experiences in the First World War to go after enlightenment…spiritual insight… the meaning of life.'

'Sounds like it might be heavy going.'

No, Lauren, not all. It's a novel about real people and their lives. Maugham's a great story-teller. He keeps your interest - no doubt about it. It's kind of like where I am.'

'How d'you mean?'

'I want to understand why I'm here.'

'*You* in particular? Sounds self-obsessed.'

'No I mean why we're all here. What's going on? What's the purpose of it all?'

'D'you think there's a purpose? Mark doesn't.'

'I know that. He takes everything at face value. Like the universe is just a big machine randomly grinding along, but he's only looking at the surface of things. He wants to know how things work, not why things work.'

'And you?'

'I'm sure life is purposeful. I can't believe that it's not all planned by some...what?...higher intelligence. I can't see life just emerging randomly out of mud and rock and sunlight. And consciousness too. Science can't explain how consciousness works or how it came about. Scientists always back away from that issue or just stay silent.'

They enter the house by the back door. Dinner's cooking but there's no one in the kitchen. They go through and up the back stairs to Mary's sitting room. The dogs follow them.

Dominic stops outside her door. 'There's a quote at the beginning of *The Razor's Edge* from an ancient Indian book called the Katha-Upanishad. It impressed me and I've memorized it: "The sharp edge of a razor is difficult to pass over; thus the wise say the path to salvation is hard."' Dominic smiles as he knocks on the door.

Lauren looks puzzled.

'Just thought you'd like to know, Sis.'

Mary calls out, 'Come in.'

Dominic follows Lauren and the dogs into the room. It's beautifully furnished and very homely. There are three armchairs around the fireplace where a small log-fire is burning. The chairs are covered with a William Morris designed floral fabric and the heavy drapes are of a similar pattern.

'Hello, you two. Come and sit down. I was just having a rest before dinner.'

Mary smiles at them as they sit down facing her. 'To what do I owe the pleasure of this visit?'

'Dom and I have been talking about Grandma.'

Mary looks uncomfortable.

'When I got home after I'd been to the hospital you said that the illness might have been triggered by Grandpa's suicide. But Bohm told me that it could be hereditary, which is worrying us both. Right, Dom?'

'Yes.'

'So we came to ask you if there is any other

history of mental illness in your side of the family. Is there?'

Mary thinks about this. She looks cornered as she stands and puts a log on the fire. 'I don't think so. But I can't be absolutely sure.'

Lauren is determined. 'Who else might know?'

Mary sits back in her chair. 'I suppose I could ask Aunty Mel.'

'Will you?'

'Yes, Dom, of course I will.'

Freddy is working in his study. The phone rings. He glances at it, waiting for someone to take the call, but no one does. Eventually with a sigh he picks up the receiver. 'Hello. Freddy Wheatcroft here. Can I help you?'

He waits then asks, 'Is there anybody there?' He listens intently. No voice comes back to him, but he can hear the Bach Prelude & Fugue faintly playing. He listens for a few seconds then slams the phone back in its cradle. He's agitated. He picks up the phone again and dials the operator. He knocks back the remaining whisky in his glass while he waits to get through.

'Ah. Hello. Good evening. This is Professor Wheatcroft, Dean of St Andrew's College. I wonder if you could trace the caller who phoned me just now…Thank you.'

He taps his fingers on the desk then pours himself another whisky from the crystal glass decanter on his desk.

'Hello again. Yes, I'm still here.' He listens to the operator. 'From overseas? Can you trace it?' He listens again. 'If you can't trace the call, can you at least say what country it came from?' Another pause. 'Mexico! Thank you. You've been most helpful.'

He puts the phone back on its cradle, drinks his whisky and leans back in his chair.

Chapter Seven
The Last Supper

The true meaning of disaster is 'to be separated from the stars' - and stars in this sense are not outer stars but the inner stars of the mind and spirit.

A few days before the end of the Michaelmas Term Mary organizes a family dinner. The twins have rooms in College so she hasn't seen much of them and feels it's high time that the family spent some time together.

Dobbo has worked especially hard to produce a sumptuous feast. The dinner is harmonious. No mention is made of Grace. However as they are finishing their dessert Dominic can contain himself no longer.

'I won't be here for Christmas this year.' All heads turn towards him.

Mary is the first to speak. 'Why not, Dom? We always spend Christmas together.'

'I know. I know. But I'm going to India and it's winter there so it won't be too hot.'

'India!' Freddy can barely believe what he's hearing.

'Yes, Dad. India.'

'But why...what?'

'Where to start?' Dominic glances at Lauren.

She smiles her encouragement. 'Well, Dad, Mum...the culture, the history and...?

'Yes?' Freddy glares at him.

Dominic glances across at his mother, hoping for her support. 'The mystical tradition.'

'The *what*?' Freddy thumps the table so hard that his empty plate jumps into the air, crashing to the floor.

'The mystical tradition, Dad.'

Mark can't suppress a sneering sigh. Mary is distressed and unsure of what to say. She'd dearly like to reestablish harmony as quickly as possible. 'But we always have Christmas together, Dom, as a family.'

'I know, Mum, but this time you'll have to spend it without me.'

Freddy manages to sputter, 'What's all this mystical tosh?'

'It may be tosh to you, Dad, but with respect it's not for me.'

Mary glances at Freddy and then looks to Dominic. 'Isn't Christianity enough for you, Dom?'

Dominic is about to reply, but Freddy cuts across him. 'Science makes it clear that there is no God, no grand master in charge of things.'

'Science?'

Mark can contain himself no longer. 'Yes, science. It explains everything.'

'You mean in terms of random mutations -

survival of the fittest?'

Yes, exactly what I mean, Bro.'

'Science may explain how things have happened the way they have, but not why.'

Freddy looks hard at Dominic. 'There is no *why*.'

'I think there is, Dad.'

'So do I', puts in Mary.

'There is no god.' Freddy thinks he has had the final word and leans back in his chair.

'You may be right, Dad, but you cannot be *sure*...anymore than I can be sure that there is.'

'There's no evidence....that there is...a creator.'

'True enough, Mark. Can't argue with that.'

Mark sighs. 'What about you, Lauren? Where do you stand in this debate? Seems like you may have the casting vote.' He laughs.

'Me? Oh, I don't know. I don't have any fixed ideas like you.'

'Ah! An agnostic. So no casting vote tonight.'

'That's right, Mark. No casting vote.'

They seem to have reached an impasse, but Dominic is not finished. 'OK, maybe your science can explain how most things got to be the way they are, but it cannot explain consciousness and how that arose out of the mud.'

'I'm sure it will,' Freddy responds, 'in due course.'

'Of course it will,' Mark snaps.

'You may both be right, but I doubt it.'

'All will be revealed.' Mark stands to leave the

54

table with a polite nod to his mother and father.

Dominic watches his brother then holds up his hand. 'Just before you go, Mark, let me just say that I was reading a paper by John Polkinghorne the other day...'

Mark stops and turns back to the table. John who?'

'Polkinghorne.'

'I know him.' Freddy stands to follow Mark out of the dining room.

'He's a Cambridge Professor of Mathematical Physics and he wrote, "We are greater than the stars because we know them and they know nothing."' Dominic smiles at Mary as Freddy and Mark leave the room together.

Chapter Eight
The Unexplained

If a tree falls in the forest and there are no living creatures to hear it, does it make a sound?

Dominic is reading in the garden. Freddy comes out of the house and carries a whicker chair over to where his son is sitting.

'Practicalities, Dominic.'

'OK. Dad.'

'Given that I've just about come to terms with your proposed trip, I want to know when you're leaving for India, how long you'll be away and how on earth you're going to pay for it. So?'

Dominic puts down his book. 'I'm flying out on 15th December and will be away for a month. I'll be back in time for the start of the Lent Term.'

'And how are you going to pay for this...holiday?'

Well...I...don't really see it as a holiday, more a voyage of exploration and discovery.'

'And just what d'you think you'll discover, Dominic?'

'I won't know that, Dad, until I've found it.'

'Riddles, riddles. I wish you were more down to earth and realistic like your brother.'

'More like my brother, huh? I know you think that. But the fact is I'm not like him even though we're twins and I never will be. You'd better get used to that.'

'I don't like your tone, boy. I'm your father. You should show more respect.'

'All right, Dad. Sorry. I'll try.'

'Good. You do that.' Freddy looks down at his hands then up to Dominic. 'So, how're you going to finance this...trip?

'I've saved everything from the month I worked for Cash's Marquees. The tips were good too. Big houses, big tents.'

'I dare say, but how much have you saved?'

Bella-Blue jumps onto Dominic's lap. He strokes her. It gives him time to collect his thoughts and prepare to make his case. Tiger-Lily sits at his feet, wagging her tail furiously. He bends down to stroke her then looks up again to Freddy.

'Enough. Syrian Arab Airways have a fantastic deal...'

'Syrian Arab Airways! Who the hell are they?'

'A cheap but respectable airline. They fly from Heathrow with one stop at Damascus then straight through to Bombay.'

'And what about when you get there? How will you eat, pay for hotels?'

'India's cheap, Dad. Once you're there.'

'How d'you know that?'

'You remember that Indian friend I had at Stowe?'

'Yes. That fellow Rupneraan.'

'Ranjit Rupneraan.'

'Right.'

'Even though his family's incredibly rich - they own half of Goa - he's traveled all over India on a very limited budget.'

'Why?'

'Because he chose to. Wanted to see what life was like for the poor - the other half or more like the other 99.9 percent.'

'Why?'

'Because he was sick of having everything and being waited on hand and foot by a gang of servants.'

'Doesn't sound so bad to me, Dominic.'

'Well, who knows, even you might tire of it.'

Freddy glares at Dominic, but lets it go.

'Ranjit gave me an idea of how much it would cost each day for food and transport. The railway system is, as you know, extensive and very cheap.'

'We gave it to 'em.'

'True. But there it is. And buses are even cheaper. He also told me that there are ashrams where...'

'Ashrams?'

'Yes, Dad. You must've heard the word before.'

'I have yes, but I don't have a clue what it means.'

'It's the name given to spiritual centres -

retreats - where visitors can stay for a few days and often eat for free.'

'And?'

'Listen to spiritual discourses from the resident...teacher.'

'And what do these spiritual teachers teach?'

'They teach an interpretation of the meaning of life and methods of enlightenment.'

'And what d'you mean by that?'

'By what?'

'By enlightenment.'

Dominic glances away from Freddy while he attempts to frame his answer. Bella-Blue looks up at him as if waiting for him to speak.

'I mean self-knowledge, Dad.'

'You've lost me there. What on earth d'you mean by self-knowledge?

Dominic struggles to find the words to express himself. He looks up at the sky, yearning for inspiration. 'Socrates said, "Know thyself." And he went on to say, "Attain self-knowledge before knowing anything else", if I remember correctly.
'

'But what is there to know?'

'To know what I am and then...why I'm here - why all of us are here. Socrates' point is that we contain everything - all knowledge, everything there is to know - within ourselves.'

'Which is patently nonsense.'

'Is it?'

'Yes, it is.'

'It makes sense to me.'

'I give up.' Freddy stands. 'Go to India. Find yourself...and good riddance.' Freddy stomps off across the garden and into the house. He slams the door behind him.

Dominic and the dogs watch him go. He is saddened, but turns back to his book. It is *The Teachings of Ramana Maharshi*. It has just been published. He reads out loud from the chapter called The Nature of Man. The dogs listen.

'The individual being, which identifies its existence with that of the life in the physical body as "I" is called the ego. The Self, which is pure consciousness, has no ego-sense. Neither can the physical body, which is inert in itself, have this ego-sense. Between the two, that is between the Self or pure consciousness and the inert physical body, there arises mysteriously the ego-sense or "I" notion, the hybrid, which is neither of them, and this flourishes as an individual being. The ego or the individual being is at the root of all that is futile and undesirable in life. Therefore it is to be destroyed by any possible means; then that whichever is alone remains resplendent. This is liberation or enlightenment or self-realization.'

Chapter Nine

Dylan

On 5th October 1962 The Beatles released *Love Me Do*, their first single.

Dominic cycles across the garden and out into Adams Road. His eye is caught by a checked peaked cap that's lying on the pavement. He stops and picks it up. It's a remarkably close match to his Harris Tweed overcoat. He looks up and down the road. There is no one in sight. He clips open the peak and tries it on. It fits. He cycles off into the city.

El Patio is a smallish coffee bar done out in the modern style with plastic tables and chairs. Abstract paintings hang on the walls. A big espresso machine dominates the entrance. The two serving staff are young and wear the latest trendy clothes - tight jeans and button-down shirts under white waiter jackets. Dominic walks on through looking for Lauren. He's arranged to meet her there and he's ten minutes late. He spots her and walks over to join her. She is at a table with Richard - the man who cycled past them on Grantchester Meadows.

'Hi, Lauren. Sorry I'm late.' He bends and kisses her on the cheek. 'I had to drop off some work to my tutor and he kept me longer than expected.'

'It's all right, Dom. Richard's been keeping me company.' She turns to Richard. He stands to greet Dominic. They shake hands.

'Dominic Wheatcroft.'

'Richard Bannerman.'

'D'you remember him, Dom? He passed us on the meadows.'

'Yes, of course I do. You were on your bike and called out Elvis is king.'

'I did indeed. And he is except that he now has a rival for my worship and affection. Elvis is about to be unseated. Let me get you a coffee and I'll tell you why. Richard heads up to the coffee machine and orders.

'I thought you said he wasn't your boyfriend.'

'He isn't.' Lauren gives her brother a sharp look.

'OK, Sis, only teasing. Did you say he's a painter?'

'That's what he tells us. I've never seen any of his work.'

'Art college?'

'Not as far as I know.'

'He'll be back in minute. Let's change the subject.'

'Yeah. Right. How's Dad?'

'Still fuming.'

'And Mum?'

'Bit weepy.'

Dominic sighs, takes off his cap and rakes his fingers through his hair.

'I like your cap, Dom. Where'd you get it?'

'Found it on the road outside our house.'

'Suits you.'

'Good. I like it. Feel a bit guilty though...'

'Don't worry about that. It's just a cap.'

'Thanks'. He smiles at her. She wants to say something. He waits.

'Look, Dom...d'you have to go to India?'

'I don't *have* to go, Sis. I want to go. Simple as that.'

'But...Christmas...'

'Oh, come on.'

Richard arrives at their table and puts a cappuccino down on the table in front of Dominic.

'Thank you.' Dominic attempts a smile. Lauren glances at him. 'I was in Millers record shop the other day with a couple of friends listening to the latest releases and the assistant asked if we'd heard the song *Love Me Do* by The Beatles.'

'The Beatles?'

'Yeah. A band from Liverpool. They're brilliant. Great sound. Really fresh. You'd like it.'

'Funny name, though, Lauren.'

'Might catch on!'

Richard sits down opposite them. He's heard the end of the conversation. 'And have *you* heard of Bob Dylan?'

Dominic shakes his head and Lauren responds,

'No, I haven't. Who's he?'

'American singer/songwriter.'

'Any good?' Dominic drinks his coffee.

'Utterly brilliant. Something totally new and amazing.'

'What's so special about him?'

'His lyrics. Like Arthur Rimbaud.'

Richard has Dominic's attention. 'I've got his first record. It's just called *Bob Dylan*. Only had it a few days but I must have listened to it a hundred times...well at least twenty. He's rather stolen my heart from Elvis. And he didn't just come suddenly from out of the blue from nowhere. He has his influences.'

'Like who?'

'Woody Guthrie, Dave Van Ronk, Joan Baez, Elvis, the blues.'

"D'you play anything, Richard?'

'Well, not really...not yet, but, yes...guitar.'

'Thought you were a painter.'

'I am, Lauren. Still. But I'm getting more and more into music.' Richard finishes his coffee stands, turns then looks back at Dominic and Lauren. 'Would you two like to come back to my place and hear the record?'

Lauren glances at Dominic. 'Yeah, why not?'

'I haven't got any lectures this afternoon, so suits me.'

'I live at my parent's house on Hills Road. We could walk there in twenty minutes or take a bus.'

'Let's walk. OK, Dom?'

'OK. Fine by me.'

Dominic and Lauren follow Richard through the front door, across the hall and down into the basement of the big Georgian house. He lets them into his room. It's simply furnished and dominated by an easel, which faces the light that comes in from two big windows. Considering it's a basement, it's bright and airy. Richard sits on the bed and gestures for Lauren and Dominic to sit on the couch opposite him.

'Coffee?'

'Yes, please.' They respond in unison and laugh.

Richard walks over to a small stove set in an alcove at the back of the room. He fills a percolator with water and pours fresh ground coffee into the holder. He turns up the heat and sets three mugs on the counter.

Dominic stands and walks round to look at the painting on the easel. It's a striking image. Thin, black swirling lines overlaid with bright swathes of colour, depicting a girl's face at once angelic, beautiful and tragic with dark, ominous undertones. Dominic is struck by its power and is momentarily taken aback. 'Are you at art college?'

'Not yet. Start next year.'

'Where?'

'RCA.'

Dominic is impressed. 'I'm no judge of painting, but this looks very good to me.'

'Thanks. It's not finished.'

'Come and see this, Lauren.'

She stands and walks to join Dominic by the easel. She studies the painting and shivers. She holds her brother's arm.

'Shall I put the record on?' Richard holds up the cover for them to see. It's very simple and unpretentious. Dylan is looking at the camera. He's wearing a black peaked cap, yellow T-shirt under a sheepskin coat. He's holding the neck of an acoustic guitar on the right of the photograph. Between his face and the guitar it says simply Bob Dylan and underneath a list of the tracks on the record.

Richard puts the disk on the turntable and carefully switches it on. The stylus moves jerkily onto the vinyl and the first song starts. She's No Good.

Lauren walks back to the couch. Dominic looks through the other canvases, stacked under the window. Richard waits for the percolator to boil. He turns up the volume and Dylan's rasping voice and easy guitar fills the room. They listen in silence.

He pours the coffee, switches off the stove and puts the mugs on the low table by the bed. He lies back to listen. Dominic sits back down next to Lauren.

'Did he write this, Richard?'

'No. This is a Jesse Fuller song, but he writes most of his own stuff. '

They listen in silence through to the end of the side.

Richard sits up. 'I guess you've both read *On the Road*?'

'Yeah. At school. Quite turned my head.'

'Me too. Dom lent me his dog-eared paperback'

'It had been around.'

'I'm sure Dylan was influenced by Jack Kerouac. What he says and his method of saying it. Stream of consciousness. Like James Joyce. And Dylan's a friend of Allen Ginsberg.'

'The America beat poet?'

'The same, Dom. *Howl*. An obscene poem! I've read it and I can't see it like that. It's certainly outspoken and direct. No question…and about homosexuality. 'His truth just gets under the skin of the conservatives. Resisting change is what they do.'

'I can't help feeling that we're all going to be part of some kind of a revolution.'

'Revolution!'

'Not to overthrow the government, Lauren. Not anarchy. More in the arts and in philosophy, psychology…in culture. In music particularly. Very immediate. Very compelling.' Richard pauses then asks, 'Would you like to smoke a joint?'

'A what?'

'A joint, Lauren. Pot. Like Kerouac.' Richard takes a brown paper bag out of his jacket pocket and puts it on the table. He picks up a packet of cigarette papers and starts to stick three of them together.

Dominic is startled, almost shocked. 'You mean marijuana?'

'Yup.'

'Uh. I don't think so. Thanks.'

'Even to follow in the footsteps of Jack, Dominic?'

'No thanks. I appreciate the offer. But...'

'What about you, Lauren?'

She's watching him, fascinated by his dexterous finger-work. His hands are delicate, his fingers long and sensual. He works deftly.

'Well, yes. I might have a puff.'

Richard smiles at her. It's sweet and open. She's charmed.

'Dylan's songs are about life, death, love...pain. All the important things. His music is for us. 'Specially for us.'

He finishes gluing the three papers together then opens the bag and crumbles the dry grass into them. He folds the papers over and licks along their length, pushing them together. He tears off a strip of post-card, which he folds into a tube and pushes into the end of the joint. He puts the joint to his lips, picks up a Zippo lighter, flicks it open and spins the drum. He lights the joint, taking a long deep drag and holding in the smoke, which he eventually blasts out in a gasping cloud of smoke. He takes another drag and passes the joint to Lauren. Their hands touch as she takes it. She takes a small draw.

'Right into your lungs and hold it as long as you can.'

Lauren follows his instructions, but soon splutters out the smoke and coughs. Her face reddens.

'And again.'

Dominic watches, fascinated, nervous. This time Lauren manages to hold in the smoke, which she eventually lets out in a thin, even stream. She hands the joint back to Richard.

'Feel anything?'

'Not yet.'

'You will.' He takes another drag and lies back on the bed.

Dominic glances at Lauren. She is looking down at her feet. She glances up at him. There's a faraway look in her eyes, which are also slightly bloodshot.

'I can see it's got to you, Lauren. Hit the spot.' Richard smiles at her.

Dominic looks concerned.

'She's OK, Dominic. There's nothing to worry

about. Really.'

'But she might get hooked.'

'No she won't. It's not addictive. Well, not like heroin. You should have a try.'

'No thanks.'

'That's OK. It's up to you.' Richard gets up, walks round to the easel and stands looking at his painting, smoking the joint. Lauren watches him. He dances back to the bed. Lauren bursts out laughing. Richard cracks up too. He hands the joint to Lauren then falls back on the bed, rolling with laughter. Dominic is uneasy. He can't see the joke.

'What's the joke?'

'There's no joke.'

'Then why are you laughing?'

Lauren throws back her head, lying back on the couch. Tears stream from her eyes. 'It's the whole thing, Dominic.'

'What whole thing?'

Richard sits up looking straight at him. 'The cosmic joke.'

'What cosmic joke?'

'The whole cosmic joke of it.'

'I don't get it. Doesn't seem like a joke to me.'

'Well, OK. It's not all a joke I grant you. There's a lot of grief in the world. But it also has its funny side. Surely you can see that.'

Dominic sighs. 'Yes, Richard. I can see that.'

Richard lies back on the bed. 'I'm so stoned.'

'Me too.'

D'you like it, Lauren?'

She sits up and glances at Richard. 'Yup. It's…'

'Isn't it?' Richard claps his hands.

'…Hard to say just what though.'

'Wanna try it, Dominic? I could roll another.'

Dominic is watching Lauren. 'Er…no thanks.'

'Frightened?'

'Not exactly. Well…maybe.'

'Nothing to fear. Eh, Lauren?'

Lauren takes a while to reply. 'Nothing.'

Dominic leans forward, puts his elbows on his knees and his hands on either side of his head as if to focus and compose himself. He looks up at Richard and then across at his sister. 'I'm going to leave you to it. Got some work to get on with in any case.'

'Up to you, Dominic. As the magician and philosopher Aleister Crowley put it, 'Do what thou wilt shall be the whole of the law'. Richard laughs again. He gets up and goes to the window. He has a half view of the front garden. A blackbird lands abruptly on the grass right in the middle of the picture he sees. It looks around nervously, its head flicking from side to side. It's very primitive. He feels like he's travelled far back in time. He feels ancient. It frightens him for a moment. The blackbird pecks at the ground. Richard shrugs as he turns back into the room. Lauren brings him the joint.

Dominic looks across at Richard then stands. He smiles at Lauren. 'Bye now.'

Lauren smiles up at him with bloodshot eyes. 'Bye, Dom.'

He walks slowly from the room without looking back.

Two hours later Lauren is walking across the quad of St Andrew's College. She has been to Dominic's rooms to reassure him about the pot smoking. She doesn't like to think of him worrying about her. She's deep in thought and doesn't notice Paul Bowler-Thompson running up behind her. He catches her arm. She stops and turns to him. He's flushed and nervous.

'Hello, Lauren. I...er...'

'Yes, Paul.'

'I would you come to my office? I have...just for a couple of minutes.'

'Why?'

'There's something I want to...discuss with you.' He looks uneasy, unsure of himself.

Lauren is puzzled. 'What is it?'

'It's about...'

'Yes?'

'Mark.'

'What about Mark?'

Paul takes a deep, shuddering breath. 'Come to my office and I'll tell you.' He leads off into the cloisters and up one flight of stairs. He opens a huge oak door and stands back to let Lauren in. He follows swiftly after her closing the door behind them. He swings round on Lauren and pushes her roughly back against the door. He gropes her, his hands roughly grabbing her breasts while he uses his body to pin her to the door. She's taken completely by surprise, horrified and almost paralyzed with shock. She tries to push him away with all her strength, but his heavy body holds her pinned. He starts to tear at her blouse and two buttons fly off across the room. He is possessed, driven by an overwhelming lust for her body. He grunts and groans as he forces his hand inside her bra. He pinches her nipple roughly. This is finally too much for Lauren and she responds. She frees one hand and hits him hard across the face with all her strength. Spit flies from his mouth as his thick cheek compresses under the blow. She pushes him away from her. He stumbles and falls to the ground with a resounding thud.

She pulls her blouse across her naked chest and gasps, 'What the hell d'you think you're doing?'

He gets up onto his knees and starts to stand. She pulls back her hand to strike him again. He stays where he is.

'Are you mad?'

He's lost for words then sputters, 'I thought when…you smiled at me at the dinner party…I thought you liked me. I thought you understood.

I...thought you wanted me.'

'Wanted you!'

'Yes.'

'Because I smiled?'

'Yes.'

'I smiled...it was a friendly gesture. I was just being kind.'

His head droops onto his chest. He holds out his hands in a pleading gesture. 'I thought you understood. I thought we had an understanding...sex...'

'You thought I wanted to have sex with you!'

'Yes.'

'Jesus, Paul! When a woman smiles at a man it does not imply...it doesn't mean she wants to give her body to...'

'I...I...'

She starts to open the door.

'Lauren! Lauren, please!'

'Please what?'

'Please forgive me. I...I'm so sorry. I didn't mean...'

'You attempted to rape me, Paul.

'No. No!'

'What then?'

'I wanted to love you. Hold you, caress you...'

'You went a funny way about it.'

'I have no experience with women. I've never...except when I've paid for it in London.'

Lauren's heart begins to soften and pity rises

up in her. She waits.

'Please don't tell anyone…anyone…about this…Freddy…Mary…it would be the end of my career.'

'You're right. It would. And prison too!'

'No…no. I can't…'

'You should've thought about it, Paul. You're not stupid.'

'I…' Still on his knees, he raises his hands in a gesture of prayer. 'Please!'

Lauren pauses and slowly starts to open the door. She looks down on him. 'I won't tell anyone, Paul.'

'Oh, thank you. Thank you…thank you.'

She turns her back on him and leaves the room, closing the door firmly behind her.

Chapter Ten
Mary and Mark

Mary and Mark are in the big sitting-room at the back of the house. Deep arm chairs and fine antique furniture float on huge Persian rugs, scattered in planned randomness across the deep-stained oak floor.

'I really don't want to get into an argument about religion with you, Mark. We won't get anywhere. We must beg to differ.'

'But, Dominic's…'

'That's enough.'

'…Going to India to visit ashrams! Dad told me.'

'Did he?'

'He's furious.'

'I know.'

'And I don't blame him. It's such utter rubbish all that guru stuff…enlightenment…'

Mark stands and strides over to the drinks cabinet. 'Isn't a bit early, Mark? It's only just gone four.'

'I need a drink, Mum.'

Mary lets it go. Mark pours himself a large whisky, adding soda from a crystal decanter.

'He could have gone after Christmas. Don't you find it selfish of him?'

'Yes, well...I would have liked to have him here of course, but things change.'

'I still think it's selfish.'

'We all are to some extent.'

'Meaning?'

'Most of us put ourselves first, don't we?'

'Yes, I suppose that we do, Mum, but surely there are people who put others first.'

'Yes. Most parents would risk their lives to protect their child. That's true.'

'What about soldiers, firemen, policemen...?'

'You have a point, Mark.'

'So I can't excuse him. Why can't he put himself out for us?'

'Have you talked to him about this?'

'Not really, no.'

'Why not?'

'He makes me so angry - messing around with all that mystical mumbo-jumbo. Gurus, self-realization! He should *realize* his responsibilities here before he goes charging off on some wild goose chase in India. It's so...childish.'

'It's very strange to me - to us - but I don't think it's childish to seek answers, explanations and meaning.'

'Yes, but can't we find that here, now, where we are?'

'Maybe not, Mark. Life's mysterious and hard to explain.'

'But we can explain it - we have with the theory

of evolution.'

'Well, you have just said it's a theory. It's not proven fact.'

'It is. For those who can see the light.'

'Is it?'

'Yes, it is. And it's staring us in the face in the fossil records.'

'Science, science, science! But what about beauty, what about...?'

'OK. The world can be beautiful - but ugly too. And meaning? There's no meaning, Mum.'

'I just can't believe that...it's all...'

Mark cuts across her. He's annoyed. 'There's meaning to us in what we do here with our lives, but as for the whole damned thing - it's meaningless.'

'Let's leave it there, Mark. As I said, we'll just have to agree to differ.'

Mark throws up his hands in exasperation. His arguments are not winning his mother's vote. It irritates him. She irritates him.

Mary looks out of the window and then back at him. 'I'm worried about Lauren. She hasn't been her usual self after she came back from her visit to Grandma.'

'Well, that's hardly surprising. What on earth tempted her to go?'

'She's naturally inquisitive and I suppose she wanted to find out for herself why her grandmother's in hospital. She came home late the other night and I had waited up for her. She was very strange, very talkative and she looked different.'

'How?'

'Her face was puffed up and her eyes were just slits and very blood-shot.'

'Did you ask where she'd been?'

'Of course. She said she'd been out with friends. They ended up at a chap called Richard's house and she said she just forgot the time.'

'Did she apologize?'

'Oh, yes. Profusely. In fact a bit too much. As if she was guilty of something.' Mary looks away from Mark. She is deep in thought.

'D'you worry about all of us, Mum?'

'Of course I do. You always worry about your children - if you're a diligent parent that is. It's natural, surely?'

'Yes, it's natural. Has to be. If we didn't look after our young we'd get wiped out.'

'And I can tell you this: once a parent, always a parent. Your children are always just that - your children. It's impossible not to be concerned about their welfare. I hope that one day you'll find this out for yourself.'

Mark smiles. 'D'you worry about us too? Dom and me?'

'I don't necessarily worry as such, but I think about you both a lot. Wondering how you are, what you're doing, if you're eating well and so on. I suppose I'll worry about Dom when he's in India. It's a country I've never been to so I don't know anything about it. I'd imagine that communicating with him might be difficult. I hope he'll manage to call us every so often.'

'He should leave us an itinerary so we know roughly where he'll be at any one time.'

'That's a very good idea. I'll ask him to do that.'

'If he knows where he's going.' Mark shrugs.

'Don't be so hard on him. You're too ready to find fault with your brother. D'you know that?'

'Well...I...'

'Well you what?'

'His head's in the clouds with his books and his modern jazz records, his poetry.'

'And you have your feet on the ground, I suppose with your science. But isn't there a place for art in your life? Art and the search for knowledge...and...'

'The only knowledge worth searching for is hard science. Theories which can be proven by experiments that can be carried out and over again and always yield up the same reliable results. The rest is just idle speculation. Beauty is truth, truth beauty. John Keats, I believe.'

'I think you're right. Keats. You surprise me. I thought you didn't read poetry.'

'I don't. I just read that quote somewhere. Don't really know what it means if I'm truthful.'

'Never mind about that. The most important

thing is that you should realize that your views are only your opinion.'

'All right they are my opinion I grant you, but not just mine of course.'

'I understand. But you should really respect the opinions of others, Mark. Don't let your arrogance get in the way of your heart. Your brother needs your support and your affection. Don't turn your back on him...please.'

Chapter Eleven

Lauren

A racing green Austin Mini Cooper is driving slowly through the village of Hemingford Grey, which lies a few miles north of Cambridge. The village sits on the bank of the Great River Ouse. Lauren visited many times with her parents in her childhood and she has a deep fondness for the spot.

She turns the Mini into Castle Street and drives down towards St James' Church. She leaves the car in the church car park, grabs her bag and walks through the graveyard down to the river. Lauren looks fresh and pretty in her light cotton, floral-patterned dress and green shoes. She walks through the graveyard and down to the river, turning right along the towpath. She stops and goes to the bank regarding her reflection in the slow-moving stream. Clouds float leisurely across the wide, deep blue sky shimmering on the water's surface. An elderly man with a bouncing Boxer puppy stops as he passes. Lauren bends down to stroke the dog, which wags its tail in appreciation. The man nods at her and walks away towards the church. Lauren strolls on and out of the village.

She walks for half a mile then sits under the

shade of a low-hanging willow. She opens her bag and takes out a leather pouch. She empties the contents on the ground beside her. Cigarette papers, a post-card and a small bag of grass. She rolls a joint, sits back against the tree and lights it. She inhales deeply, the smoke curls and swirls around her. Leaves rustle, birds sing and a dog barks in the distance. Lauren smiles contentedly. She lies back on the bank. Her hand strokes through the grass. She closes her eyes.

Footsteps approach along the tow-path. They stop as they reach her.

'Hello Lauren. Sorry I'm late.' Richard sits down beside her. He takes her hand and she squeezes his, opening her eyes to look up to him.

'Hi. You OK?'

'Sure. The bus came late.'

'It doesn't matter, Richard. I'm fine.'

'So I see.' He laughs. 'Good grass, eh?'

'Certainly is.' Lauren sits up. 'Where d'you get it?'

Richard thinks about this, looking out across the river. 'You don't need to know.'

'I suppose not.' She looks a little disappointed. They sit in silence soaking up the gentleness of the afternoon.

'How're things? How's Dominic?'

'Could be better.'

'Why?'

'It may seem trivial to you, but my parents and

Dom's brother are very upset that he won't be home for Christmas this year.'

'And why's that?'

'He's going to India.'

'India!'

'Yes.'

'Sounds amazing to me.'

'Me too. I'm very envious, but it's causing a lot of friction at home especially as he's not going as a normal tourist - just to see the sights.'

'What's he going for then? The cheap grass?'

'You're joking. Not his cup of tea as you may remember.'

'Oh yeah, yeah. Of course.' Richard laughs and lies down on the bank beside Lauren. 'I've missed you, Lauren.' He turns on his side to look at her.

'I've missed you too.' She turns his face to him and they kiss, rolling their bodies together. A woman with two young children approaches and they pull apart unwillingly.

'So, why's your bro' going to India?'

'Not quite sure how to put it. I guess you could say that he's looking for wisdom and insight.'

'Insight into what?'

'He would say the big questions.'

'Which are?'

'Oh, you know. Why am I here? What's the point of it all? What's the whole thing mean?'

'Why go to India though?'

'Well, he says that there are teachers there - gurus - who know about these things.'

'Like - uh - swamis, mystics?'

Yup. Like that. Thing is it's like a red rag to a bull as far as my father and his brother are concerned. They are devout atheists. They believe that science can - or will - explain everything. Gurus and swamis are deluded as far as they're concerned. What d'you think?'

'Dunno. What about you?'

'Don't know either. I just want to have fun and enjoy life. Just make the most of what I have and what I can do.'

'What d'you want to do?'

'Don't know. Well, not yet. But I could say I want to be happy.'

'Are you happy now?'

'With you, yes. But not about Dom or...'

'Yes? Or?'

Lauren ponders his question while she makes up her mind whether or not to tell him about Grace and her visit to the mental hospital. Richard watches her, waiting.

'I...umm. There's something I want to talk about. Something I can't discuss with my family...except Dom. I can talk to him, but he has enough on his plate right now with his journey to India and Daddy and Mummy's hostility.'

'Well, you can tell me Lauren. I'm a good

listener.'

She smiles. 'I'm sure you are, Richard, but this will probably be as incomprehensible to you as it is to me. And I don't expect you to have any answers. I just want to talk about it.'

'OK, well, try me.'

'A couple of weeks ago I went to Marchman House.'

'The nut house?'

'That's right. The nut house. Though I don't like that expression.'

'OK, Lauren. But why d'you go there?'

'To visit my grandmother.' Lauren stops, unsure of how to proceed.

'Does she work there?'

'No, Richard. She doesn't. She's a...she's a patient.'

'A patient? A mental patient?'

'That's right.'

'How...?'

'She's been there for years. Locked up. Locked away.' Lauren starts to choke, trying to hold back her tears.

'It's all right, Lauren. It's all right.' He puts his arm round her and she puts her head on his chest. Her sobbing increases as she lets out her pain. He holds her close to him and rocks her gently in his arms. She starts to calm.

'I...'

'No rush.'

'Daddy and Mummy won't talk about her. It's as if they want to pretend that she's not there, that she doesn't exist even.'

'Let's walk, Lauren.' He stands and helps to her feet. They stroll on up the towpath. He puts his arm around her and she leans against him.

'She was frightening - violent. And she didn't even recognize me. Thought I was a biblical figure. The doctor had warned me, but...I had no idea.'

'Well, you couldn't.'

'What d'you mean?'

'Is she manic-depressive?'

Lauren is taken aback. 'How...how did you know?'

'I don't know. Just guessing.'

'How come? I mean, what d'you know about mental illness, Richard?'

'Not a lot, I admit. But something.'

'How's that?'

'How's what?'

'How do you know something...anything about it?'

'I have an uncle who spends time in Melford Hospital. A lot of the time he's well - normal - but he swings up and down and he's caused his family a lot of trouble. I haven't seen him for years, but I've heard my folks talking about his manic-depression. He's in there when he's up and he's in there when he's low. They're going to try electro-convulsive therapy I believe.'

'That sounds terrifying. Some of the people at Grandma's hospital want to try that, but her doctor doesn't believe in it.'

'I know nothing about it, but I don't like the sound of it either.'

They arrive back at the church. 'Shall we go back into Cambridge? My car - my father's car - is here.'

'Yes, if you want. Can you come back to mine?'

'I want to.'

'Good. I hoped you say yes.' They kiss again and walk into the churchyard up to the green Mini. Richard walks round it admiringly.

'Nice car. Mini Cooper?'

'Yes. Daddy's a bit of a car fanatic.'

'Could say. Must be pretty nippy.'

'Fast enough for me.' Lauren laughs, unlocks the driver's door, gets in and slides over to unlock the passenger side. Richard climbs in and looks around the interior.

'I wouldn't have expected you to have an interest in cars.'

'Why not?'

'Being an artist...'

'But *this* is art. Practical art. Like you, Lauren, it's exquisite to look at and no doubt runs beautifully.'

Lauren flushes.

'You're blushing.'

'Only a bit. Don't embarrass me, Richard.'

'But you are beautiful. No getting away from that fact, my dear girl.'

'You are most kind, sir.'

'My pleasure, ma'am.' They kiss again then Lauren puts the key in the ignition and starts the car. She drives out of the car park. Richard pulls a pre-rolled joint and a lighter out of his inside pocket. 'Want to smoke a joint?'

'Yeah, let's.'

Richard lights up, takes two big drags and passes the joint to Lauren. He opens the window. 'Don't drive too fast. Don't want to get stopped by the cops with this.'

Lauren takes a deep drag. 'You know sometimes I forget it's illegal.' She takes another smoke. 'Why is it illegal anyway?' The both laugh.

'God knows. Probably pressure from the alcohol industry. Stop them losing sales to a drug that doesn't even need to be processed and does less harm.'

'Seems crazy to me.' She passes the joint back to Richard.

'It is. Like so much else in this warped society, in which we live and have our being.'

'But, d'you think there might be any long-term bad effects?'

'Like rot your brain?'

'Yes.'

'Don't think so. Don't know of course. But I

don't really care. Keep your eye on the road though. I don't wanna die yet.'

They laugh again.

It's dark when Lauren leaves Richard's parents' house. She drives slowly through the town. It has started to rain and the streets shine dully in the light from the street lamps. She looks thoughtful and stoned.

She parks the car in the garage and enters the house through the front door. The phone rings as she goes into the entrance hall. She looks around and waits. No one answers it. She picks up the receiver. 'Hello. Professor Wheatcroft's house.' She listens for a response. There is none. 'Hello. Is there anyone there?' She listens intently then puts the phone back on its cradle as Mary comes out of the sitting room.

'Who was it, dear?'

'I don't know Mummy. There didn't seem to be anybody there. All I could hear was distant organ music. It sounded like Bach.'

Chapter Twelve
The Great Nostalgia

'All the books in the world will not give you happiness.
In yourself there is everything you need: sun moon stars.
Because the light you are looking for lives within you.
The wisdom you've been looking for a long time in the library
now shines on every page because it is now yours'.
Hermann Hesse

Freddy, Mary and Lauren are having dinner later that night. They are finishing their dessert. Freddy leans back in his chair. 'I saw Mark today. He's settled in well and he's enjoying his course. I'm not so sure about Dom. Haven't seen him for over a week. Have you?'

'No, Daddy. I haven't. But I'm sure he's fine.'

'I bumped into him in Joshua Taylor's the other day. He was in a rush, getting ready for India.'

Freddy scowls at Mary and pours himself another glass of wine. 'That boy irritates me.'

'And Mark doesn't?'

'No, Lauren. He does not. He has his feet on the ground. Dominic is frankly away with the fairies. He's not going anywhere.'

'I wouldn't be too sure about that, Daddy.'

'Ha!'

They lapse into silence. Mary speaks eventually. Her voice is thin and weak. 'You should still support him, Freddy.'

'Support him! I do support him. I pay for his education, his clothes, the food he eats.'

'I meant, dear, emotionally, spir...'

'My God!' The irony is lost on Freddy, but Lauren smiles.

'And what are you laughing at, young lady?'

'I'm not laughing, Daddy. I just thought it was odd that you should call on God on like that.'

'I did not call on God. I took his name in vain.' Freddy pushes back his chair abruptly and gets up, glaring first at Lauren and then at Mary. 'I'm going to take the dogs for a walk.' He walks out, slamming the door behind him.

The two women are stunned and neither speaks for a few minutes.

'Why's Daddy got it in for Dominic?'

Mary looks sad and lost. 'I don't think he has, dear.'

'He has. He's always favoured Mark.'

'Has he?'

'Yes, Mummy. You know he has.'

'I'm...'

'Why?'

'Mark is more athletic, more of a man's man. Dom is...what...deep and that's always irritated Daddy in some way I can't understand.'

'Nor can I. I love them both. I don't discriminate...favour one more than the other. It's not right to do that.'

'It isn't right. It makes me sad.'

'Well, say something Mummy.'

Mary wriggles uncomfortably. 'I can't.'

'You can. Well, you could.'

'He won't listen to me.'

'He should. You're wiser than him.'

Mary laughs, a light, twinkling ripple. 'D'you really think so?'

'Yes. I do.' For all his grand position and his power he really is a simple man. He's a bigot and a bully.'

'Really, Lauren! You shouldn't talk about your father like that.'

'Why not when it's true? You know it is.'

'I don't want to be disloyal.'

'You aren't. You never are. You stick by him through thick and thin. You never criticize him. And yet he feels fully justified to criticize anyone and everyone.'

'Don't be too hard on him. He means well.'

'Does he? I sometimes wonder.'

Dobbo comes into the dining room to clear the table.

'Thank you, Dobbo.' Mary smiles at her. She looks uneasy.

'What is it, Dobbo? What's the matter?'

Dobbo pulls back her shoulders, gathering her

93

strength. 'Can I have a day off next week, Madam?'

'Of course you can. D'you mind if I ask why?'

'My sister Crisp is in hospital in Bedford. She's...' Dobbo is lost for words.

'Yes?'

'She's having an operation next week and I'd like to go and see her when it's done.'

'Well, yes, you must go. May I ask if it's serious?'

'It is, Madam. Yes. Very. She has cancer. A tumor in her stomach. They don't even know if she'll live through the operation.'

'How terrible...for you.'

'More terrible for her, if I might say, Madam.'

'Of course. You're right. Which day would you like to go?'

'Wednesday, please, Madam.'

'That'll be fine, Dobbo. I think Professor Wheatcroft will be in London that day and will probably be staying the night. So that's a good day.'

'Thank you, Madam. Now if I may...'

'Yes, please carry on.' Mary glances at Lauren. 'We were just going for a walk in the garden.' She stands. Lauren gets up too.

'You'll need coats. It's getting colder out these evenings.'

'Ah, yes. Autumn's on the way.' She turns to Lauren. 'Let's get our coats.'

The two women walk through the hall, gather

their overcoats and walk out into the garden. A light breeze flutters through the trees, rustling the dying leaves, which fall to the ground without ceasing.

'Sad, isn't it?'

'What Mummy?'

'The autumn - the end of summer, shorter days.'

'The Chinese don't see it like that. To them it's the beginning of a new cycle of life.'

'How's that?'

'Seeds fall and new life starts to happen.'

Mary ponders this as they walk.

'Dominic was here the other day.'

'Oh. Did you see him?'

'No, Mummy.'

'How d'you know he was here then?'

'He left me a book.'

'A book?'

'*The Razor's Edge*. Have you read it?'

Mary looks puzzled.

'Somerset Maugham.'

'No, I haven't.'

'I've started it. It's a good story.'

'Why d'you think he left it for you to read.'

'It made a big impression on him and, I suppose, he just wanted to share it with me.'

'What's so special about it?'

'I think Dom sees himself as being like the hero of the novel, who turns his back on society to go on a quest for enlightenment. You know...'

'Like his visit to India.'

'Yes. Just like that. In fact Larry, the hero, does go to India. He visits a guru called Ramana Maharshi. I think Dom wants to meet him too.'

Mary doesn't respond. They sit on a bench beside the pond. Lauren takes a deep breath. 'I rang Dr Bohm yesterday.'

'Why?'

'To see how Grandma is.'

'And what did he tell you?' Mary looks uncomfortable.

'He said that she was a lot better and he suggested that I should visit her again.'

'Oh dear.' Mary sighs, picks up a ball and throws it in the pond.

'Why do you say that - *oh dear*?'

'It's just that you were so upset last time and Daddy...'

'Daddy! It's got nothing to do with him.'

'He won't like it.'

'Don't tell him then.'

'But I...'

'You should stand up to him Mummy. Don't let him bully you. He's just a man. He's not a god, you know.'

'I can't stand up to him. I've never been able to.'

'And you've given him all the power.'

'I never had any, Lauren.'

'Well now's the time to start. I'm going to.'

'You already do.'

'Well, I'm going to do it more in future. I won't let him lord it over me. He has no right to.'

'*He* is your father.'

'And I am *me*. I am my own person.'

'But you're a woman.'

'So?'

'It's a man's world.'

'Maybe it has been and maybe it is now, but not forever. Mother nature, mother earth. What about that?'

'I don't know about that.'

'Well, think about it, Mummy. We could have the power. We do have the babies after all. That's power, surely?'

'I've never looked at it like that.'

'Well it's certainly worth thinking about. And, anyway, he's not as strong as he'd like us to believe. Bullies are always insecure underneath, you know.'

'Are they?'

'Oh, yes.' Lauren stands. 'I am going to see Grandma and I don't give a fig if Daddy finds out.'

Chapter Thirteen
On The Trail

*"The cosmos is within you. We're made of star
stuff. We are a way for the cosmos to know itself."*
Carl Sagan, Astronomer.

The day of Dominic's departure for India starts
badly, but quickly improves the further he gets
away from home. He wishes that Lauren was
with him, but is glad to see the back of his father
and Mark. Freddy was icy cold when Dominic
had visited him in his study to say goodbye. No
hug and hardly a handshake. Mark was almost
equally unfriendly and hostile. Dominic is
puzzled by their behaviour. It's hard to explain
- it's almost, he feels, a conspiracy. He's always
known that his father favours his brother for
reasons beyond his understanding but he's
never had the courage to address the issue
head-on. His father is not an emotionally
demonstrative man. Never has been. But still…

Mary was loving and tearful and at a polar
extreme to the two men. Her warmth and
affection was almost uncomfortable and too
clingy. But Lauren was perfect as usual. He
adores his sister and they have always been
close. Her pot smoking is difficult for him to
accept, but he has let it go. His love goes way

beyond his incomprehension.

The train from Cambridge is on time. Dominic finds an empty compartment and heaves his rucksack into the luggage compartment. He pulls a small, battered pamphlet out of a side pocket before he sits down to watch Cambridge slide away through the dirty window. The booklet is called *Who am I?* It is by Bhagavan Sri Ramana Maharshi. Dominic opens and reads: At the deepest level of Spirit, we know that we all come from the same source, at the same time, by the same word of creation that created all. It is clear that the primary motivation and energy behind Creation can be narrowed down to one single word – Love. Love is the cement that binds all together. Love is the force that is primal in nature. The nature of awareness is truth-consciousness-bliss. Sat, chit, ananda.

He looks up from the booklet at the passing woods and fields. He thinks about Lauren and he smiles. He ponders too his father's aggression and his anger. Like his sister he appreciates that his father is a bully and that his position in the college gives him a sense of power and inflated importance, which he allows to spill over into his family life. Like Lauren he wishes that his mother would stand up to him. He can see that Mary has always taken a submissive position in the family hierarchy and that this will be hard to change and will probably never be possible.

He can see that the situation is unhealthy and that it leads - has led - to all kinds of problems. The train pulls into Liverpool Street and Dominic makes his way to the underground. He takes the tube out to Heathrow. He checks in, passes through passport control and into the departure lounge. He goes to a public phone, puts in money and calls home, hoping his father won't pick up. Fortunately it's Lauren who answers.

Hi, Sis. It's me. I'm at Heathrow.'

'Everything OK?'

'Yeah. I've checked in. I think we'll be boarding in about half an hour.'

'How d'you feel about going now?'

'I'm excited. Pleased to be going, but I miss you already. How's Mum?'

'Bit tearful.'

'Oh. dear.'

'You mustn't worry about her, Dom. She'll be OK and you're only away for a month. It'll fly by. I'm going to take her shopping tomorrow. We'll have a nice girls' day out.'

'That's good. Dad was very…cold to me when I said goodbye.' He pauses. 'I've just read, "Love is the cement that binds all together". Pity he doesn't realize this.'

'Isn't it?'

'You know I get the feeling that something is bothering him, nagging away at him, and I don't think it's me. It's almost like he's hiding something or not facing up to something.'

'I don't know…'

'He's so angry and his hostility towards me just doesn't make sense. It seems like maybe I'm just a scapegoat.'

'Yes, Dom, you may well be right about that.'

'Well, look Sis, I'm going to say goodbye now. I love you.

'I love you too. Look after yourself and don't forget to write.'

'I won't. 'Bye'

'Bye, Dom.'

Dominic replaces the phone and walks over to the observation window. There is a Syrian Arab Tristar airliner on the tarmac beneath the window. Ground crew are loading luggage into the hold. The aircraft is an ugly beast with a fourth engine half way up the tail fin. Dominic sits down and takes out the booklet to start reading again.

Twenty minutes later his flight is called and Dominic takes his place in the queue to go out to the aircraft. Once aboard he finds his window seat and sits down to wait for take-off. The aircraft taxis out then turns to face down the runway and the engines roar. The plane moves off slowly, quickly picks up speed and leaves the ground. Dominic is committed. He watches London slip by beneath him and is soon over the

English Channel flying into the dawn.

The flight makes a scheduled stop in Bahrain for refueling and to pick up more passengers. Once they are in the air again Dominic dozes until supper is served.

When Dominic steps onto the tarmac at Bombay Airport he is hit by a firewall. The heat is overwhelming. The air is thick with the smells of India: wood-smoke, incense, exhaust fumes and human waste. 'If this is winter,' Dominic ponders to himself, 'what the hell is the summer like? And hell,' he thinks, 'is most likely the appropriate word for it!'

He queues for what seems like hours at immigration, eventually gets through, collects his rucksack, changes some money and, after much hassling, staggers out to the front of the airport to find a taxi. He is immediately surrounded by taxi touts, desperately trying to win his business. He hangs on tight to his rucksack as brown hands pull him this way and that. He pushes through the hustlers to the taxi queue and a cab immediately pulls up in front of him. He opens the door, throws his bag on the seat and climbs in.

'Ashoka Hotel, Bellasis Road, please. It's block A, number 43.' The car lurches away from the curb as a gaggle of beggars closes in on it.

'Is this your first visit to India, Sir?'

'Yes.'

'I thought so. You looked, if I might say, a little stunned.'

'I was...I am.' Dominic looks back over his shoulder at the fast receding airport. 'Your English is very good.'

'Ah, yes. Thank you, Sir. I was living in UK for two years. I worked as hospital porter and I lived in Southall. I had a room in a bungalow on the corner of Beaconsfield Road and Woodlands Road. Very nice.'

Dominic is unsure how to respond.

'Do you know that bungalow, Sir?'

Dominic stifles a laugh. 'Uhh...no.'

'Very nice bungalow, Sir. I am surprised you are not knowing it.'

'I don't live in London.'

'And which city do you hail from, Sir?'

'Cambridge.'

'Ah. Very fine city it is too.'

'You've been there?'

'My uncle has driven me there. In one day - there and back. He has a very fine car. An Austin A40. You know this car, Sir?'

'Yes, I know it.'

Dominic doesn't want the conversation to continue. The driver steers like a madman through the traffic, swerving to avoid oncoming cars, lorries, coaches and the deep potholes in the road. To Dominic he seems to be unsure of which side of the road he should be driving on.

They careen onto Bellasis Road half an hour later and the driver peers through his filthy windscreen, scanning for the hotel.

'There it is, Sir. Right where I thought it would be.' He swerves the cab across the road narrowly missing two cyclists and another cab, and pulls up outside the hotel.

'Are you sure you want to stay here, Sir? I know another hotel that's better and cheaper.'

'How d'you know it's cheaper?'

The driver has no ready answer.

'How much do I owe you?' Dominic notices that the meter has not been on and is in fact hanging off its hinges.

'That will be 450 rupees, Sir. Very good rate, Sir.'

'I'm sure it is. Thank you.' Dominic pays him with an extra fifty rupees. The driver is delighted and runs around the car to open the door for him. He attempts to carry Dominic's rucksack. Dominic keeps hold of it and walks into the hotel reception. There is no lighting.

'Good day, Sir.' A voice comes out of the darkness.

'Where are you? I can't see you.'

'Over here, Sir. Walk straight ahead.'

Dominic's eyes are adjusting to the gloom. 'Ah, yes. I can see you now. Why are all the lights off?'

'Power cut. Usually around this time, Sir.'

'Every day...like this?'

'For just an hour or two.'

Dominic reaches the reception desk. 'I'm Dominic Wheatcroft. I wrote to you to reserve a room for tonight.'

The receptionist pushes a ledger towards Dominic. 'Yes, we have your letter, Sir. And we have set aside a very good room for you. The very best.'

'Thank you.'

'Just sign here, please Sir.'

Dominic signs at the spot where a finger is pointing.

'We have torches, Sir. Follow me and I will take you to your room. Guaranteed, you'll like it very much. Guaranteed.'

Dominic follows the receptionist's torch beam. He stumbles on the first step. He is jet-lagged and tired.

'Oh, I'm so sorry, Sir. Let me take your bag.'

'No. It's alright I can manage.'

The receptionist leads him to do a door on the first floor, which he throws open with a flourish. Dominic follows him into the room.

'Very best room, Sir.'

'I'll take your word for it. I can't see much.'

Dominic jumps as the lights come on.

'Ah, Sir. That's better.'

Dominic blinks and looks around, taking in the very basic and untidy room, the dirty windows and the worn carpet. Dust covers everything. The receptionist beams at him. In the bright light Dominic is struck by the man's elegance. He's dressed in a cream silk shirt and narrow trousers. He has a neat moustache which cuts across his noble face and enormous smile. Dominic attempts to focus.

'Can I help you, Sir?'

'Uhh...yes, you can. I'm leaving Bombay tomorrow. I'm going to Tiruvannamalai.'

'That is very long journey. You must go by way of Madras and change trains. Probably three days it will be. You'd be advised to go by first class air-conditioned sleeper car.'

'Yes. I know it's a long way, but I've never been to India before and I want to see the country.'

'You will certainly be doing that.' The receptionist steps over to the bed to straighten the counterpane. 'You'll be needing some help to buy your ticket and make your reservation. It's complicated. I will dispatch to the railway station to place an order for you now and I will send a boy with you tomorrow to collect your tickets for very small fee.'

'Ah, yes. I've been told by an Indian friend that buying tickets here is not a straight-forward process.'

'Indeed, it is not, Sir.'

Chapter Fourteen
Sri Ramana Maharshi

'For as long as man continues to be the ruthless destroyer of lower living beings, he will never know health or peace. For as long as men massacre animals, they will kill each other. Indeed, he who sows the seeds of murder and pain cannot reap joy and love.'
Pythagoras

Dominic stands to the side of the ticket hall at the station as he watches the hotel's boy hustle for his ticket. After twenty minutes the boy runs over to him waving a clutch of documents in his hand.

'I have them, Sir.' He holds the documents out to Dominic. 'This is your first class air-conditioned sleeper ticket and reservation to Madras and this is your ticket for Tiruvannamalai.' You'll have about twenty-five hours' journey to Madras and then eight hours on the train to your destination. You'll wait ten hours for your connection to Tiruvannamalai.'

Dominic takes the documents and gives the boy one hundred rupees. 'Thank you.'

'And thank you too, Sir. I hope you have pleasant journey.' He steps back and disappears into the crowd.

Dominic wakes in the night still jet-lagged. He

climbs out of his bunk and goes to a seat by the window. He tries to peer through the dusty, smudged glass. They've stopped at a station, but he can't tell where they are. The platform is crowded with food vendors and what appear like piles of rags, but when he looks more carefully he can see that the heaps of cloth are actually sleeping people. He eats the sandwiches and fruit he'd brought with him from the hotel. Even though he also has two bottles of water, he is tempted to buy a mug of tea. He leans out of the train window and a vendor is quickly to hand to sell him chai. He sips the delicious hot, sweet liquid and holds the mug out of the window for the chai wallah to take back from him, which he does with many thanks and bows. Dominic makes his way to the toilet, recoiling at the door as the stench of the latrine hits him. He puts his hand over his nose, takes a deep breath, and enters.

He goes back to his compartment and dozes until the train pulls into Madras Station. It's on time. The platform is a seething mass of humanity: porters, vendors, travelers, beggars. Dominic doesn't look forward to spending ten hours at the station and then finding the train to Tiruvannamalai and his reserved seat. He makes his way to the booking hall and sees his departure listed on a battered and barely readable display. He walks out on the street and is quickly surrounded by touts and beggars. He ends up giving away most of his change. Annoyingly this only increases the number of supplicants. They pull at his arms, tugging his shirt and trousers. He starts to feel angry and decides to find a taxi to take him to a hotel before he loses it. Eventually he pays a porter to show him the way to a cab rank. He manages to convey that he would like to be a taken to a decent hotel near the station. He feels suddenly lost, overwhelmed and very lonely, wondering if he's done the right thing coming to this mad, chaotic country and if it was worth upsetting his parents and missing the family Christmas. Homesickness tugs at his heart.

Though the bed is as hard as a rock the room is better than he expected. He puts down his rucksack, goes to the window and looks down on the street. The sight that greets his eyes makes his head spin. The cars weave through the swirling mass of pedestrians, cyclists and carts. The air is grey and thick with exhaust fumes. He turns away, disgusted, and throws himself on the bed, too tired to wash. He tosses and turns unable to rest, unable to sleep. He gets up, goes to his bag and pulls out his tattered paperback copy of *The Razor's Edge*. He props up the thin pillow and lies down again. He reads and eventually he drops off.

The waiting room is only available to passengers

with a ticket. Once inside he finds he's in a calm oasis of the affluent. He wonders what Lauren would make of this place. He misses her. He has no doubt about what Mark would think and he doesn't miss him. His heart warms when he recalls his mother.

He quickly finds himself the centre of attention. It seems that all the travelers want to talk to him especially when it comes out that he is from the UK - and Cambridge. Several people want to know his destination. When he explains that he's on his way to the Ramana Maharshi Ashram a chubby little man with a big smile introduces himself and offers to travel with him as he too is on his way there. Dominic is delighted to be befriended.

'My name is Bunty Bharatram. I hail from Jaipur. D'you know the Pink City?'

'No. I've never been there, but I've heard of it.'

'You'd like it. Very beautiful place. Very spiritual.' Bunty pauses, regarding Dominic. 'What is your name?'

'Dominic. Dominic Wheatcroft. No alliteration there, I'm afraid.' Bunty laughs and shakes Dominic's hand vigorously. Dominic takes an instant liking to this little smiling man and is confident that he can trust him. He feels his loneliness and sense of isolation start to drain away. 'Are you a disciple of Sri Ramana Maharshi?'

'Oh no, Dominic. The Bhagwan wasn't my guru. He died before my time. My master's in Rajasthan. His ashram is just outside the Pink City.'

'May I ask his name?'

'Of course. Of course.' Bunty closes his eyes and is silent for a few seconds. When he opens them again they are shining. 'He is called Swami Satchit Ananda.'

Dominic smiles. 'I've not heard of him.'

'And why should you? He doesn't advertise himself and we're encouraged to keep our discipleship to ourselves.'

'You were happy though to tell *me* his name.'

'That's true, Dominic. It's because he wants you to know his name.'

'Why?'

'I don't know, brother. But he knows best.' He points at the ceiling.

They sit in silence for a while, nursing their new-found friendship. Dominic speaks first. 'So, may I ask why you're traveling all this way to the Sri Ramana Maharshi Ashram?'

'It's seva, Dominic. I'm doing this for my master. It's my service and I do it willingly.'

'What is it you're doing for him?'

'I am carrying in this bag some documents for the ashram management.' He taps the bag that hangs around his neck and looks up at the huge clock on the opposite wall. 'Come, brother, there's still time for us to eat before the departure of our train.'

The train arrives at Tiruvannamalai station in the early hours of the morning. Although Dominic had managed a few hours sleep he's still exhausted and disorientated. Bunty helps him off the train and onto the platform where they're met by a representative from the ashram. Few words are spoken as they're led to an Ambassador saloon. The air is thick with fragrant wood smoke and incense. Dominic is beginning to warm to India. They drive in silence. Bunty is lost in his own thoughts and Dominic watches the world go by.

As they approach Mount Arunachala Bunty says, 'Over the centuries, many saints and sages have been drawn to this hill. In the 15th century, Guhai Namasivaya, Guru Namasivaya and Virupaksha Deva came from Karnataka and settled on Arunachala. Saint Namasivaya lived in one of Arunachala's caves, which is still known by his name. Also Virupaksha Deva lived in an OM-shaped cave higher up on the hill and this cave still bears his name. You'll find it on the southeast slope of Arunachala. This was the very cave that Sri Ramana Maharshi lived in from 1899 to 1916.'

They pass under an arch, which displays the name of the ashram, and park in a large open courtyard flanked by shady trees. As they get out of the car Bunty says, 'That tree is an Iluppai, Dominic, and it's over 400 years old.'

'It's certainly beautiful.'

'It's also useful. We call it The Indian Butter Tree because of its yellow fruit, which we use for the care of the skin and for manufacturing soaps and detergents. Also some use it as a vegetable butter. So it's a wonderful tree.'

'I'm impressed.'

Bunty bows slightly. 'Follow me please and we'll sign you in and then they'll take you to your guest room while I deliver these documents.'

Once Dominic has signed in he's taken to his room. It's clean and simple. It has a bathroom, an overhead fan and screened windows.

Over the next two days he explores the ashram. He particularly likes the small Nirvana room where Ramana Maharshi spent his last days. He spends time in the library reading the *Book of Mirdad* by Mikhail Naimy, which Bunty has recommended to him. He buys a copy of a new book on Ramana Maharshi by Arthur Osborne from the bookstall.

He writes a letter to Lauren, telling her that all is well and that he's arrived safely at the first ashram he intends to visit. He quotes from the Mikhael Naimy's *The Book of Mirdad*:

Much like an eagle hatched by a backyard hen and cooped up with the brood of that hen is the man with the Great Nostalgia among his fellow-men. His brother-chicks and mother-hen would have the young eagle as one of them, possessed of their nature and habits, and living as they live; and he would have them like himself - dreamers of the freer air and skies illimitable. But soon he finds him a stranger and a pariah among them; and he is pecked by all - even his mother. But the call of the summits is loud in his blood and the stench of the coop exasperating to his nose. Yet does he suffer it all in silence until he is fully fledged. And then he mounts the air and casts a loving farewell look upon his erstwhile brothers and their mother, who merrily cackle on as they dig in the earth for more seeds and worms.

Then he adds 'I don't count you among those brother-chicks, Lauren. I believe that you, like me, have that Great Nostalgia though. Am I right?'

Bunty returns to Dominic's room. 'I've come to say goodbye and to give you the address of my master.' He hands a slip of paper to Dominic. 'You remember his name?'

Uhh. Honestly…no I don't.'

'It is Swami Satchit Ananda. I can assure you he'll be pleased to see you and will want to share his hospitality with you.'

'Thank you, Bunty. Will I see you there?'

'If I'm not doing my traveling seva - then I'll be there. It's my home.'

'I hope you're there.'

'You will come then?'

'Yes, I think I will. But first I'll visit Meher Baba.'

'Ah, Meher Baba! A great man, a great saint. You'll receive much benefit from being in his presence.'

'Is it true he doesn't speak?'

'That's so. He has kept silent since 1925.'

'So how does he communicate with his followers?'

'He uses an alphabet board and hand gestures. It's not hard to understand him. He's spent many years in seclusion, but he's traveled widely too, holding gatherings. He's known for his charity, working with lepers, the poor and even the mentally ill.'

'Is it worth my while to visit him?'

'Oh, yes. It is. But may I ask you if you gained anything from your visit to this place?'

'Not really. D'you mean gained some insight…spiritual?'

'Yes.'

'No. But I've enjoyed my time here. I like the atmosphere and I'd read about Ramana

Maharshi and wanted to...walk on the same ground, touch the same walls.'

'Where did you read about him, Dominic?'

'In Somerset Maugham's *The Razor's Edge*.'

'Ah yes. I too have read that book.'

'You have?'

'Of course. You sound surprised. Why?'

'No, no. I'm not surprised that *you've* read it, Bunty. I didn't mean to be rude. It's just that most people I know haven't.'

Bunty smiles. 'You weren't rude.'

'Good.' Dominic looks relieved. They walk out onto the small verandah. 'What d'you think I'll learn from Meher Baba?'

'That, my friend, depends on what you're looking for. Can you put that into words?'

'Knowledge.   Insight.   Wisdom...an explanation.'

'Well, my friend you're certainly aiming high.' He laughs. 'And that's a good thing.'

'What will Meher Baba offer me?'

'The same as all true saints offer.'

'And what's that?'

'He'll tell you that at the deepest level of Spirit we know that we all came from the same source, at the same time, by the same word of creation that created all.' Bunty pauses, taking Dominic's arm, he leads him out into the garden. 'It's clear to me that the primary motivation and energy behind this creation can be narrowed down to one single word – Love. Love is the cement that binds all together. Love is the primal force in the universe. Before we came into this world we existed together in the potentiality of love in the glorious love of God for eternity. We can remember at the level of the soul how we felt when we were aware of our oneness with all that is. These moments of transcending the physical bonds of Earth are just a glimpse of the unimaginable bliss and feeling of all-encompassing love that we'll feel when our souls finally complete their journey on Earth and rise up again into eternity.'

'That's quite a speech, Bunty.'

'It's my, how you say, set piece.' He smiles.

'Well, it's good. I like it.'

'Thank you.' He turns to go then stops abruptly. 'My master's name, as I have told you, is Satchit Ananda. Do you know what that means, Dominic?'

'No.'

'It means truth, knowledge, bliss. The truth consciousness bliss of the Self. And that is really, as they say, my parting shot!' He laughs, shakes Dominic's hand, then turns and walks away across the courtyard. Dominic watches the rotund little man disappear and leans back against the wall. He's filled with a deep sadness and an overwhelming desolation. Loneliness consumes him. His mouth pulls down at the corners and he sobs, thinking of Lauren and his mother how he much misses them and home.

Chapter Fifteen
Living at Home

'Greater love hath no man than this, that he lay down his life for his friends.'
John 15. 13

It's a cold morning in Cambridge. Lauren sits in the garden on a bench surrounded by a rich and colourful carpet of fallen leaves. The sun shines brightly, but it's cold. She is reading Dominic's letter for the umpteenth time. She has also read *The Razor's Edge* and been deeply affected by it, trying to imagine Dominic in India. She found a copy of Maugham's diary in the reference library and copied out this passage from his meeting with Ramana Maharshi:

He bore himself with naturalness and at the same time with dignity. His mien was cheerful smiling, polite; he did not give the impression of a scholar, but rather of a sweet-natured old peasant. He uttered a few words of cordial greeting and sat on the ground not far from the pallet on which I lay. After the first few minutes during which his eyes with a gentle benignity rested on my face, he ceased to look at me, but, with a sidelong stare of peculiar fixity, gazed, as it were, over my shoulder. His body was absolutely still, but now and then one of his feet tapped lightly on the earthen floor. He remained thus, motionless, for perhaps a quarter of an hour; and they told me later that he was concentrating in meditation upon me. Then he came to, if I may so put it, and again looked at me. He asked me if I wished to say anything to him, or ask any question. I was feeling weak and ill and said so; whereupon he smiled and said, 'Silence is also conversation'. He turned his head away slightly and resumed his concentrated meditation, again looking, as it were, over my shoulder. No one said a word; the other persons in the hut, standing by the door, kept their eyes riveted upon him. After another quarter of an hour, he got up bowed, smiled farewell, and slowly, leaning on his stick, followed by his disciples, he limped out of the hut.

This helps her to get a picture of the ashram. She's taken out an illustrated guide to India and she opens that again. She studies the pictures intently, but they do nothing to convey the heat and the atmosphere. Nonetheless she shudders and, gathering her coat around her, she goes into the house. As she crosses the hall Freddy comes out his study, carrying a coffee mug.

'Good morning, Lauren.'

'Hello, Daddy. I was reading in the garden, but it was too cold. Autumn's beautiful, but summer's better.'

'Though, as you say, autumn has its charm.' He glances at the book in Lauren's hand. 'What's that you're reading?'

'It's an illustrated guide.'

'For what?'

'India.'

'Not thinking of going to join your brother, are you?' He half jokes.

'Oh, no! I just wanted to get an idea of what Dom might be experiencing.'

'And?'

'It looks thrilling. Different from here...Cambridge. I still can't imagine what it must be like to actually be there.'

'I'm sure he'll tell you all when he gets home. Oh, by the way, when's he due back?'

'Not for over two weeks.'

'Can't wait,' he sneers.

'Oh, Daddy.'

'Sorry, Lauren. You know how I feel about his trip and all that mystical mumbo-jumbo.'

'Judge not that ye be not judged.'

'I beg your pardon, young lady.'

'Sorry, Daddy, but I do feel you could be more open-minded and supportive.'

'Do you, indeed!' Freddy is irritated and Lauren is starting to lose her temper.

'I'm going out,' Lauren responds, just keeping herself in check. 'I'll be back tonight.' She turns away from her father and runs up the stairs.

'You're not to take the Mini. Is that clear?'

Lauren turns and glares at Freddy. 'That's

clear.' She is almost in tears.

Richard is rolling a joint. He's wearing skin-tight jeans and a white t-shirt, singing along with Gene Vincent's *Be-Bop-A-Lula*. There's a new painting on the easel. Lauren watches him work. She has regained her poise and looks at ease. 'I had a letter from Dominic. It sounds like he's having quite a time.'

'Where is he?'

'Place called Arunachala. It's some kind of sacred mountain.'

'Whereabouts?'

'Southern India. Near Madras, I think.'

'What's he doing there?'

'Well, it's a kind of a pilgrimage for him. It's a place he read about in a book by Somerset Maugham.'

'Called?'

'The Razor's Edge.'

'Good title.' Richard lights the joint, takes a deep drag and hands it to Lauren.

'Good book.' Lauren smokes the joint with some elegance.

Richard smiles at her. 'You've read it?'

'Course.' She hands the joint back to Richard.

'Nice grass.'

'Phew! You could say.'

'D'you want to go for a walk?'

'Maybe.'

'Well, d'you want to?'

'I'm so stoned, Richard, I really don't mind what we do.'

'Let's walk then.'

Lauren stands and goes over to the easel. 'What's it called...this painting?'

'Don't know yet. Maybe I should call it Pilgrimage.' They both laugh.

They are strolling down Brooklands Avenue towards Coe Fen. Their breath hangs frostily in the cold night air. Richard has his arm around Lauren. She snuggles up to him.

'We keep getting strange phone calls.'

'Strange? Why?'

'When you pick up the phone there's no one there - just organ music. Bach's Prelude & Fugue.'

'That's cool.'

'Cool?'

'That's what they say now when something's good.'

'There nothing good about the calls, Richard. They're weird. Disconcerting too.'

'But the music's good.'

'I agree. But cool is a funny was to describe something you like. Sounds kind of cold, icy.'

'Not cold, not icy. Cool.'

They laugh again as they reach Trumpington Road. Richard takes her hand as they cross onto the fen. A thin mist swirls across the grass, rolling up from the river. Lauren stops and holds

Richard back.

'You should paint this. It's ethereal.'

'I could.'

'Could you?'

'Well, maybe not. It would be difficult for me. I find abstracts easier. I admit it would be a real challenge for me.'

'Be challenged then. For *me*.'

'For you, Lauren, maybe I'll try.'

She kisses him gently and pulls back to look at him. 'I'm going to see my grandmother tomorrow.'

'In the hospital?'

'Of course. Yes. D'you want to come with me?'

'D'you want me to come?'

'Yes. I wouldn't ask if I didn't want. I could do with your support. It's a frightening place.'

'I don't know much about mental illness.'

'But you guessed she was a manic-depressive.'

'It was just a lucky guess.'

'Not lucky for her.'

'No, but the guess was.'

They walk on through the mist towards the river and go onto the bridge. Richard points upstream. 'You know someone drowned over there last summer. He dived in and got caught up in the weeds and no one noticed he was in trouble.'

'I'd hate to drown.'

'Better than being burnt to death, don't you

think?'

'Well, yes. But isn't it strange that we all have to die?'

'How d'you mean strange?'

'Well, you know…we don't have any idea what happens to us when we die.'

'It's just the end. Lights out.'

'I can't believe it's like that. Just fini. I mean what about the immortal soul?'

'What's that - the immortal soul?'

'I don't know *what* it is, Richard, but it's what they talk about in religion. In the Bible.'

'Religion pisses me off.'

'Why.'

'Causes war and bigotry and fear.'

'That's true, but there might be something true behind what the books say.'

'Books are just books. What you need to do is speak to the people who actually wrote 'em.'

'Yeah, fine, if you could. And I guess that's why Dominic's gone to India…to speak to a real live mystic. You know, get it from the horse's mouth.'

'As they say.' Richard points across the fen where three horses are grazing. 'Might just as well ask them in my opinion.'

'And it's only your opinion.'

'Fair enough.' Richard takes another joint and a lighter out of his denim jacket pocket. He lights up, leaning back on the side of the bridge. 'But again, who can say? I mean who can remember what it was like before they were born?'

Lauren shrugs.

'And has anyone to your knowledge come back from being dead to tell us what goes on?'

'Not that I know of, but that doesn't mean you should discount the possibility that life, awareness, call it what you will, dies when the body dies.'

'Well, I won't then. But this discussion isn't going anywhere, is it?'

'You're right. Let's walk on.' They take the path along the riverbank towards Cambridge.

'Hey, Lauren, you know what?'

'What?'

'It's Wednesday.'

'And?'

'If it's Wednesday it's Miller's Jazz Club. Ever been?'

'No. Where is it?'

'Over the record shop in Sidney Street and it's really good. Modern jazz. I mean it's not trad jazz.'

'Dominic likes that kind of music - free-form improvisation...'

'Just so.'

Chapter Sixteen
Two Steps Forward and One Step Back

Lauren and Richard sit in the hospital reception like two lost souls, waiting to be taken up to see Grace. Richard squirms in his seat and would very much prefer to be somewhere else. Anywhere else. Because Lauren knows what to expect she's taking it more in her stride. She holds Richard's hand and squeezes it encouragingly. A middle-aged couple cross reception on their way to the main door. They both look distressed. The woman's high heels clack loudly on the parquet floor. Richard welcomes the distraction. The same dour receptionist, pretending to read, watches them over his newspaper. Richard catches his eye and winks. The man looks away without a smile. Bohm's secretary comes down the stairs with measured steps. Lauren stands to meet her.

'Dr. Bohm will see you now. Please follow me.'

Richard and Lauren tail meekly behind her as she leads them to Bohm's office. He meets them at the door and shows them in.

'Good morning, Miss Wheatcroft and...?'

'This is Richard Bannerman, Dr Bohm. He's a

friend of mine.'

Bohm shakes Richard's hand. 'Pleased to meet you.'

'Likewise.'

'Have a seat.' Bohm points to two empty chairs. 'You'll find your grandmother in a very different and more agreeable state than when you were last here I'm pleased to say.'

Lauren and Richard sit down. 'That's good news. I don't think I could really bear to see her again like she was.'

'I have to remind you, Miss Wheatcroft, that Grace isn't well. You'll find her subdued now. Morose. She's in the depressed phase of her cycle. She is, how you say, withdrawn and uncommunicative. Having said that, I'm very glad that you - both of you - have come to visit her. It's important that deep down she knows that someone cares for her and that she's not forgotten.' Bohm moves to his desk and sits on the corner.

Richard has been listening intently and asks, 'How do we…behave with her? I mean, what do we say to her?'

'It's not easy for me to give you clear and sensible guidance, Mr Bannerman. We're all human and yet, at the risk of stating the obvious, we're all different. I would suggest that you play it by ear and take her as you find her. Be kind, be friendly and please don't get angry with her or show your frustration. That is, if you are frustrated by her, which I hope you won't be.'

He makes an open hand gesture. 'Are you ready to see her now?'

'Yes, I think so. Richard?'

'Yes. As ready as I'll ever be.'

'I'll take you to her room, but this time I won't come in with you if you're happy with that.'

'I'm OK with that and I've Richard to support me this time.' She takes Richard's hand and they follow Bohm out of his office to Grace's room. 'This time she's not in a secure unit. She's not a danger to herself or others.'

Richard looks pale and nervous.

Lauren sees this. 'It's OK, Richard. Really don't worry. They know what they're doing.'

'Do they?'

Bohm turns to Richard and replies decisively. 'Yes, Mr Bannerman. I believe we do.' He opens the door for them then steps back and leaves.

'Spooky guy.'

'I think he's OK. He's been very supportive.' Lauren steps into Grace's room and Richard follows. He's still uneasy.

Grace is lying on her bed with her back turned to the door. She is facing a window, which looks out the park. It is barred. Richard glances at the trees, not wanting to look at Grace. Lauren moves towards her grandmother and goes round the bed to stand in front of her. Grace raises her head and looks at her. 'Lauren?'

'Yes, Grandma, it's me.'

Grace stares at her, trying hard to focus. 'Have I seen you recently?'

'Yes, I was here a few weeks ago.'

'Was I...?'

'You were upset, Grandma.'

Grace looks at her, struggling to find words to express herself. 'Why am I here? Why aren't I at home?' She sobs. 'I want to go home.'

Lauren glances at Richard. He's still looking out of the window. He clearly doesn't want to be in this room, with this woman. Lauren goes to stand beside him and puts her arm round him. 'This is my friend, Richard, Grandma. He wanted to come with me to see you.'

Grace glances at Richard. She looks confused. 'Do I...should I know him.'

'No, you don't know him. I only met him a little while ago.'

Grace closes her eyes. She slumps. 'I...'

'Don't worry, Grandma.'

Richard and Lauren look out over the park.

'Can we go now?' He glances back at Grace.

'Soon.' She walks to the bed and sits on the edge of it. She takes her grandmother's hand and squeezes it gently. Grace looks up at her. There is a far-away look in her eyes. They are cloudy and dim. Lauren feels lost and frustrated that there is nothing she can do to help, to change the way things are. Life appears suddenly too difficult and overwhelming for her. She wants to go, to smoke another joint and forget this sad old lady.

'Let's go, Richard. There's nothing...' She stands and walks to the door. 'Goodbye, Grandma. I'm sorry...I...'

Grace doesn't respond. She stares blankly at the window. Richard and Lauren leave the room, closing the door quietly behind them. Richard sighs. Lauren glances at him. She is almost in tears. They walk off down the corridor, descend the stairs and go out into the park. It feels like the sun is struggling to find a gap in the clouds. The wind lifts their hair and their coats billow. Lauren pulls Richard to her and kisses him.

'She must've been very beautiful once.'

'She was...you can see that?'

'Oh, yes. She looks like you, Lauren.'

'You're too kind, gallant sir knight...to both of us.'

'But you are very beautiful. And not just physically either. Your spirit is beautiful too.'

They walk on hand in hand to a seat under a gigantic ewe.

Lauren stares up into deep tangle of branches. 'This tree is ancient. It was here before we were born - even thought of - and it'll be here long after we're gone.'

They sit in silence. 'What'll become of your

grandmother?'

'Bohm says she's not likely to ever be capable of living out in the world.'

Richard shivers. 'A fate worse than death.'

'Oh, I wouldn't say that…go that far.'

'I would. I don't like this place. It doesn't feel good.'

'What d'you expect? It's a mental hospital for God's sake!'

'I know it's a hospital, but why does it have to be so grim? Why do these people have to be locked away?'

'Don't be stupid, Richard.'

He is taken aback by her vehement response.

'What would you do? Let them run wild in the world?'

'Yes.'

'You can't mean that. You're being stupid.'

'And you're being a boring conformist.'

'Am I?'

'Yes.'

Lauren stands. She wants to hit him. All her rage and despair rush to the surface. She needs to smash him, smash herself apart. She is shaking. 'Fuck you, Richard.'

'Fuck you too.' He turns his back on her and she strides off across the park and out onto the road. She reaches a bus stop just as one turns up. She climbs aboard without looking back and slumps into a seat. She is ashen and still shaking.

Richard is devastated, realizing too late what he's done. He runs after her, but he's way too late. Appropriately it starts to rain.

Chapter Seventeen
Meher Baba

'A lot of power comes with being a mystic. They can be corrupted by money and sex.'
Andrew Rawlinson

Dominic retraces his path back across India to Bombay. The journey is uneventful, but hot and fraught with frustrations. Apart from meeting Bunty he feels that the journey so far has been fruitless and is not going anywhere. The fact that he's heading back the way he came doesn't help, but he has to go to Bombay to take a bus to Ahmednagar.

The Bombay bus station is hot and chaotic, but Dominic eventually manages to book a seat with a company called Royal Travels. The bus is due to leave in 15 minutes. It only remains to find the departure point, which turns out to be far harder than he could have imagined. But he finds the coach with two minutes to spare and gets on board, having watched his rucksack heaved onto the roof. It looks precarious. He has no choice but to trust in the rack's ability to hold onto his bag. His reservation turns out to be meaningless and he has to squeeze into a seat by a window next to a woman of enormous proportions, but she is cheerful and smiles benignly at Dominic as he shoe-horns his way in. The coach continues to fill for the next 10 minutes. There seems to be no limit to the number of people the driver is prepared to take on board. Dominic feels blessed to have found a seat. It's a 12 hour journey. The bus is like a furnace so he is relieved when the diesel engine belches and sparks into life and it lumbers out of the terminal. They swerve and weave through the Bombay streets, but eventually make it into open country. Dominic is grateful for the small breeze that finds its way in through the open windows. For all that the stench of human and animal bodies is potent and takes some getting used to.

He dozes fitfully until the bus makes a scheduled stop to refuel. The passengers scramble off to buy water, food and relieve themselves by the side of the road. Dominic takes his chances with the rest. The woman beside him is staying on board and promises to hold his seat for him. There is a God! He buys water, two bottles of *Thumbs-up*, some cooked food and has a pee in a small glade of sad, dust-covered trees. Crows wheel overhead crying with a fierce, ugly sound like sheets of corrugated iron being rubbed to together. Dominic's skin prickles and he recoils from the sound.

He has an abrupt memory of a disturbing

conversation he had with Lauren when she told him about the mysterious phone call with only the sound of the Bach Prelude & Fugue. It disturbed him then and it disturbs him again now but he's not sure why. He does his best to put it out of his mind and returns to the bus. He can see that his rucksack is still on the roof and breathes a sigh of relief, half expecting it to have fallen off or to have been stolen. He clambers aboard, finds that his seat has been kept for him, squeezes in and sits down. The air is thick and hot. His throat is dry and rasping from the dust thrown up by the brightly decorated passing lorries. He is sweating and waits impatiently for the bus to get going. It becomes apparent that the woman in the seat next to him doesn't want to open a conversation. She sleeps through most of the journey. Dominic is grateful for this even though her head constantly flops onto his chest, which he considers a small price for her silence. His thoughts are still focused on home and on what he might expect when he meets Meher Baba.

He recalls that in 1954 Meher Baba declared publicly that he was the Avatar of the age. Dominic feels that this is something of a grand claim, given the number of gurus to be found in India. It smacks of self-aggrandizement, but he tries to keep an open mind and not rush into making a judgment of his own until he has met the man face-to-face.

Having avoided a dozen potentially fatal collisions they finally roll into Ahmednagar bus terminal. They are three hours late, which Dominic takes as something approaching a miracle. He stumbles off the bus, collects his rucksack and finds a taxi rank. He's shattered. Hot and dirty. The road is dusty and swollen with cars, lorries, donkey carts and cyclists, all fighting for space. They pass several sugar factories bathed in steam. They don't smell good.

The taxi drops Dominic at the gate of the ashram. He walks in unsteadily feeling the worse for wear. He is greeted by an elegant Indian woman. She leads him to a small room. It is clean and tidy. He asks her when it will be possible for him to have an audience with Meher Baba. She considers this for a few seconds then tells him that she can probably arrange this for later in the day and that she will send a messenger to find him half an hour before he can see the guru. She tells him that refreshments will be served for him in the dining hall when he's ready and that board and lodging will cost him just five hundred rupees a day. She bows and leaves and Dominic throws himself on the bed. He contemplates the ceiling, wondering why he is here in this place.

An hour later after he has washed and changed he makes his way to the dining room, which is clearly signposted. The room is large and simply furnished with basic tables and chairs. He makes his way to a long table covered with a clean white cloth. There is a flask. He pours out a mug of milky chai and is struck by its pleasant spicy aroma. There is also a plate of sandwiches and Dominic takes one. He sits down at the nearest table and is joined by a tall, blonde man with long curly hair.

'Hi, I'm Marco.' He offers his hand to Dominic. They shake.

'Dominic.' He looks at the man and asks, 'Are you American?'

'Yup. From Petaluma. Been there?'

'No, no. I've never been to the USA.'

'First time in India?'

'Yes.' Dominic sips his tea.

'What d'you think of it?'

Dominic considers the question. 'Takes a bit of getting used to.'

'Doesn't it just!'

'It's all overwhelming. The heat. The noise. The traffic!'

'Yeah, the roads sure are scary. You travelin' alone?'

'Yes I am. Are you?'

'No. I'm here with a couple of friends. Safety in numbers.' Marco regards Dominic. 'You're English?

'Yes. I am. From Cambridge.'

'I like your accent. Sounds...cool. Real old world.'

Dominic smiles and bites into his sandwich. By the colour of the filling it is clearly supposed to be strawberry, but has a synthetic, plastic flavor.

'Not so good, huh?'

'Pretty disgusting, but I'm hungry so I'll eat it.'

'Strange, ain't it, when they could make it with real fruit.'

'It is. I had one of those *Thumbs Up* on the bus over here and that was totally awful. Synthetic and sugary.'

'You had one of those! You're a brave man. Your teeth'll most likely fall out. Indians sure like sugar and toxic additives. You noticed that?'

'I'm beginning to.'

'We're going out later. Wanna join us?'

'Where?'

'Take a car into town. Sometimes it can get oppressive in this place.'

'How long have you been here?'

''Bout a week.'

'What do you think of Meher Baba?'

'Oh, he's a cool dude.'

'Cool?'

'He don't speak.'

'Is that cool?'

'Sure is. We all talk too much. Yak, yak, yak. Don't'cha think?'

'Never really thought about it, Marco.'

'Well, now's your chance while you're here with Baba.' Marco stands. He taps Dominic on the shoulder. 'You goin' to come with us?'

'Uhmm…not tonight. Too tired.'

'OK. Say, I can't believe you came over here by bus.'

'Didn't you?'

'No way. We hired a car and driver. It's real cheap. 'Specially if there's three a' ya.'

'Wish I'd thought of that.'

'Live and learn, man. Live and learn.' Marco leaves Dominic and walks out of the dining room.

Dominic chokes down his sandwich and washes it away with chai. He picks up a packet of sweet biscuits. He walks out into the burning sunlight and munches on them as he strolls around the compound. He finds the atmosphere here very different from Ramana Maharshi's ashram. He realizes that this is because there's a living guru present. There's an almost humming silence. There are some western visitors sitting quietly reading in wicker chairs on the manicured lawns. Most ignore him. Some look at him and wave or smile. Dominic likes the atmosphere and looks forward to his meeting with the guru. He goes back to his room to rest.

The call comes from Meher Baba about an hour later. Dominic silently follows the same elegant woman through the ashram. He is led into a

140

modestly furnished waiting room and he takes a chair. She leaves, returning five minutes later. She leads Dominic into the audience room then sits next to Meher Baba. He is seated cross-legged on small raised dais. He smiles benignly at Dominic and indicates that he should sit on the floor in front of him. Baba regards him intently for a minute, then picks up an alphabet board. He spells out: 'I hope you are comfortable here and your needs have been attended to.' It is a slow and laborious procedure, but it allows Dominic time to study the guru.

Dominic replies, 'Yes, Sir. Thank you.'

Baba spells out: 'Have you any questions?'

Dominic thinks about this carefully then says, 'Yes. How would you...what is your message, your advice for me?'

Baba spells out: 'Don't worry. Be happy.' He smiles benignly.

Dominic smiles in return.

Baba spells out: 'All things are as they should be. Have no fear.' He looks long and hard at Dominic then puts his palms together like a Christian in prayer and bows his head 'Namaste'. Dominic follows suit, understanding that the audience is over. He stands and the Indian woman leads him from the room, closing the door behind her.

Outside she turns to him and, without expression says, 'Dinner is at six. You will hear

a bell. Please make your way to the dining room.'
She bows with the same hand gesture, which
Dominic reciprocates. She turns and walks away
without another word. Dominic admires her
poise and graceful movements.

As much as he's been inspired by the audience
and the guru's benevolence he feels dissatisfied.
He walk slowly back to his room, picks up *The
Razor's Edge*. Taking a chair outside, he sits on it
under a tree. He doesn't open the book
immediately, but ponders the meaning and
import of Baba's simple message. He finds it
challenging. 'Don't worry. Be happy.' Easier said
than done, he thinks. He dozes and is woken by
the dinner bell. He returns to his room with the
chair and his book. He washes then strolls over
to the dining room. Inside it is humming with
the murmur of quiet chatter. There are about 30
other guests. Some collecting their food, others
already eating. Dominic picks up a plate and
stands in line. One of the guests in the queue
ahead of him, a plainly attired woman in a
simple white dress turns to him and asks, 'How
d'you like the food here?' Dominic doesn't
recognize her accent, but thinks it must be either
Swedish or Danish.

'I haven't eaten here yet. Well, only the tea-time
sandwich and to be honest I didn't think much
of the jam.'

She throws back her head and laughs. 'Yes.

Horrible that Indian so-called jam. Have you been long on the vegetarian diet?'

'No, not really. Only since I arrived in India a few days ago. I know it's a prerequisite of the spiritual path here and I thought it would be safer anyway in India.'

'Prerequisite? I don't know this word.'

'Requirement.'

'Ah yes.' She ponders. 'It is.'

They stand in silence for a few seconds as the queue inches forward.

'Have you met Baba yet?'

'Yes, I had brief audience this afternoon.'

'And how did you find it - him?'

'Short and sweet I'd say.'

She laughs. 'He's certainly sweet."

'Is he your guru?'

'Oh, yes. I've been his disciple for over ten years. He changed my life. He saved my life.'

'How's that.'

'I was lost and confused. I felt my life was going nowhere. I think you say in English.'

'Yes. We say that. And I know the feeling.'

'He gave me back my confidence and my direction.'

'My sense of direction.'

Ah, yes. Just so.'

'What's your name?'

'Dorthe. Dorthe Wallander.'

'And where're you from, Dorthe?'

'Can't you tell?'

'Honestly no. I can't.'

'Sweden. And you are?'

'Dominic Wheatcroft. And I'm from England.'

'I guessed that Dominic.'

Dorthe reaches the head of the queue and holds out her plate while it is filled. As she leaves the line Dominic does the same and follows her to a table by the window. They sit opposite each other. He finds that he is very hungry and eats with great pleasure. He stops for a moment and looks up at Dorthe. 'This food is excellent. Truly delicious.'

'It is, isn't it? Most of it's grown here in the gardens and it's all given to us for very little. Baba is very generous with his wisdom and his love.'

'Apart from the charge, don't you have to give something else in return?'

'Yes, of course.'

'What?'

'Our love first, then if you care to, you can do seva - work in the garden, housekeeping - that kind of thing.'

'And what about money? Where does that come from? I mean, how does the ashram pay its way if we're only giving five hundred rupees a day?'

'I don't know everything about it, Dominic, but we're encouraged to give whatever we can

144

afford.'

Dominic thinks about this and they eat in silence. The food is excellent, wholesome and well-prepared.

Dorthe takes her empty plate to the kitchen. Dominic sits where he is, looking out of the window. His eye is caught by a tribe of monkeys as the swing into the compound. They settle in a tree and go about stripping it bare. He watches them as they eat and scramble squealing from branch to branch. When not one leaf remains they leave, whooping into the distance. No one has attempted to stop them or drive them away. Dominic is impressed and, at the same time, puzzled. He expected India to be a land of mystery. That's what he read in the travel brochures at home. But it also had turned out to be a land of extremes and paradox.

The following day Dominic goes to the morning meeting. Sitting next to Meher Baba, a middle-aged man in white pyjamas gives a talk on Baba's philosophy. The essential message he gives is that at the core of the teachings is the importance of daily meditation as instructed by Baba. He also stresses the importance of putting trust in Baba's ability to help the aspiring mystic on his inner journey, asserting that Baba has completed the inner journey back to the source of consciousness and is enlightened. Baba smiles encouragingly throughout the discourse. As they file out of the meeting hall Marco comes up to Dominic.

'Wanna come out tonight? We got a car picking us up the main gate at seven.'

Dominic accepts the invitation this time, fancying a break from the rarefied somewhat cloying and stifling atmosphere of the ashram.

'Yes, I'll join you tonight if that's OK.'

'Sure, man. You're welcome. See you later.' He strolls off to join a couple, who are talking on the lawn. Dominic goes back to his room thinking over the talk. He is not convinced that Meher Baba is what his disciples believe him to be. He realizes that he has no way of telling if the guru is an enlightened being or not.

Just before seven Dominic is at the gate. The sun is setting. The light dances in the dust and smoke. The white painted buildings of the ashram glow like gold.

Marco arrives at the gate with two other people. A man and a woman. 'Hi Dominic. This is Jessica and Troy.'

They shake hands. Jessica is very thin and flat-chested with a long face, reminding Dominic of a horse. Troy is very different. He is short and plump with a round, cheery face. The taxi arrives and the four of them clamber in.

The drive into the city is hair-raising. The traffic is wildly uncontrolled. Cars, buses and trucks swerve and weave as if rules of the road are only there to be ignored or disobeyed. Dominic sees potential collisions wherever he looks and is amazed. Ahmednagar is noisy and dirty and smells of factory effluent. Marco leans across the front seat to talk to the driver. 'Take us to the fort, please.'

The driver makes an abrupt right turn throwing the three passengers across the back seat of the cab and into a heap on the driver's side.

'Holy shit!' Troy exclaims from the bottom of the pile of bodies.

They spread out again across the back seat. The plastic is hot - wet and slippery with sweat. Jessica is miserable. Dominic looks away and out of the window. The sight that greets him is neither attractive nor reassuring. Beggars and whole families, camped out in makeshift homes, fill the litter-strewn pavements. Men pull carts precariously swollen with merchandise along the pot-holed road, bouncing and swaying from side to side. For a minute Dominic wishes with all his heart that he was somewhere else as the taxi pulls up abruptly by the small park in front of the fort. Marco pays the driver and they get out. They stand and look up at the fort. A massive curtain wall, built of cut stone masonry, rises above them. They cross the moat, which surrounds the fort. It's in good condition. It's under military control so it's well maintained. Lush green babul trees hang down from the walls on either side of the main gate. A sculpture of a tiger trampling on an elephant looms over them. The stone path is hot under their feet, burning through the soles of their shoes. They climb up onto the ramparts and Marco breaks out a joint and some matches from his shoulder bag. He lights up and sits on the wall. He takes a drag then passes the joint to Troy, who puffs it and hands it on to Jessica. Dominic watches them unsure how he will react when it's his turn. In any event he takes the joint and draws in the smoke, holding it in his lungs just as Richard had instructed Lauren to do.

He leans back against the castle wall as he's infused with a warm, sensuous glow, which spreads out around his body. He closes his eyes. There is a faint ringing in him and, coupled with this, an enhancement of the sounds around him. He opens his eyes. The light is almost blinding. The world has become, lighter, brighter and more meaningful. He is filled with wonder and an overwhelming feeling of love. He glances at Marco, who's watching him.

'You OK, Dom?'

'Yeah, yeah. I'm...cool.' His voice sounds lower, slower, his words more loaded with meaning and import.

'Thought you might be having a bad trip.'

'Why?'

'Well you looked kinda out of it.'

'I am out of it.'

Jessica stands. She looks at Dominic. 'You look pretty stoned.'

Dominic considers the meaning of this. 'Yes, I'd say I am pretty stoned. Very stoned in fact. I've never felt as...like this before.'

Troy turns to him. 'Well, you ain't tried acid then I guess.'

'Acid?'

' Lysergic Acid Diethylamide 25.'

'I'm none the wiser.'

'The ultimate trip. Total ego loss. From here to infinity, my man.'

'Back in April '43 a Swiss chemist called Albert Hoffman was working at Sandoz Labs with ergot, synthesizing LSD and he got some on his fingertips and...'

Marco takes up the story. 'He had the trip of lifetime and when he came down he knew he'd really hit on something.'

Jessica looks up into the branches of the babul tree. 'I guess it's what brought us all to India.'

'How d'you mean?'

'I mean we want to be in that state of awareness the whole time and you just can't go on taking acid every day. Too exhausting. And anyway after a while the body adjusts and you don't get completely out there.'

Marco goes to stand in front of Dominic. 'We wanted a way to get there naturally and we believe that meditation can get us there.'

'By Baba's method?'

'No. I think Baba's a bit of a fraud. A victim of his own self-belief. He's got a bit carried away with all that Avatar of the age stuff. I think his power's corrupted him. When you set yourself up as God incarnate, you lose humility and your sense of perspective. His followers in the beginning were Indian. They tend to be easily influenced - just believing rather than questioning.'

Troy chimes in, 'Look at some of his western followers too. They're so far up their own arses they've lost any discrimination. They're so gone on Baba they've lost touch with reality. Off with the fairies.'

Marco walks on through the gate. 'Let's go look round before it's too dark to see.' The other three follow him.

Next morning Dominic feels fine. Bright and alert with no hangover. He's relieved. As he's finishing his breakfast he's handed a letter. He opens it eagerly, recognizing the writing immediately. It's from Lauren. He goes out into the garden and sits on the grass under the shade of a eucalyptus tree to read it. She tells him that they're all well at home and that she's still seeing

Richard, which is going OK. But the mysterious phone calls continue and it bothers her. Mark and Mary have both heard the Bach too. There's something very strange going on and it's unnerving. There's no direct threat, but she can't get the calls out of her mind.

She writes that she's finished *The Razor's Edge* and is now half way through Maugham's *Of Human Bondage*. She's very impressed by his work and can understand why Dominic wanted to go to India and at least visit Ramana Maharshi's ashram. She wants to know where else he's been and where he intends to go before he returns home.

Dominic decides to move on and go up to Rajasthan. He packs his bag, tracks down Dorthe and his other three friends and says his farewells. He doesn't hire a driver, but takes the bus. His journey back to Bombay is hot, sweaty and uneventful. From the bus terminal he takes a cab straight out to the airport and books himself onto the next flight up to Delhi.

Chapter Eighteen

Freddy

'It's better to shut up and appear stupid than open your mouth and remove all doubt.'
Mark Twain.

Freddy and Mark are in the showers. They've just come off the squash court at St Andrew's College. As usual Freddy has won. Mark never ceases to be surprised that his father can beat him so easily. There's something humiliating about his father, who's more than 25 years his senior, winning every game. They are both highly competitive and very good players. Mark is pleased for his father, but unsatisfied with his own performance. Dominic never stands a chance against either of them.

'I've booked us a table at The Bath Hotel for seven thirty. So let's get a move on.'

'OK, Dad. Thanks.'

Freddy drinks heavily and steadily throughout the meal. Mark notices that he stands unsteadily as he pays the bill and starts to go through to the bar. Mark attempts to steady him, but Freddy shakes him off his arm.

'Maybe we should go home now, Dad…'

'Won't hear of it. The night is young, my boy.'

Freddy lurches to the bar and rudely waves to the barman. 'Two large brandies.'

'Uhh...not for me, Dad. I've had enough.'

'Two large brandies.' He turns to Mark. 'Don't be wet. You must hold your drink like a man.'

Mark is not impressed. Clearly his father is not holding his. 'If you insist.'

'I do.'

The brandies arrive and Freddy knocks his back in one slug. Mark sips his.

'Barman. Two more of the same. Drink up, boy.'

Mark takes another sip.

'Have you heard from that brother of yours?'

'No, but Lauren showed me a letter he'd written her.'

'Read it?'

'Yes.'

'What'd it say?'

'Said he was well and enjoying it there apart from the heat and dust.'

'Say anything about those bloody ashrams?'

'Uhh, Yes.' Mark is hesitant, convinced himself that Dominic is wasting his time and money on a fruitless quest.

'What'd he say?' Freddy presses on.

'That he found the one he had visited inspiring, but that he was moving on to visit a guru who doesn't speak.'

'Doesn't speak! What's the hell's the point of visiting someone who doesn't speak?'

'I don't know, Dad.'

'I'm sure you don't. Bloody wild goose chase!'

Mark finds himself taking his brother's side. His father's drunken state annoys and embarrasses him.

'We should give him the benefit of the doubt. He's very sincere about what he's doing...what he's looking for.'

'Fuckin' rubbish!' Freddy is shouting. Several heads turn to look at him.

'Steady on, Dad.'

The barman brings two more brandies. Freddy grabs one, throws back his head, loses his balance and topples from his stool. He crashes sideways to the ground, landing in a heap at Mark's feet. A woman cries out and two men rush to help him to his feet. They heave him upright. Mark pushes them away without a word of thanks then steadies Freddy and leads him out of the bar, through the hotel and onto the street. Freddy can barely walk.

'Where'sa car?'

'Let's leave it here, Dad, and get a taxi.'

'Bugger'at. I can drive. Know what I'm doing.'

'No, Dad, you can't...shouldn't.'

'Don'chu answer me back, boy. I'm your father. Where'sa car?'

'I'll drive, Dad.'

Freddy turns on him and screams, spitting in his face. 'I drive. Clear?'

'Oh, Dad.' Mark despairs. 'You can't. You mustn't!'

'Will. Can. Where'sa car?'

Freddy falls forward tearing away from Mark's steadying arms. He hits the pavement hard. Mark hears the crack of his father's head hitting the pavement. Freddy groans, but makes no effort to get up again. Mark can see blood on the concrete. He panics and, leaving his father where he lies, he runs back to The Bath Hotel. He bursts into reception. Even though it's been a short run he's out of breath and shaking.

'Ambulance. Please. Quick...999.'

Lauren arrives at Addenbrooke's Hospital the next morning full of trepidation. She's been told that her father is concussed but not in any danger. The hospital reminds her of Grace and she feels guilty for not visiting her again.

Freddy looks terrible. His head is bandaged. His eyes are bloodshot and swollen. He can barely look at Lauren. He can't remember much of the events of last night, but knows he has made a fool of himself. He's ashamed and for once is lost for words.

'Hello Daddy?'

He turns away from her.

'Are you all right?'

'Uhhm...my head hurts. I have some stitches.'

'And a hang-over most likely from what Mark

tells me.'

Freddy looks round at her. 'What did Mark tell you...exactly?'

'Well, you know, Daddy...he's very loyal. Just said you had too much to drink.'

'Yes, yes. I did.'

'He said you wanted to drive home.'

'Did I?'

'He said you did. And er...'

'Yes?'

'It's not like you to be so...irresponsible.'

'That sounds like you're judging me, Lauren.'

'Yes, I am, Daddy, given your position in the college, in the community. It'll get around you know. It won't be well received, will it?'

'Why will it get around?'

'Cambridge is a small place and there were a lot of...what shall I say...important people in The Bath Hotel last night.'

Freddy groans and clutches his head. 'Oh, God. It's a mess.'

'Yes, it's a mess.' Lauren considers carefully what to say next. 'Lady Plimworth called Mummy this morning.'

'She's heard about it?'

'Yes. She's heard.'

'What did...? How is Mummy?'

'Naturally she's very upset.'

Freddy pulls himself into an upright position. 'Why isn't Mummy here now?'

156

'She couldn't face it. Doesn't know how to handle it. She's ashamed, I think.'

'Really, Lauren, there's nothing to be ashamed about.'

'But she *is* ashamed.'

Lauren sits on the bed and takes her father's hand. 'The Cambridge Evening News called this morning. They'd been in touch with the hotel manager.'

'What!'

'They're going to put it in the paper.'

'On no. It's just...not fair.'

'Fair or not it'll probably...'

'But it was only a few drinks.'

'A few drinks too many by the sound of it, Daddy.'

He nods his agreement then asks, 'And Mark?'

'He can't show his face in the college.'

Freddy groans. He looks defeated. Lauren's heart goes out to him and she squeezes his hand.

Mark walks unwillingly across the ward to his father's bedside. 'Hi, Dad.'

Freddy is snoozing and opens his eyes slowly. 'Hello, Mark.'

'How're you feeling?'

'Physically?'

'Yeah.'

'OK. I had some stitches and they want me to stay here under observation for another day.'

157

'And otherwise?'

'Frankly I'd rather stay here until this…thing blows over.'

'There was a piece in the paper.'

'Lauren said there would be.'

'Have you heard from the college?'

'Yes. Paul came to visit me.'

'What'd he say?'

'That it wouldn't affect my position, but that it'd undermine my authority somewhat. Make my position difficult. Not untenable, but difficult. Of course there are those who'll try and take some advantage from what's happened to advance themselves. I don't need to tell you that there are enormous jealousies in the college body. A lot of envy and power-play. But beyond all that there's loyalty. You know sticking together for the good of the college.'

'I'm glad…relieved that Paul came to see you.'

'So was I, Mark, so was I.'

Mark sits on the bedside chair.

'And what about you, Mark?'

'Oh, that's not important.'

'It is, Mark. It is to me. Lauren said you didn't want to go into college to begin with. Have you been yet?'

'Yes.'

'And how was it?'

'Not too pleasant to be honest. Lot of snide looks and some sniggering, but interest in it seems to be on the wane.'

'Time will do its work. Paul suggests I take a sabbatical.'

'And will you?'

'I don't know.' Freddy glances down at his hands, clasped together on the top of the bed. 'Part of me feels I should go back as soon as I'm out of here and the other part feels it would be good to stay away at least for a little while.'

'What does Mummy think?'

'She came in last night by the way.'

'I know.'

'She doesn't know what to think. In a way she can't really deal with it. It's out of her league.'

'Lauren's spending a lot of time with her. She persuaded her to go into town and brave the day...show her face to the world.'

'How was that?'

'She looked tired and strained when she got home, but all we can say is that she got through it. Should be easier each time she goes out.'

'Should be.'

'Oh and Lady Mel's coming round tonight for supper. She's being very supportive and steering clear of gossip, she says.'

'She's a good friend.'

'Yes, I know. Mark's body language betrays his desire to leave and be on his way.'

'D'you want to go now, Mark?'

Ah, yes, Dad. I've got some things to

do…work…an essay. You know.'

'Life must go on. Off you go.'

'OK, Dad.'

Mark stands, unsure of how to make his farewells. He steels himself, pulling back his shoulders. 'There was something I wanted to tell you about.'

'What's that, Mark?'

His courage deserts him. 'Oh…not now, Dad. Some other time.'

'As you wish.' They shake hands and Mark turns on his heels and walks away off the ward. Freddy rolls over to face the wall.

Chapter Nineteen
Swami Satchit Ananda
मत् चित् आनान्द्

Dominic is sick in spades when he finally arrives by taxi at The Imperial Hotel in Delhi. He manages to check in and just makes it to his room before he gushes out of both ends for the tenth time. He throws himself on the bed, groaning, tossing and turning. It's a long time since he's felt so wretched and he assumes it's caused by something he's eaten. The thought of food is repulsive and makes him heave even more. Then he remembers his moment of stupidity when he dropped his guard and bought a ham roll at a grubby little stall outside Delhi airport. He knew he was probably making a mistake at the time, but he was very hungry and there wasn't a lot of choice. He ate the whole thing. As he recalls the taste he's sick again and can't believe there's anything more to come up. In fact there isn't anything much, just burning bile.

Somehow he gets through the night. His thirst is unquenchable. He has to call room service three times to bring him more bottled water.

Down it goes and up it comes. It's a good thing, he thinks, that the bathroom is tiled - floor and walls.

He dozes on and off for most of the day, finally getting up and washing in the late afternoon. He's still not hungry. He walks through the hotel. The main corridor is wide with wooden panel walls and a deep traditionally patterned carpet. Hotel staff, some in white jackets carrying trays and some in exotic uniforms go busily about their tasks. He goes through the glass-roofed terrace and into the garden. The heat and the roar of the traffic belt into him. He staggers and blinks in the light. There are peacocks strutting across the lush green and close-cropped lawn and guests sit on white wicker chairs sipping tea from glass-topped tables. Waiters hover and buzz around like busy white butterflies. Dominic sits on a low wall and contemplates the scene.

Eventually he feels steady enough to go through to reception and book his ticket on a mid-morning Pink Train to Jaipur. As he goes back up the big corridor he notices the gift shops on either side selling local works of arts - paintings, clothing, stationary, cushions. He decides to visit the shops on his way back from Jaipur to buy gifts for his family, Dobbo and Jack.

He books a return train ticket to Jaipur in first class and changes a small amount of money to top up his supply of rupees. He wanders out through the hotel car park and out onto Janpath where he is immediately set upon by vendors of one kind or another, including drug-pushers. Hustle, hustle, hustle. He pushes through and, setting a good pace, he strides off.

'Hey, Dominic.' Marco ducks and weaves across Janpath, calling out at the top of his voice. He comes up to Dominic panting from the brief exertion and the heat. 'How you doin', man?' Marco slaps him on the shoulder.

'OK now, Marco, thanks. But I've been very sick - vomiting and...you know.'

'Ah, yeah. Delhi-belly.'

'That sort of thing.'

'Where you goin?'

'Nowhere special. Just strolling, looking around.'

'Wanna go for a smoke? He points out over the road. 'In the park.'

'Err...no. Don't think so. I'm still feeling a bit sick.'

'Help to settle your stomach.'

'May do that...but, no thanks.'

'OK, Dom. So where're you stayin'?'

'Over there at the Imperial.'

'Nice. Bit colonial, British Raj for me. But OK for you I guess, being a Brit and all.' They laugh. 'So where next for you, Dom?'

'Rajasthan. Jaipur. I'm going there tomorrow

on the Pink Train.'

'What's up there for you?'

'A man called Swami Satchit Ananda.'

'Never heard of him.'

'I take that to be good sign.'

'Why, because *I* haven't heard of him?'

'No, no sorry. I didn't mean that. I just meant that he's not well known. So...'

'OK, Dom. Yup. Well, fine. You take care of yourself. I hope you find what you're looking for.'

'Yes, so do I.'

'Bye now.'

'Goodbye, Marco. Give my best to Troy and Jessica.'

'Would do, man, if I knew where they were.' He slaps Dominic on the shoulder again and disappears into the swirling, churning mass of humanity that is Janpath.

The following morning Dominic takes a taxi to the railway station. He is early, having misjudged the time it would take to go from the Imperial Hotel to the station. Sitting in the waiting room before he boards the train he finishes his letter to Lauren. He has so much to share with her that he hardly knows how to finish. He tells her about Meher Baba and his extraordinary audiences with him, his meeting with Marco and smoking the joint at the fort and his journey back to Delhi. He doesn't mention being sick. He doesn't want to worry her or the rest of the family. The night before he wrote post-cards for Freddy, Mary and Mark, which he encloses with his letter. He buys a stamp and posts the letter before he goes to board the train. It's a five hour journey and he's looking forward to chugging out of the filth and squalor of the city into the desert landscape of Rajasthan. The Pink City beckons.

In between watching the world go by he reads at random from the Osborne book *The Teachings of Ramana Maharshi.* He's full of anticipation when he thinks of meeting the Swami. It's an exciting prospect. *Maybe* he'll find what he's looking for.

He takes a taxi from Jaipur railway station out to the ashram. It's sweltering. They travel through the centre of the city. It's stunning and it is pink. He takes an immediate liking to the place and starts to feel better about being in India and so far away from home.

The ashram is small. It is called The Sat Nam Centre. It stands on a low hill overlooking the beautiful Jal Mahal Palace, which sits majestically in the midst of the tranquil Man Sagar Lake. It was built by the British Army in the local architectural style to disguise its purpose, which was for training specialists for the intelligence corps - a well-kept secret.

Dominic's taxi swings through a broad gateway into the courtyard. A tall Sikh steps out from an office and comes to meet Dominic as he pays the taxi driver. With his hands pressed together palm-flat in front of him the Sikh bows, 'Namaste'.

Dominic echoes the greeting. He's getting used to doing this and enjoys it.

'You are Mr Wheatcroft, yes?'

Dominic is taken aback. 'I am, yes. How did you know?'

'Mr Bharatram said you would be coming. He's reserved a room for you overlooking the lake.' The Sikh smiles kindly and, taking Dominic's bag, he leads him across the courtyard and under an arch framed by vivid purple bougainvillea. Dominic is impressed.

'Is Mr Bharatram here?'

'Oh yes, sir. He's asked that you come to his office when you are washed and have taken some refreshment. You will get tea over there in the dining room.' He points towards a cloister, also hung with bougainvillea. The Sikh walks on, leading Dominic along a cool, dark tunnel and into another courtyard with small, brightly painted doors on all four sides. He shows Dominic to a green painted door, which he unlocks and opens, gesturing for Dominic to enter. Inside it is refreshingly cool.

'If you would care to come back to the

reception when you're ready I'll show you to Mr Bharatram's office where you can take tea.'

'Thank you.'

The Sikh bows and leaves. Dominic unpacks his rucksack. He feels at ease, elated even. He washes in the small bathroom, changes his clothes and sets off for reception.

The Sikh is sitting outside on a white wicker chair, obviously waiting for Dominic's appearance. He stands and bows. 'Please follow me, Mr Wheatcroft.' He leads Dominic across the courtyard to a door marked: Secretary Sri B. Bharatram. The Sikh knocks gently on the door and waits.

A voice from within, 'Come in, please, Mr Wheatcroft.'

Dominic opens the door and enters a neat, tidy office. The walls are covered by shelves filled by files and books.

Bunty stands. His knees crack. He is beaming. 'Dominic, I am so pleased to see you again and here - at this place.'

'Thank you.'

'You are most welcome, most welcome. Swami Ji's been expecting you. He said you would come and as usual he's right. Have a seat, please, while I go and announce your arrival and arrange a time for you to meet the Master.'

'Before you go, Bunty, may I ask you something?

'Of course.'

'What does namaste mean?'

Bunty thinks about this. He puts his palms together and bows. 'It means I honour that place in you where the entire universe resides. I honour that place in you, where, if you are in that place in you, and I am in that place in me, there is only one of us.' He smiles. 'OK?'

Dominic is impressed, only able to respond with, 'OK. Thanks.'

'My pleasure.'

Dominic sits as Bunty leaves the room. He's impatient and apprehensive at the same time. He notes that his hands are shaking. He claps them together to still them and he thinks of Lauren. It warms his heart. He wishes that she could be with him for his first meeting with Satchit Ananda. Dominic feels that this day is going to be a major turning point for him and one that may determine the future course of his life.

Bunty returns to his office with a wide smile on his face. His eyes are twinkling. 'The Master will see you now.' He stands in the portal, holding the door open for Dominic, who follows him to the bottom of some stone steps. Bunty gestures that Dominic should go on up without him. He climbs up to the first floor. The landing opens out to a shaded balcony lit up in the red and orange of the sinking sun.

'You are most welcome.' Satchit stands to greet Dominic with a bowing namaste. He sits again, gesturing to Dominic that he should sit in the chair opposite. Satchit is a man of medium height. He is slim and elegant, charming and self-assured. He has a noble air about him - unpretentious and open - and he smiles gently at Dominic. Most of that smile is in his eyes and they sparkle with humour and humble self-assurance.

'Have you taken refreshment?'

'Yes, Sir. I have. Thank you.'

'And are you rested after your journey?'

'Yes. I feel...it wasn't a long journey and the train was comfortable. I enjoyed it.'

'And are you happy to be here?'

'Certainly I am. It's a great privilege...'

Satchit holds up his hands with his palms open and towards Dominic. He nods his head to one side.

'We will see, Dominic, if it is indeed a privilege in the fullness of time.'

Dominic is starting to relax. He feels safe in the Master's presence.

'Have you any questions you want to ask me?'

'I have, yes. Many.'

'Go ahead. Let us get started.'

Dominic takes a deep breath then asks, 'Why is there so much pain and suffering in the world?'

Satchit laughs. 'Well, Dominic, you certainly

get very directly to the point.' Satchit regards Dominic for a few seconds before he answers. 'It is indeed mysterious, I agree. A Sufi mystic put it like this: 'I was a hidden treasure and I desired to be known. Therefore I created creation in order that I might know myself.' He pauses then goes on, 'Before creation God existed as undifferentiated unity. Because of the one reality's wish to know itself the world of differentiation and duality was created. When we human beings can at last see ourselves and the universe as none other than divine reality, but rather as its reflection, then we experience that reality as it is.' He pauses. 'Does this make sense to you?'

Dominic has been listening intently. He finds that he cannot take his eyes off the Master. He knows he is staring at him, but can't do anything about it. 'I...I read somewhere that the medieval alchemist Paracelsus wrote in a text: "Solve et Coagulum".'

'I am not familiar with Latin, Dominic. How d'you translate that?'

'Well, loosely translated it means he separates in order to unite.'

'Just so. That's well put. Thank you.'

Dominic smiles. 'My pleasure, Sir.'

'There is a great saint in Northern India called Maharaj Charan Singh. He has written:

The Lord has fashioned this world for both

pleasure and pain. You will never find a
person who has experienced pain and
misery without the respite of at least a few
moments of happiness. Similarly, no one
ever experiences only happiness without
ever having to face pain. For example, if
you experience ten days of happiness,
after that you are likely to suffer some
pain; if you undergo ten days of suffering,
a breathing space with some degree of
happiness is sure to follow.'

Satchit nods and looks hard at Dominic. 'So I
will ask you, Dominic, what is the source of our
pain? What is the well-source of our misery?'

Dominic is not sure how to respond. He doesn't
know if Satchit is actually asking him for an
answer or if the question is rhetorical.

Satchit looks into his eyes. 'Well, brother, our
pain is caused by our attachment to the people,
ideas and the objects of this world. It's our
attachments and our expectations that bring us
pain. They let us down because they don't live
up to our needs as we see them. When we put
all of our thought, our love and our attention
into this world, we become utterly and
completely lost in it and are swept hither and
thither by the unpredictable currents and forces
at work here. We cannot steer our vessel. We
cannot see our way. But still we devote ourselves
to trying to manipulate people and events to suit

171

our selfish personal ends. This is a vain undertaking and a waste of our life's energy. It's no-win situation, Dominic. We're pouring all our strength and power out into the world, instead of inwards towards the Master. The more we throw ourselves into our worldly pursuits and games, the more we become lost to the Lord.'

'I still don't see why the creator made the world this way? It's hard to understand.' He leans back in his chair for the first time, still keeping his eyes fixed on the Master's.

'Dominic I would suggest that you stay here at the ashram for a couple of weeks so that these issues may become clearer to you and so you can decide if this is the right path for you and if you would like me to initiate you.'

'I would love to do that. But...'

'Yes?'

'How can I pay...I mean is there a fee?'

'No there is no fee.'

'What about board and lodging? Can I pay for those?'

'No, Dominic, you can't. I - we - do not want any money from you. There's no charge.'

'Well, Sir, what *can* I do for - give - you?'

'You need only give me your love and your devotion to the path. And, please, don't call me "sir".' Satchit laughs.

'What do I call you then? What is the correct way to address you?'

172

'You can call me Swami Ji if it suits you and if you're happy with that.'

'I'm fine with that.'

'Good. Now I want you to attend the morning Satsang meetings and the discussion groups, which we hold here every evening. Will you do that?'

'Of course. I'll do whatever you want...whatever you suggest.'

'Well, Dominic, we'll see about *that* in due course!' Satchit looks hard at Dominic. 'If you're happy with me and the teachings after two weeks have passed I'll initiate you into the path and teach you how to meditate according to the system we have here.'

'Thank you, Swami Ji.'

'Don't thank me. Thank Him. It's all His grace.' Satchit stands and Dominic does too. 'I'll see you again at the Satsang tomorrow morning.'

'Yes. You will. And again thank...' Dominic catches himself and laughs as he steps from the balcony and descends the stairs. He is walking on air. His spirit is lifted up. It's been a long, long time since he has felt so good.

Chapter Twenty
Mark

It's a dull, cold day. A bitter wind is sweeping in over Cambridge from the fens. Cows are grazing on the lush green abundance of Grantchester Meadows.

Mary and Mark are lunching at The Orchard. It's a pleasant venue - relaxed and homely - and the staff are polite and friendly. But neither Mary nor Mark is at ease. Troubles seem to be pressing in on them. Mary is worried about Lauren and Dominic and they are both worried about Freddy. Since his release from hospital he's taken to drinking more and more often. It appears that the only way he can deal with life now - with his disgrace and hospitalization - is to mask it with more alcohol. It's a vicious downward spiral and he's taking his family with him.

'He won't discuss it with me.'

'Nor me, Mum.'

'It's not just his place at the college that's threatened. It's his health too. He looks awful.'

'What about Dr Anderson? Would he listen to him?'

'He might, Mark. He respects him enormously, but will he go and see him?'

'I doubt it, Mum, but we can try.'

'Will you ask him?'

'I think it'd be better coming from you.'

Their food arrives. The waitress is very pretty. She gives Mark a big come-on smile, but he takes no notice of her.

'She's a pretty girl.'

Mark glances at the girl and then at Mary. 'Is she? Oh, I didn't notice.'

'You didn't notice how she *looked* at you, Mark?'

'No.'

Mary starts to eat then pauses. 'When are you going to get a girl-friend?'

Mark looks awkward and studies his food. 'I...erm...I don't have time for girls, Mum. I'm too busy what with one thing and another.'

'Well, it would be nice for you...some companionship, you know.'

'Yes, I know, Mum, but...'

He picks at his food.

'Aren't you hungry?'

'Not very. I...'

Mary looks up at him. She can see he's struggling to say something. 'What is it, Mark? What's the matter?'

'I don't know how to say this, how to put it...how to tell you.'

Mary waits. He looks down at the table.

'Tell me what, darling?'

'Thing is I don't how you'll take this - how you'll be able to handle it.'

'I am your mother, Mark.'

He looks up at her. 'Mum I'm a...'

'Yes?'

'I'm a homosexual.'

'A what?

'I'm homosexual. I'm a queer.'

Mary is lost for words. Mark wants to leave, to run from the room, but he keeps his seat.

'How...how can that be?'

'I don't know how it can be. But it is. It just is.'

Once more Mary is dumbstruck. They stare at each other, trying to find a way to proceed.

Mary breaks the silence, 'How long?'

'Always, Mum. All my life.'

'But you're so masculine, so good at sport and...'

'So are women good at sport. So what? That just doesn't mean anything.'

Mary shivers, puts down her knife and fork as she tries hard to get a handle on what she's just been told. The wind beats around the building, reflecting the storm within. Mark doesn't know what else he can say to help Mary understand something he's never understood himself. How could he be in a man's body yet crave the love of men. It makes no sense, but it's a fact and has always been so for as long as he can remember. Strange, weird and inexplicable. Confessing to his mother has lifted the weight off his shoulders just a little, but of what might happen next he has no idea. He's sick and tired of lying, cheating and deceiving, pretending to be what he isn't - a man in a man's world. He often wonders if it 'shows' and if he really gets away with it. His tendency is to over-compensate - to be more masculine than his peers.

Mary finds her voice again. 'What can be done?'

'What on earth do you mean, Mum?'

'Can you be helped to change? Can't you find a way to...like women?'

'I don't think you understand.'

'No, I don't understand. I just don't understand.' She breaks down and starts to sob.

Mark glances around him suddenly very aware of the other diners in the room. 'Not here, please. We should...er...we should leave.'

Mary is unable to move. She doesn't want to stay or to leave. She wants more than anything for this nightmare to end, for this conversation to have been a dream, from which she can wake up and be just as she was. She controls her tears, wipes her eyes and looks up at Mark. He's staring out of the window. Under the table his hands are gripped tightly together. He wishes that things with him were other than they are. What puzzles him is the place of homosexuality in the scheme of nature and evolution. He can't comprehend what part it plays.

As he understands it the purpose of physical love between a man and woman is for procreation. It is nature's way of ensuring that the species will continue and not die out. Two men or two women having sex together cannot reproduce. If everyone were homosexual the species would rapidly die and disappear from the face of the planet. So, why? It feels literally fruitless and meaningless. And yet he has it. It's strong in him. He desires men. He desires men physically and he craves the companionship of men. He wants a loving relationship. From time to time he wishes that it all - his life - would end.

He often finds himself reflecting too on the mystery of infectious diseases and what part they might play in evolution. He had been reading recently about the so-called Spanish flu pandemic of 1918-'19, which killed something in the region of 50 million people. He wonders what on earth can be the point of that. What purpose could it serve? Then he catches himself thinking about purpose. Does the universe have a purpose? His scientific mind says, no. There is no purpose, no meaning, no goal, no intent. And yet…he wonders about beauty, about truth, about love, about how we value one thing over another. It puzzles him, nags at him. He can't quite put his finger on what it is, but…

Mary watches him in silence then waves to the pretty waitress, signaling that she wants her bill. 'Mark.'

He doesn't respond.

'I am your mother, Mark, and I'll always love

you whatever happens, whatever you are.'

He turns to look at her and smiles. 'Thank you, Mum. I believe you.'

'You should. I'll never turn my back on you, never let you down or stop loving you. You're my son. That's just the way it is and it will *always* be so.'

They sit in silence until the waitress arrives with their bill. Mark looks at her and smiles. She blushes and looks away. He can see that she is very attractive and charming too, but it doesn't stir him. Mary watches them both as she pays the bill.

Outside they gather their coats around them as they stride off across the meadows towards Cambridge through the wind and the light rain that begun to fall.

'How d'you think Lauren is these days, Mark? Does she seem different to you?'

'Different? How different?'

'She seems to be in the clouds - vague and distant.'

'I haven't noticed any vagueness. She doesn't seem distant to me. I know she misses Dominic. Maybe that has something to do with it.'

'I wonder how he is. I miss him too.'

'Well, Mum, he'll be home soon.'

'And with a tale to tell.'

'No doubt.' A sneering note has crept back into his voice.

'Why are so critical of him, Mark? Why so skeptical?'

'Ohh,' he groans. 'Mysticism! It's for the birds.'

'How can you be so sure?'

'Science, Mum. Science shows us the way. It's all there. It's staring us in the face.'

'Yes, OK, but, as Dom says, science can explain how things occur, but not why.

'There is no why. There just is. There's nothing behind it. It is what it is. There's no big bearded man in the sky pulling strings. That's all mumbo-jumbo.'

'Might be a she…no beard!'

They laugh. She takes Mark's hand. He doesn't object.

'I shouldn't say anything about what you told me just now to Daddy.'

'I won't. Don't worry. He'd go through the roof.'

'He certainly would. Especially with things as they are now. It'd be that last straw.'

'And the camel's back would be broken.'

Mary stops and turns to Mark, 'I wish he wouldn't drink so much.'

'I guess he'll drink less when this whole thing blows over.'

'I hope so. I do so hope. I suppose that one day it will blow over.'

'I'm sure it will, Mum.' Mark does his best to reassure Mary, but he's not very convincing.

They walk on in silence along the bank of the

Cam, lost in their own private thoughts and struggles. The sun shines distantly through the clouds and a faint rainbow arches across the sky while raindrops dance on the surface of the green waters of the river. Two swans swim calmly and with regal indifference through the centre of the stream. Mary stares out over the water. A tight frown is etched across her brow.

'Have you met Lauren's boyfriend?'

'No, but Dom has.'

'Did he say anything about him?'

'Not much. He lives in his parents' house and he's a painter.'

'A house painter?'

Mark laughs. 'No, no, Mum. He's an artist. Dom says he's good.'

'I hope he doesn't let her down.'

'It's not as if they're a couple yet.'

'But still, if she's fond of him...'

'That's a risk we have to take, isn't it?'

'I suppose it is.' Mary stops and turns to Mark. 'D'you have a...?'

'Boyfriend?'

Mary flinches. Mark pretends not to notice.

'I don't, Mum. We...queers have to be careful. It's against the law.'

'And against nature?'

'I don't know about that. The feelings I have are *natural* to me.'

'Sorry. I didn't mean...I don't want to hurt you.'

'I know you don't, Mum.'

'I just have to get used to the idea.'

'I understand. Maybe you can. Maybe you will.'

Chapter Twenty One
The Collapse of the Wave Function

'The evolution of the world may be compared to a display of fireworks, which has just ended. Only some few red wisps of ashes and smoke remain. Standing here on this cooling sphere, we see the slow fading of the suns as we try to recall the vanished brilliance of the origin of the worlds.'
Abbé Georges Lemaître
Astrophysicist and Theologian

One evening Dominic walks down into Jaipur. He takes a taxi five miles out of the city on Bhawani Singh Road to the Rambagh Palace Hotel. He has read that it's the former residence of the Maharaja of Jaipur and is now a luxury Taj Palace Hotel, widely considered to be one of the best hotels in the world. In 1887, during the reign of Maharaja Sawai Madho Singh, it was converted into a modest royal hunting lodge. The house stood in the midst of a thick forest. In the early 20th century, it was expanded into a palace by Sir Samuel Swinton Jacob. Maharajah Sawai Man Singh II made it his principal home, adding several royal suites in 1931. By the 1950s, the royal family felt that the upkeep of the palace and its 47 acres of gardens were becoming too expensive. In 1957 they decided to convert it into a luxury hotel.

Dominic is wandering through the gardens, lit in the silver glow of the full moon. He is in a grove of thick overhanging trees and is startled when a small man springs out of the darkness and confronts him with the challenging statement, 'Snake eye, tiger eye!'

Dominic jumps and steps back. 'What!'

The man smiles. He's not threatening and repeats, 'Snake eye, tiger eye.'

Dominic finds his voice. 'What d'you mean?'

'Come, sit down.' He leads Dominic to a stone seat in a dimly-lit alcove. 'I cannot say. It's for you to consider and act on.'

'Don't know what you mean.'

'It is not about what I mean. It comes from Him.' He points at the sky and his smile beams wider.'

Dominic cannot resist. He smiles back.

The man takes Dominic's right hand and studies it. 'Your father's name is Freedy.'

Dominic is taken aback and can only respond with, 'It's Freddy actually, not Freedy.'

The man shrugs, turning over Dominic's hand. 'Your father is professor. Yes?'

'Yes.'

'I see that he has some disgrace.'

'Perhaps. Not that I'm aware of.'

'His future. It's smeared. In flux.'

The man goes silent and Dominic waits. He's unsure about him and very puzzled that he appears to know Freddy's name.

'Your father will partly recover from this recent incident, but there is worse to come.'

Dominic sags onto the back of the seat, wondering what he means by recent incident. 'Are you sure about this?'

'Yes. It is clear.'

Dominic is lost. His head is spinning. 'I...I can't be sure of you.'

'Sure of me?' He shugs. 'D'you mean: am I telling truth?'

'That's what I mean.'

'I am what I am. You can believe me if you want to or you can choose to not trust me.'

Dominic stands. The man continues to sit. 'The choice is yours, Sir.'

Dominic turns to leave.

'The old lady in the hospital for the insane wishes that you tell your sister that all will be well.'

'The old lady...yes, there is an old lady and she is ill.'

'I see that. But her future is unclear. I understand that the phone calls you've been receiving with the music are puzzling you.'

'Puzzling everyone.'

'Your father will be hurt when they stop.'

'Why?'

'Because he will know.'

'What?'

'Where the music is coming from.' The man takes a plain white card from his pocket and writes a few words on it. He holds it out to Dominic as he stands. Dominic takes it. The man removes a small red and black amulet from his pocket. He also hands this to Dominic. 'That is my address. You can write to me for advice at any time and I will make a small charge for my reply. If you tell anyone about our meeting tonight you will lose that piece of paper and the charm. D'you understand?'

'I understand that but I don't understand how...' Dominic opens his arms with his hands palm upwards in a gesture of defeat.

'There is nothing to lose. There is nowhere to go.' He bows to Dominic. 'Namaste.' He turns, steps back into the thick foliage and is gone in the rustling leaves.

For a few moments Dominic is rooted to the spot. But then he shivers, turns abruptly and walks back to the front of the hotel. He finds it hard to calm down on his way back to the ashram. He goes to his room, washes and puts the note and the amulet in a safe place. He then heads straight to Bunty's office. The light is still on. He knocks and hears Bunty call, 'Come in.'

Dominic takes a seat while Bunty finishes his work. Eventually he looks up, 'Now, what can I do for you, Dominic? You look agitated.'

'I am agitated. I've had a remarkable experience in the garden of the Rambagh Palace.'

'And what was that?'

'I...er...I was walking through the gardens when a youngish man, slight build, jumped out of the shadows and accosted me with, 'Snake-eye, tiger-eye.' I was startled. He couldn't really explain what he meant, but he went on rapidly telling me things about my family that he couldn't possibly know like my father's name and the fact that my grandmother is in hospital. Is it real or is it a trick - an illusion?'

Bunty thinks carefully before he replies. 'There are many, many are men and women in India, who have attained these powers. They do it by learning to focus their attention on specific chakras to develop and build the energies in that region. When performed successfully these ascetics can release enormous energy from these centres, giving them access to a variety of powers.'

'Really?' Dominic shakes his head in disbelief.

'Oh, yes.'

'So you think that the man who stopped me was a genuine savant?'

'From what you tell me it would certainly appear to be the case.'

'Well, I'll be...was he waiting for me? Did he know I was coming?

'Probably, you see, he would be able to use his abilities to tap into the minds of others - anyone, not just you. But then again, he might have singled you out. We may never know.'

'I have his address. I can keep in touch. He said that I could pay him for the next consultation.'

'And that is how he makes his living.'

Dominic shakes his head again in wonderment. India never ceases to surprise him.

'You must remember, Dominic, that the path to spiritual enlightenment is fraught with dangers. It's rife with temptations for the powerful being who seeks but more power. The Master advises us to forgo these powers when they are offered to us along the way. We are encouraged to think of the Master, dwell on the Master, relying only on his protection and guidance.'

The following morning after Dominic has dressed he decides to look at his two mementoes. He looks behind the curtain where he left them, but they're not there. He checks all around the window frame and the nearby floor, but without success. He looks under the bed and goes through all the pockets of his clothes. There's no sign of them. He goes through the bathroom, looks in all the drawers and his rucksack. He cannot believe that they've been spirited away. He seeks a rational explanation, but none is forthcoming. He is yet more confused than he was last night. He sits on the bed trying to gather his thoughts.

After breakfast Dominic is still dazed and puzzled by his experience of the previous night. He goes into the garden to think. Green parrots flitter among the branches of the trees. He picks up and opens the small pamphlet that Bunty had loaned to him after their talk. It is called *The Path* and was written by an American philosopher called Del Brotman. He reads:

The physical universe is an illusion. How can we say this? How can this be true? The physical universe is a wave function. Light is waves. Sound is waves. Our senses detect the waves and then collapse them into particles. With sound, the waves are collapsed into individual notes or words. With light, the waves are collapsed into individual images. It is the mind, which creates the illusion in which we all share. Though, to be sure, we can never be certain of what another human being's perception is. We can never be certain that it matches our own perception. What is 'red' - the colour 'red'? What is it? What do we mean by

this? Do we all mean the same thing? Do
we really all see the same thing?
Indeed what is it that we see? We see a
wave - light at a specific wavelength. So,
what is real about the pictures that we
see? In the end, they are in the mind. It
is there that we actually see. We see the
world one way, insects see it another, and
artists in yet other ways. A bee can see
ultra violet, and flowers look very
different to them. The visions of artists
are amazingly varied. Is reality
'pointillise' as Seaurat painted it, or
glowing light as Turner saw it? What is
out there? What does out there mean? Is
there any out there, at all?

Swami Ji initiates Dominic and gives him his
mantra and meditation technique. The technique
is known as Bhakti Yoga or the path of
surrender. Its goal is fostering love, utter faith
and surrender to God. Swami Ji explains that
this method is the easiest way for the man in the
street to raise his consciousness and attain God-
realisation. It is a path of devotion to the guru,
the guide, the helper. This sits well with Dominic
and he trusts Swami Ji. He can believe in him.
He feels in one way like the father that Dominic
never had, the father who loves him without
judgement or condition. He inspires him. Sadly

Freddy was never any of these things for him. Dominic grins up at the parrots in the tree above him. Everything's falling into place and he's in the right place at the right time.

Bunty walks across the garden. He picks up a chair and takes it over to Dominic. He carries a small package. He sits. 'You look well, Dominic.'

'And I feel well, Bunty.'

'Are you leaving today?'

'I am, yes. My bag's packed. I was just going to call on you.'

'Ah, well, I've beaten you to it then.' They laugh.

'Are you pleased you came here?'

'Of course. Can't you tell?'

'Well, yes I can. It shows on your face and…in your posture. You look somehow taller and certainly brighter.'

'I certainly feel a lot brighter than when I first arrived here, but taller?' They laugh again and after a short pause Bunty turns to Dominic. 'As I understand it there are not so many vegetarians in your country. Will you be OK with the diet?'

'I will be fine. We have an excellent cook at home and more and more people are cutting out meat and fish. So, I'd say that the diet is catching on slowly'

'That's most gratifying to learn.' Bunty hands the package to Dominic, who opens it and takes out a slim, plain booklet. He studies the title: *The Collected Poems of Seyyid Syfullah Nizamoglu.*

'Thank you, Bunty. You're very kind.'

'Please. It is my pleasure to share this with you.'

'I have never heard of this man.'

'That's hardly surprising. He was a Sufi mystic and poet, who lived in the sixteenth century. He was a leader in the Helveti Sufi order. I would guess that he is not known at all in the West save for a very few scholars. But among the Sufis he is revered and highly respected. Let me recite a poem for you as we go to reception to order a taxi. I know most of his poems by heart.'

They stand and walk. Bunty takes Dominic's arm as they stroll beneath the sheltering trees in and out of the flickering sunlight.

'The poem I'm going to recite is called *The Path of Amazement* and it goes like this:

I cannot say who it is I am.
I am amazed, I am amazed!
I cannot call this self myself.
I am amazed, I am amazed!
Who is in my eyes seeing?
Who is in my heart enduring?
Who is inhaling and exhaling?
I am amazed, I am amazed!
Who is speaking with my tongue?
Who is listening with my ears?
Who is understanding with my mind?
I am amazed, I am amazed!

Who is stepping with these feet?
Who is tasting with my mouth?
Who is chewing and who swallowing?
I am amazed, I am amazed!
Who holds these riches in his hand?
Who is the one throwing them away?
Who is buying and who selling?
I am amazed, I am amazed!
Why is there life coursing below my
skin?
Why are my eyes bloodshot from
crying?
Why this religion, why this faith?
I am amazed, I am amazed!
Everything comes from the One.
Abandon yourself to this mighty
beauty.
I am amazed, I am amazed!'

Bunty's voice has a soft, gentle ring and Dominic is enchanted. 'That's truly beautiful, Bunty. Thank you.'

'Don't thank me. Thank him.' He points up to the sky and smiles benignly at Dominic. 'It's profound and very deep.'

'It is indeed.'

They arrive at reception and enter.

Two hours later Dominic is boarding the Pink Train and heading back to Delhi, its mayhem and its madness. He's sad to be leaving Bunty and Swami Ji, but at the same time thrilled at the prospect of going home again. He misses his family - particularly his mother and Lauren. He knows that when he's home he'll miss Swami Ji very much for his inspiring presence and Bunty too.

Chapter Twenty Two
The Ritz Hotel

'And what you ask is the beginning of it all? And it is this: Existence that multiplied itself for sheer delight of being so that it might find itself innumerably.'
Sri Aurobindo

Dominic's Syrian Arab flight is at noon so he's up early to prepare for the journey. He finds his passport, but cannot lay his hands on his airline ticket. He tips the contents of his rucksack onto the bed and desperately goes through it. No sign. He feels echoes of the amulet and the note and is shaken. He separates everything out and anxiously checks through his clothes and toiletries, but without success. His good mood evaporates and his heart sinks. He's at loss to come up with a solution. He can't face calling home for support. Too humiliating after all his brave talk. He calls reception to see if anyone has found the ticket and handed it in. The answer is no. He goes through his stuff again, checking every pocket of his rucksack again and then again.

Out of the blue he has a brainwave. Ranjit Rupneraan. He has his address and phone number in Calcutta. He gets an outside line and dials. After an interminable wait the phone is answered.

'Hello. Can I speak to Ranjit, please.'

'He's not at home now, Sir, but will be here in two hours. Can I take a message?'

'Yes, you can. Please ask him to call Dominic Wheatcroft as soon as he can. I'm staying at the Imperial Hotel in Delhi and my room number is 43.'

'I have made a note of that, Sir. I will pass your request to Mr Rupneraan as soon as he returns home.'

Dominic puts down the phone and flops onto the bed. He is restless. He picks up a notebook from among his possessions. He flicks through it until he finds a page headed with the title *The Cloud of Unknowing*. He reads his comment followed by the text:

> *Of the two currents running through this world, the one that carries the soul down and the other that carries the soul up, there is a beautiful description in The Cloud of Unknowing. This is a fourteenth century text of unknown authorship.*
>
> *'Work hard and with all speed in this nothing and this nowhere, and put on one side your outward physical way of knowing and going about things, for I can tell you that this sort of work cannot be understood by such means. With your*

eyes you can only understand a thing by its appearance, whether it is long or broad, or small or large or round or square or coloured. With your ears you understand by noise and sound; with your nose by the stench or scent; with your taste whether it is sour or sweet, salty or fresh, bitter or pleasant; with your touch whether it is hot or cold, hard or soft, blunt or sharp.

But God and spiritual things have none of these varied attributes. Therefore, leave all outer knowledge gained through the senses; do not work with the senses at all, either objectively or subjectively. For the natural order is that by the senses we should gain our knowledge of the outward material world, but not thereby gain our knowledge of things spiritual. So crush all knowledge and experience of created things and of yourself above all for it is on your own self-knowledge and experience that the knowledge and experience of everything else depends. If you will take the trouble to test it, you will find that when other things and activities have been forgotten there still remains between you and God the stark awareness of your own existence. And this awareness too must go before you experience meditation in its perfection.

Dominic ponders this and underlines the phrase: '...*there still remains between you and God the stark awareness of your own existence.*' He falls into a fitful doze, awaking abruptly when the phone rings. For a moment he doesn't know where he is. He grabs the phone as his plight comes back and hits him hard.

'Hello.'

'That you, Dom?'

'Yes...Ranjit. It's me. Thanks for calling back.'

'What's up?'

'I'm in Delhi and...'

'You're in India?'

'Yup.'

'You're in India and you didn't come and see me.'

'Been south and west - nowhere near Calcutta.'

'Where to?'

'Coupla ashrams.'

'Ashrams!'

'Yup.'

'Any good?'

'Yeah, great. Found an amazing guy in Jaipur called Satchit Ananda.'

There is a pause on the line.

'So what's up?'

'Lost my flight ticket home and I've got no lolly left. Don't know what to do.'

'What about your parents?'

'No go there, Ranjit. My Dad didn't want me to come here and it would really piss him off. I'd rather not ask.'

'OK. I've had a thought. A friend of mine's father runs a small airline out of Delhi. It's called Brothers Air Services. They fly to London and they're very cheap.'

'How much.'

'Very cheap.'

'But I have next to nothing left and nothing in my bank.'

'Well, OK, Dom. I could help you out and you can settle up when we're back in college.'

'You're a star.'

'Thanks. Look, I'll make a couple of calls and get back to you later. When d'you want to fly?'

'Today.'

'Too soon. Maybe I could get you fixed up for tomorrow.'

'That'd be brilliant.'

'Stay by your phone and I'll call you soon.'

'I'll do that.'

'OK, Dom. Take it easy. Don't worry.'

'Thanks.'

'My pleasure.'

Dominic puts the phone back on its cradle and falls back on the bed with a sigh. He sits up and placing the pillows up against the wall, he crosses his legs, straightens his back, closes his eyes and meditates.

An hour or so later he is still meditating when the phone rings.

'Hello Ranjit.'

'Hello Dom. I've fixed things for you. Plane leaves tomorrow at three pm.'

'That's great. Thank you so much. How much is it going to cost?'

'Only 90 quid.'

'So cheap! I'll pay you back next term.'

'Thanks, Dom. But no rush.'

'You're a pal.'

'Now what you've got to do is go to room 104 at the Ritz Hotel to collect your ticket.'

'At a hotel.' Are you sure about that?'

'Yes. That's the place. They don't have an office yet, but they have a suite up there.'

'OK. When can I pick up the ticket?'

'It'll be ready for you to collect in an hour. All paid for.'

'Thanks so much, Ranjit. Dinner on me when we get back next term.'

'Offer accepted. See you then. Have a good flight. Bye, Dom.'

'Bye, Ranjit.

Dominic checks in at two pm the following day, having collected his ticket from the Ritz Hotel. He was concerned and unsure. It all seemed a touch shady and temporary, but his ticket is accepted and he goes through passport control and into the departure lounge. He walks to the viewing window and can see the Brothers Air Services aircraft on the tarmac below. He is taken aback when he sees that the plane is a twin prop Douglas DC3. It's a vintage aircraft, the workhorse of the World War II. But there it is, and ground crew are loading luggage into the hold.

Inside the aircraft it's very basic: blue canvas fabric seats strung across spindly metal frames. The pretty air hostess smiles reassuringly as she helps the passengers to their seats. The aircraft is only half full, which doesn't surprise Dominic. Once they are seated the pilot addresses the passengers in English and in Hindi. He explains that it will be an 18 hour flight, allowing for refuelling stops at Karachi, Tehran, Rome and Brussels.

The flight is uneventful and the stops allow the passengers to stretch their legs and stroll through the airports' duty free areas. Dominic is not convinced that the aircraft is 100% airworthy. He can see oil streaming back along the cowling of the port engine, but he thinks of Swami Ji and manages to reassure himself that all will be well. In fact they make it to Brussels without incident, having passed through hair-raising patches of turbulence, which the plane bucks, drops and weaves through but without falling out of the sky.

The aircraft taxis towards the terminal. Two vehicles sweep out and block the path of the Dakota, which shudders to a halt. The passenger door is opened and a ladder is brought out from the terminal. The passengers and crew disembark and they are led to a bus, which ferries them mysteriously to a Nissen hut out on the perimeter of the airfield. They are taken into the hut. The door is closed and bolted from the outside. While they wait a well-spoken Indian man gives them some background on the airline. He explains that an affluent family bought the aircraft from Aden Air, a liquidated British company and that they have been flying out of Delhi for the past two years.

After an hour or so the door of the Nissen hut opens and two officials enter. They explain in English that the plane is not airworthy and will be grounded at the airport until it can be repaired and considered fit to fly. In the meantime they would be all flown free of charge to Heathrow by Sabena Airlines. Smiles all round and Dominic makes it back to Blighty with a light heart and full of excitement at the thought of being home again in the bosom of the family. He's not aware of his father's unfortunate debacle and his humiliation by the press. All will be revealed once he gets back to Adams Road. He phones home to announce his safe landing. Dobbo takes the call and almost weeps when she

hears his voice again. He takes the tube into
London with butterflies in his stomach.

Chapter Twenty Three
The Mysterious

'The most beautiful thing we can experience is the mysterious.
It is the source of all true art and science.'
Albert Einstein

Lauren collects Dominic from Cambridge Station and drives him home in the Mini Cooper. On the way she tells him about Freddy's misfortune before she asks him about his adventures in the east. He is shocked, but does his best to avoid being angry with Mark for letting it happen. They agree to go out for a drink later so he can tell her in peace all about his guru hunt and the outcome.

Mary meets them at the front door when they arrive home. She hugs Dominic passionately. She's so relieved to have him back in one piece looking tanned and well. She almost weeps for joy. Lauren watches them with quiet pleasure. She can intuit that Dominic's return will put back some balance and order into the disturbed family dynamic.

Freddy is in Oxford at a conference so the three of them go through to the lounge to talk. There is a log fire burning and they draw up chairs around it. Mary tells Dominic the story of the drunken evening at The Bath Hotel as Mark had related it to them. He listens carefully, but without commenting until she has brought him right up to date. When she's finished both women turn to Dominic to hear his reaction.

'I find it difficult to understand that Dad would allow himself to get so drunk unless...there's some problem he wants to escape from. It's out of character.'

'To be honest, Dom, Mummy and I've noticed that he has been drinking more.'

'That's very puzzling given his recent promotion and the importance of his job to him. He knows too how crucial it is that he behaves with decorum and sets a good example to the staff and students.'

'He's aware of that. No doubt about it,' Mary responds.

'Has anything happened to upset him?'

Both women consider this question carefully before Lauren speaks. 'There have been several of those odd phone calls. I mentioned it to Daddy and he flew off the handle for no apparent reason. He said he'd never had the experience himself, but something told me he was lying and that he had taken one or more of those calls.'

'Why would he lie?'

'I don't know, but he was very flustered. Seemed lost for words. It was odd. I picked up the phone once and got the silent treatment with only the Bach Prelude & Fugue playing faintly in the background. It's disconcerting, I agree, but nothing to get so steamed up about. Daddy's reaction was…inappropriate, out of proportion.'

'And that's all there's been that's out of the ordinary?'

Mary responds, 'As far as we know unless something's happened at work. I know the college is a seething mass of jealousy and envy but Daddy's always been able to handle that. It's what you expect in a place like that - everyone vying for the top job and more status.'

'Typical men!' Lauren smiles.

'And women too, Lauren.'

Yes, OK, Dom, but not to the same degree.'

'Women *are* competitive. They want to be boss.'

'Some are competitive, I grant you, but boss?'

'You're a woman, Lauren, so you can't see how bossy your kind are.'

'Mummy doesn't boss Daddy.'

'She couldn't. He's a power-mad tyrant.'

'Steady on, Dominic. Don't be too hard on him.'

'Why not? He's hard on us.'

'True.'

'Thanks, Sis.' Dominic smiles at her and takes her hand.

'But what about, Daddy? He won't see a doctor…'

'I don't know, Mum.'

'Neither do I.' Lauren shrugs. Hey, we haven't given Dom a chance to say anything about India.'

'Sorry, darling. I was just so pleased to have you back safe and sound that I forgot to ask.'

'Well, it was hot, crowded and mostly very poor.'

'But did you find what you wanted?'

'I did, Mum.'

'What did you find?'

'I found a teacher I could trust.'

'A guru?'

'Yes, a guru.'

'What did he...?'

'Give me?'

'Yes.'

'He gave me hope, confidence and a meditation technique.'

'What did all that cost?'

'Nothing, Mum. It was all free.'

'All free?'

'Yes...all. I stayed in his ashram for two weeks and they didn't ask for any money.'

'Food?'

'Yes, everything. Food, lodging, instruction...everything.'

'Astonishing.'

'Yes, it was, Mum. I offered to pay, but he wouldn't have it.'

'He...what's his name?'

'Swami Satchit Ananda.'

'Swami what?'

'Satchit Ananda, Mum, which translate as truth, knowledge and bliss.'

'And the other bit?'

'In Hindi swami means master, lord or prince. He likes to be called Swami Ji. Ji is a term of endearment. He calls his disciples - followers - brother or sister. He doesn't lord it over people.'

'He sounds like an astonishing man, Dominic.'

'He is, Mum. Astonishing and inspiring. I wish you could meet him. And you too, Lauren. On the day I was…initiated I thought of you and wished that you could've been there with me.'

'Oh, Dom, how sweet of you to think of me…there'

'I mean it, Sis. I always think of you. I missed you both so much.'

Mary is touched. She has to choke back her tears, but one unavoidably rolls down her cheek. She wipes it away discreetly, hoping that the children haven't seen. But they have. Lauren finds it hard to hold back her tears too.

Dobbo knocks on the door and comes in to announce that dinner is ready. Over their meal Dominic tells them more about his experiences in India, leaving out the story of his journey home.

After they've eaten Lauren and Dominic walk over to The Granta pub for a drink. They stand on the bridge over the millpond to watch the water flowing and the ducks and swans bobbing in the turbulence. As children they did this, staring down at the water until they felt that they were moving and the water was standing still. Dominic's happy to be back here again. He realizes how fond he is of Cambridge and how attached he is to the city and his family.

'Got it. I'm moving.

'Me too, Dom. They laugh and hold hands.

'Love you.'

'Love you too.'

They both look up from the river and smile.

'Let's go in, Dom.'

They walk into the pub hand in hand and go up to the bar.

'I'm buying. What'd you like, Sis?'

'Gin and tonic, please.'

The barmaid walks over to them.

'One gin and tonic, please, and a Coke.

'Coke!'

'Yup. I promised Swami Ji I wouldn't drink or take drugs.'

'Why?'

'He told me that if I want this meditation thing to be effective I have to keep my head clear.'

'D'you mind?'

'Not at all. I want the meditation to work.'

'What'll happen if it does work?'

'Hard to explain. I could start with what Sophocles said.'

'And what'd he say.'

'Know thyself. He meant get right inside yourself.'

'And?'

'Well, Lauren, as Jesus Christ said, "The kingdom of heaven is within you."'

'And what is the kingdom of heaven exactly?'

Dominic laughs. 'I don't know exactly. I've never been there...as far as I know'

'What d'you think it is?'

'Swami Ji says that we contain everything within ourselves and that we can get in touch with the life force itself. Jesus also said that "If therefore thine eye be single thy whole body shall be full of light."'

'You certainly know your Bible, Dom.'

'Swami Ji quotes from it a lot.'

'Really?'

'Yup. He's well read.'

'You know, Dom, I don't think I could do this. I like to drink too much and I just love smoking grass.'

'You still do?'

'Yes, whenever I can.'

'With Richard?'

'Uhm. I'm still going out with him.'

They take their drinks and go to a table by a window overlooking the millpond. Night has fallen and the street light reflections shimmer on the water's surface. They sit in silence for a while.

'D'you like him?'

'Oh, yes, sure.'

'Are you in love with him?'

'I don't know. I mean I don't exactly know what love is and what it would feel like if I was in love.'

'I think you would. You wouldn't be able to think of anything else.'

'God, Dom. You're such a romantic!'

'Am I?'

'Always have been and that's what I like about you. Mark is cold compared to you - just like his science.'

'Einstein was a scientist and he wasn't cold. He was passionate about life. I read somewhere that he said, "The most beautiful thing we can experience is the mysterious. It is the source of all true art and science."'

'I like that. But so what?'

'So life excited him…he wasn't cold, without passion.'

'I've always felt that Mark's holding something back. He won't let himself go. He seems to be hiding something…holding back on his enthusiasm.'

'I know what you mean. But he's always been like that…restrained in some way.'

'Well, I guess you know him best, Dom.'

'True, but we've never been as close as twins might be, which is sad, I guess.' He smiles. 'But

I have *you*.'

Chapter Twenty Four
Rubbing Along Together

It's spring and it's 1963. The day dawns bright and clear and the family are all at home. Lent term has finished. They are breakfasting together. On the surface things are calm and they are getting along. Lauren feels groggy. She's been up most of the night getting very stoned with Richard and his artist friends. Freddy looks bloated, following a heavy night on the booze. If he's not out with friends and colleagues he drinks alone. Mary as usual is doing her best to keep things smooth and sweet.

Mark is buttering his toast. He turns to Dominic. 'Done your meditation today, Dom?'

Dominic does not rise to the bait. 'Yeah, I have a little.'

'Got any results?'

'That depends on what you mean by results, Bro.'

'I mean, does it work?'

'It works. Yes. I like it.'

'What happens?'

'Nothing *happens*.'

'Nothing?' So why d'you do it?'

'Rome wasn't built in a day, Mark.'

'OK. Point taken.'

The conversation dips and they eat in silence. Mary breaks the spell. 'Are you going into college today, Freddy?'

'Yes, I've…a meeting at ten.' He looks distracted and leaves the table and his unfinished breakfast. He goes to his study. He sits down at his desk and pulls open a drawer. He lifts out a half bottle of whisky. He takes a deep slug, puts the bottle on the table for a few seconds then drinks again. He leans back in his chair and closes his eyes. He shakes his head, puts the bottle back in the drawer and leaves the room.

Later that morning Dominic is in the lounge He is alone in the house with the dogs. He is reading *The Times* when the phone rings. He picks it up from the table beside him. Silence except for the Bach Prelude & Fugue.

'Hello…is there anybody there?' He waits then almost shouts, 'I suggest you stop this nonsense. It's very irritating. And some of us here are finding it very distressing. My advice to you is *fuck off*. Got that?' He slams the phone down and goes back to his paper. The dogs look up at him, alerted by the vehemence in his voice and the sound of the phone crashing back onto the cradle. Dominic's not distressed but he is angry.

When Mark comes home for lunch he joins Dominic in the lounge. He grabs the paper and sits. 'How're things, Dom?'

"All right thanks.' Dominic stands and goes to the French windows to look out over the garden. 'That phone call came again.'

'What phone call?'

'The one when you can only hear Bach. It's damned annoying. What d'you think's going on?'

'No idea. Does it matter?'

Dominic turns back into the room. 'Not sure. Maybe. Mum doesn't like it nor does Lauren.'

'I know. And nor does Dad.'

'So it does matter then.'

'I suppose it does.'

Neither man speaks. Dominic turns from the window and looks back into the room, waiting for Mark to add something. Mark stands.

Dominic watches him. 'Dad's changed recently, don't you think?'

Yeah…he's certainly drinking a lot more than he used to.'

'And you'd know all about that, Mark.'

'Look it wasn't my fault he got so pissed that night.' Mark is getting angry and going on the defensive.

'Well, whose fault was it?'

'His.'

'But *you* were there.'

'OK. But what could I do? He wouldn't listen to me. 'I - we - are just children to him.'

'Yeah, well, Mark, I agree he's pretty

dominating.'

'If we're honest we could say he's a bloody tyrant!'

Dominic is taken aback. 'I had no idea you felt so strongly...'

'I'm beginning to wake up.'

'OK, but take it easy. There's nothing we can do about it.'

'No. Nothing...'

'I'm puzzled, Mark, I thought you and he were pretty close...what with your science and all.'

'To be honest that's all we do have in common.'

'Really?'

'Yes really.'

Dominic is moved, touched by his brothers' sudden honesty. 'You know, I've always felt he liked you more than he liked me.'

'I don't know. I think it's just about impossible for him to show his feelings...stiff upper lip and all that bollocks.'

'Yeah, well, he has been through World War II...saw some hardship, lost friends, family.'

'Yes, and what did he do in the war? Never went into battle...just sat in some country house torturing German POWs.'

'Not exactly torturing.'

'How do you know?'

'Because he told me, Mark.'

'Because he told you! And you believed him?'

'Why shouldn't I?'

It's Mark's turn to go to the window. He hits the glass with a dull thud. 'And what did he tell you?'

'That he - they- used techniques like telling blind-folded prisoners they were going to burn them and then putting iced cold bars on their backs where they couldn't tell hot from cold. Things like that...not actually harming them.'

'Still torture though.'

'OK. Fair enough.' They fall silent, pondering. After a while Dominic breaks the silence. 'You know, it's years since we talked...like this.'

'True. Funny...'

'I'm glad.'

'Me too, Dom.'

Mark walks back to his chair, but he doesn't sit. 'Look, Dad and I are going up to London to The Royal Society for a lecture by Peter Mansell on evolution. Would you like to come? I'm sure I could get you a ticket.'

'Thanks, Mark. Nice thought, but I don't think it would be a good idea. Sounds like a subject we might disagree on.'

'You're probably right. Don't fancy it much myself. Not the lecture, but being with *him* for an evening. Better go though.'

'Yeah, you go.'

'OK. Nice talk. See you later, Bro.' He walks to the French windows, opens the door and steps out into the garden.

Dominic gets up to go through to the kitchen. As he passes the front door a letter falls on the mat. He stops to pick it up. It's from India. He turns it over and there in elegant script is Bunty's name and address. He is uplifted immediately and he smiles as he carries on through to the kitchen. He fills a kettle and sets it to boil on the Aga stove. He sits at the table and opens the letter, careful not to rip the delicate envelope.

The letter begins with polite pleasantries. Bunty hopes that he had a comfortable and easy journey home, which makes Dominic smile when he thinks back to the madness of Brothers Air Services, the Dakota and the Nissen hut at Brussels Airport. Bunty gets down to the heart of the matter and he writes:

Swami Ji says that when we go inside we don't experience blankness or emptiness. Inside it will in fact be full and that's because all desire dissolves there. It'll be something that once seen there will be nothing more to see. Once we have become that there will be nothing more to become. When we have known that there will be nothing more to know. It is that sat, chit, ananda: truth, knowledge, bliss. It is that which has no other. It is endless, eternal, infinite - one and one alone. It is an everlasting, continuous experience. It is the permanent in the midst of impermanence,

the imperishable amidst the perishable.
Swami Ji says that this realm is beyond the
senses and beyond even the mind. And this
is why its existence cannot be proved by
scientific experiment. It is purely a matter
of faith and Swami Ji questions the atheist,
who asks for proof of the existence of God.
He asks that atheist if he can prove that there
is no God and asserts that no one has yet
proved the non-existence of God.

Dominic looks up from the letter, he smiles and
his gaze wanders up to the window above the
range. Clouds race across the bright blue sky.
The bare trees shiver in the breeze, their
branches like the bifurcating blood vessels of the
human body. He's inspired. His spirit soars as
he thinks of Swami Ji and feels that love once
more.

The back door opens and Lauren slips into the
kitchen. She's surprised to see Dominic sitting
there with a far-away look in his eyes.

He turns to her and smiles. 'Hi, Sis.'

'Hello, Dom.' She continues on her way
through the kitchen without stopping.

'Hold on. Why don't you sit with me for a bit?
I just had an amazing letter from my friend
Bunty in India. Want to read it?'

'Sure, if you don't mind.'

'I wouldn't ask you if I did, would I?'

'I suppose not.' She takes the letter from

Dominic and sits on one of the kitchen chairs opposite him.

He studies her as she reads, watching for her reaction.

She looks up. 'Wow! That's some letter.'

'Isn't it?'

'So that's where your meditation's supposed to take you.'

'Yup.'

'Would be something.'

'Wouldn't it.' He smiles. 'You're stoned, aren't you?'

'No…yes…very. How'd you know?'

'It's not rocket science, Lauren. Your eyes are like shining rubies.'

'How'd you know what that means?'

'I've been in India remember. I smoked a joint or two there.'

'Ah, yeah. Right.'

'You know it grows wild there along the sides of the roads.'

'You mean it's free?'

'Yes, more or less. Of course you've got to pick, dry it, roll it up.'

'Wish I lived there!'

'You like grass a lot?'

'Love it.'

'You should be careful, you know.'

'Why? It's not addictive.'

'I know that. But it affects the mind and no one

knows yet the long term effects it might have on the brain.'

'Not going to worry 'bout that.'

'I suppose not. But take my advice...and that's free too.' He laughs. 'Just don't overdo it for your own good. OK?'

'OK, Dom. Got the picture. Now, if the lecture's finished I'm going up to my room.' She stands and goes to the door then turns back. 'Thanks for letting me read your letter. It's powerful stuff.'

'It is, Lauren.'

'I can see why you went there.' She leaves the kitchen.

Dominic picks up Bunty's letter from the kitchen table and reads it again. When he's finished he puts it back in its envelope and calls the dogs. They run excitedly into the kitchen and follow him out of the house and into the garden. He plays chase with them for a few minutes then strolls out onto Adams Road with the dogs at his heels. He walks into Cambridge and through the town to his college. Term starts in two days and he wonders if Ranjit has arrived yet.

He goes into the Porters' Lodge. The bowler-hatted head porter looks up from his paper and stands to greet Dominic.

'Good afternoon, Mr Wheatcroft.'

'Good afternoon, Simms. Any mail for me?

Simms looks in Dominic's pigeon-hole. 'No, Sir. Nothing.'

'Thanks. Is Mr Rupneraan in college yet?'

'He is, Sir. Arrived this morning.'

'Thank you, Simms.'

Dominic crosses the quad with the dogs in tow. He passes the 16th century chapel, glances up at the glorious stained-glass windows, and enters staircase eight. He climbs up the well-worn steps to the first floor and Ranjit's rooms. He knocks on the door.

'Enter.'

Dominic goes into a small, cozy room, furnished with antique brown leather armchairs. A low fire burns in the grate. The room is warm and smoky. Ranjit bounds across the room and shakes Dominic's hand with great enthusiasm.

'Dominic, my dear fellow.'

'Hello, Ranjit. Good to see you again.'

The dogs fuss around the Indian's feet and he acknowledges them, rubbing their heads and backs.

'Likewise.'

Dominic immediately takes in the fact that Ranjit's not alone. A stunning, dark-haired girl in an elegant fur coat is perched on one of the armchairs. She smiles at Dominic and waves a delicate manicured hand.

'Rebecca meet Dominic. My best chum.'

She stands and walks over to the two men to shake Dominic's hand. 'Pleased to meet you. Ranjit was just talking about you. He said you'd been in India recently but didn't go to the bother of looking him up.'

Dominic looks shame-faced. 'I...I'm sorry, Ranjit. I was nowhere near Calcutta.'

'As you've already told me, dear boy. Come, let's sit down. Sherry?'

'No thanks.'

'Tea, then?'

'Please.'

Ranjit goes through to the small scullery and puts the kettle on. Rebecca sits on the arm of the chair opposite Dominic. 'So why'd you go to India?'

'It's a long story.'

'I've got the time.'

'OK. We could start where I started with Somerset Maugham's novel *The Razor's Edge*. Read it?'

'Can't say I have.'

'Read any of his books?'

'No.'

'It's a book about a disillusioned man searching for meaning and direction in his life, who goes to India to find a teacher.'

'So you went there to find a...teacher?'

'Yup.'

'And did you find one.'

'On my third attempt.'

Ranjit comes and sits beside them, putting a tray on a small table beside him. He starts to prepare the tea. 'I know Dom takes his tea with milk and no sugar. How about you, Rebecca?'

'Black, please.'

'Extreme.'

She laughs. 'If you say so.'

While Ranjit pours the tea Rebecca watches him and Dominic watches Rebecca. He finds her very attractive. Ranjit hands the teacups round.

'When I get my allowance I'll pay you back half of what I owe you, Ranjit. Should be in the next couple of days. I'll get a job in the vac and pay you the rest.'

'Thanks, Dom, but there's really no rush. I'm not hard up.'

'In fact, Rebecca, he's very rich.' He teases Ranjit.

'Oh, yes. Very, very rich.' Ranjit chuckles.

Dominic watches Rebecca sip her tea. He is fascinated by her and this doesn't go unnoticed by Ranjit. He knocks back his tea and announces, 'I've got a meeting with the college sports club secretary in five minutes. I won't be long.' He gets up and springs across the room. 'See you soon. I'm sure you can amuse yourselves while I'm away.'

Rebecca sinks into the empty armchair and Tiger-Lily jumps onto her lap. She strokes the dog's ears. 'D'you play squash?'

'Uhm, No. I'm not very keen on sport to be honest.'

'Me neither. But you look like the sporty

type...fit and athletic.'

'It's only skin deep, Rebecca.'

She laughs and Dominic's eyes are drawn to her mouth and her snow-white teeth.

'I've never liked sport either. Seems like a waste of time to me.'

'Me too.'

'So what d'you like to do, Dominic?'

'Well, reading, talking, walking the dogs, going to the cinema.'

'I love the cinema.'

'Thought you might.'

'Oh yeah. Why?'

'You dress like a film-star.' He laughs.

'The fur coat?'

'Yes.'

'Not real.'

'Whatever. It looks good on you.'

'You're too kind, gallant sir.' It's her turn to laugh. 'And what are you going to do when you grow up, Dominic?'

'Be a rich and famous film-star.'

'You're probably joking, but you've got the looks to carry that off.'

'You are too kind, fair maiden.'

'Touché. And seriously?'

'I'd like to write, but I don't know yet if I've got it in me. Maybe a journalist or work in television. Well, anyway, something in the arts. How 'bout you?'

'I'm reading Biology. I wanted to be a doctor. Now I'm more drawn to the law and fashion.'

'Big difference between those two.'

'Yes, but how're we supposed to know what we want to do until we've lived a bit and tried some things out.'

'I dunno. It's puzzling, but I do know I've always liked books, words, language.'

'So what are you reading?'

'Guess.'

'English Lit.'

'Right first time, Rebecca.' Dominic puts coal on the fire. Rebecca picks up Bella-Blue and puts the dog on her lap next to Tiger-Lily. 'Where do you live?'

'Here. In Cambridge.'

'And you?'

'London. Kensington...round the back of the Albert Hall.'

'Must be fun up in the big city.'

'It is, but I prefer it here in Cambridge. It's a beautiful place with the colleges and all.'

'So you like architecture too?'

'Yes I do. 'Specially Kings College Chapel.'

'Yeah. It's awesome. Do you know how they built it?'

'No. Not really I confess.'

'Well, they didn't use scaffolding.'

'How then?'

'They put down the foundations then one level

of stonework. Next they moved in soil and built a low hill all round the building then put in the next level of stonework. More soil, more soil...up and up and up... until the building was inside an enormous hill. And when it was done they took the hill away and voilà - a completed chapel.'

'Well, I never knew that.'

'Thought not. Most people don't. It's just history and doesn't change things much. But we don't build 'em like that anymore.'

Rebecca takes his cup. 'Might be a bit strong and cold, but d'you want some more?'

'Please.'

She pours the tea and hands his cup back to him. 'Tell me more about your teacher.'

'What d'you want to know?'

'His name. Where he lives. What he teaches.'

'The first two are easy. The third might take longer to answer.'

'Let's start then.'

'OK. His name is Swami Satchit Ananda and he lives just outside Jaipur in Rajasthan.'

'The Pink City.'

'How'd you know that?'

'Read about it somewhere. Looks nice.'

'It is - very - and it's a lot quieter than your average Indian city.'

'So you went there and met the Swami?'

'I did.'

'And what did you think of him?'

'He's an impressive man. He inspired me.'

'To do what?'

'To follow him and his teachings.'

'And what does he teach?'

'A meditation technique.'

'Is that it? You went all that way to be shown how to sit still and contemplate your navel.'

'There's more to it than that.'

'Only kidding.' Rebecca smiles at him. Dominic melts and his stomach flutters. They hear footsteps pounding up the stairs and Ranjit bursts into the room. Dominic pulls himself together.

'How'd the meeting go?'

'Oh, you know, usual damned thing…bureaucracy comes first and then the fun and games can begin. You two OK?'

Rebecca answers. 'Sure we were just discussing India. Couldn't really do that with you here…preaching to the converted…kind of thing.' They all laugh.

Chapter Twenty Five
The Royal Society

'Happiness is the interval between periods of unhappiness.'
Don Marquis

The silver Bentley pulls out from the drive and onto Adams Road. Jack is driving. Freddy and Mark are together in the back. Freddy pulls a crumpled program out of his jacket pocket and hands it to Mark. 'Mansell is a good speaker and a sound evolutionist. He puts up an effective and clear argument. I would've liked Dominic to hear it. Might've dispelled some of his foundationless beliefs.'

'I did ask him if he'd like to go, Dad, but he said no.'

'What's he doing?'

'Getting ready for the start of term I'd imagine. He'll have plenty to talk about with his friend Rupneraan.'

'Rich family that. I'd like to have some of their money. His father has promised to make an endowment when his son graduates. The college can always do with more money. So much needs to be done on the maintenance side. A lot of the roofing is badly in need of renovation and we just don't have the funds. Could be embarrassing if the leaks get any worse.'

The car rolls off Fen Causeway and onto Trumpington Road. The traffic is light and they make good progress. They soon leave Cambridge behind, bowling smoothly down the A10 to London.

As they approach The Royal Society Jack swings the car into Carlton Gardens. He spots a parking space and eases the car into it. He's a good driver. He gets out and opens the door for Freddy. Mark climbs out and joins his father. Freddy strides off without a word to Jack. Mark makes a point of thanking him.

'See you later, Jack. Round about ten I should think.'

'Thank you, Sir.'

Mark strides off after Freddy and catches him up. 'Why didn't you thank Jack or at least say something to him?'

'Why should I? He's just a servant.'

'He's a human being too. He has feelings.'

'Mind your own business, Mark. Not mine. I do what I want.'

'So I've noticed.'

'And what does that mean?'

'Never mind, Dad.

'Don't worry, I won't. I need a drink.' Freddy strides off purposefully and ducks into the pub on the corner. Mark follows him in. Freddy is already at the bar ordering a double scotch. 'What d'you want, Mark?' he asks without even looking at his son.

'Pint of bitter, please Dad.'

Freddy orders for Mark when his whisky arrives. He knocks it back in one slug and orders another. Mark shakes his head in disbelief. Freddy doesn't notice or else ignores it. Mark leans on the bar to take his beer from the barman. 'I had a good heart-to-heart with Dominic today. First decent chat I've had with him in a long, long time.'

'And?'

'We talked about this and that.'

Freddy knocks back his second whisky and looks at Mark. 'Exactly?'

'We discussed the mysterious phone calls with the Bach in the background.'

Freddy does a double take. 'Not much mystery about them!' He looks away and waves the barman over. 'Same again.'

Mark is shocked, but presses on. 'Don't you think?'

'What?'

'They're a little mysterious.'

'Nah. Just some prankster messing around.' Freddy's words are starting to slur.

'He's - or she's very persistent though.'

'Maybe...persistent but it doesn't mean anything.'

Mark sips from his beer.

'D'you talk about me?

'You were mentioned.'

'And?'

Mark takes a deep breath. 'You drink too much.'

'None of your business.'

'It is when you make an ass of yourself.'

'Ass?'

'Yes, like at The Bath Hotel.'

'Oh, that?'

'Yes, that.'

'Ancient history. College's forgotten all 'bout it.'

'I wouldn't be so sure about that.'

'What you heard?'

'Nothing…but…'

'What?'

'These things just don't get swept under the carpet. Some people have long memories.'

Freddy draws himself up. He glances at this watch. 'Time to go. Lecture's starting in…' He looks at his watch again, 'Ten minutes.'

'All right. Let's go.'

Freddy is unsteady and when Mark tries to help him he pushes him aside. 'Don't need help. Thank you very much.'

They leave the pub and make slow progress to The Royal Society. Freddy fumbles in his pocket for their invitations. He goes through all his pockets and eventually finds them. They walk up the steps to the main door. Freddy almost falls backwards as they enter the building. Mark steadies him and this time he doesn't resist. A smiling receptionist checks their invitations and they go into the hall and take their seats.

The lecture is well presented but doesn't come up with any new insights, merely reinforcing the views that Freddy and Mark already hold. Freddy dozes on and off throughout the presentation and Mark only has to nudge him once as he slumps sideways across him. As they descend to the bar they feel that their beliefs have once more been vindicated. They take the offered glasses of wine and circulate through the thong, nodding to acquaintances and colleagues. Mark stays close to Freddy afraid that he may do or say something stupid and out of order. In any event they leave without incident and walk back to the Bentley. Jack sees them coming and gets out of the car to open a rear door for them but Freddy doesn't get in. He stands, swaying slightly and leaning on the car and then he speaks.

'I'm driving back to Cambridge.' He pulls his wallet out of his jacket pocket and hands a ten pound note to Jack. 'Here. Take a cab and catch the train back to Cambridge.'

Jacks looks concerned. 'Are you sure, Sir?'

'I am sure...and don't answer back. Get going.'

Jack hesitates.

Mark's heart sinks when he thinks back to the incident after the squash game and where that led. He feels trapped in a repeating and nightmarish cycle. He calls on all his courage and manages to assert himself. 'I'm going with Jack.'

'No, you're not. You're coming with me…enjoy the drive.'

Freddy gets into the driver's seat. Mark and Jack look at each other. Both hesitate.

'In the car, Mark. We're going.'

'I'm not. I'm going on the train with Jack.'

'No, you're not. You're coming with me.'

Jack walks away and Mark starts to follow him.

'Do as you're told and get in the car.'

Mark glances at Jack and shrugs. 'Maybe I should go with him.' He walks round the car to the passenger side. 'See you later, Jack.' Mark gets into the car and Jack sets off, hailing a cab. Freddy starts the car, grinding into first gear. He pulls out from the kerb without checking the rearview mirror. A passing car successfully avoids hitting the Bentley. A horn blasts and Freddy shrugs.

'Bloody fool!' Mark takes a deep breath, wishing he were anywhere but here, in this car. Freddy switches on the car radio. With a crackle and bump the Bach Prelude & Fugue comes through loud and clear.

'Fuck!' Freddy spins the tuning dial, taking his eyes off the road, creaming through a red light. Mark gasps and Freddy scowls at him. 'Pull yourself together, boy.' Mark does a double-take. He's angry, but makes no comment. Freddy finds a light music station and hums along.

They manage to get out of London without further incident. It's a dark, overcast night. The road is not well illuminated but this does not prevent Freddy from driving fast and overtaking every car and lorry that slows his pace. He seems to be enjoying himself. The speed appears to energize him. Mark keeps his eyes closed and wishes he could doze but he can't.

Just north of Broxbourne the road curves to the right and Freddy loses control of the Bentley. It hurtles off the road and crashes through a hedge. It hits a rise and rolls. Mark is thrown from the car, hitting the ground hard, dislocating his shoulder, breaking his arm in two places and badly grazing his face. It all happens in slow-motion. Time is stretched out. Seconds feel like minutes and he is strangely detached and fearless. It's as if it is happening to someone else. He has got off lightly, but not so Freddy. He is flung through the windscreen, fracturing his skull and breaking his back. His right eyeball pops from its socket and falls into the mud. His right foot has been sheared clean and his blood pumps into the furrows of the field. The car ploughs into the ground and comes to a grinding halt. It steams as the water system spews its heat into the night. Mark is stunned, but remains conscious. Freddy is alive but dead to the world.

There were witnesses to the accident and the police are on the scene within 15 minutes. An ambulance arrives a little later and Freddy's life is saved - just.

Mary is concerned but not alarmed when the big clock in the hall chimes midnight. She assumes that Freddy and Mark will have gone to dine after the lecture and will be home at any minute. Lauren is asleep. Dominic is in college. When the phone rings an hour later she half expects another mystery phone call but not Addenbrookes hospital.

'Mrs Wheatcroft?'

'Yes.'

'Good evening. This is Addenbrookes hospital. I am Dr. Moorcock. I'm afraid I have some bad news for you.'

Mary sways and sits down.

'Hello? Are you there?'

'I am.'

'There's been an accident. Your husband and your son were admitted here an hour ago. Your son has minor injuries and is recovering well. I'm afraid that I cannot say the same for your husband. He's unconscious and is seriously injured.'

Mary lapses into stunned silence. She is ashen. The front door bell rings once, then again and then a third time.

'Mrs Wheatcroft? Are you there?'

'Yes, yes I am.'

'We are doing everything we can for your husband, but he's in a dangerous condition. You should come to the hospital as soon as you can.'

Mary manages a weak, 'Thank you. My daughter is…she can drive me.' She puts down the phone. She's in shock. Immobilized. She doesn't respond when the front door bell rings once, then again and then a third time.

Lauren comes down the stairs in her dressing-gown. She glances at Mary and goes to open the front door. She stands back to let two policemen into the hall. She glances from them to her mother. She is frightened.

The policemen remove their helmets and wait awkwardly by the door. 'We have some bad news.'

'I know.' Mary stands then falls back in the chair. Lauren goes to her. 'The hospital rang…just now.' She turns to Lauren. 'Daddy and Mark have been in an accident. Mark is…Daddy's in danger…go now to Addenbrookes…we…'

Lauren goes to Mary, puts her arm around her and looks back at the two policemen.

'There's been a car accident in Broxbourne. As far as we know no other car was involved…but the car…' He glances at his notes. 'The Bentley left the road. We don't know why yet.' The policeman looks uncomfortable.

Lauren gathers herself. 'Thank you, officer. We'll go to the hospital.'

'Very well, Madam. We'll be in touch again when the facts of the incident have been established.' The policemen turn and leave. Mary breaks down. She can no longer contain herself. Lauren hugs her.

'We have to go now, Mummy...face this...whatever...I'll get your coat and dress then I'll get the Mini.' Lauren puts on a bold front. Inside she's cracking, but to support her mother, she displays remarkable courage. Courage she was not aware she had.

Lauren gives Mary her coat then runs upstairs, changes her clothes and returns to the hall after a couple of minutes and helps Mary to put on her coat. She takes the car keys off a hook by the front door and goes out to the garage. Mary hears the car start up and gathering herself she walks shakily out onto the front drive. Lauren helps her into the Mini. They don't speak. Neither knows what to say. Lauren thinks of Dominic and wonders if she should have phoned him. She resolves to call the college when they reach the hospital.

The drive across the city is painful. Both women are full of fear and trepidation. They don't speak. They want to get to the hospital, but are dreading what they'll find. Lauren swings the car into the hospital car park. She switches off the engine and they sit in silence, frozen.

'Come on, Mummy. We've got to go in. We can't just sit here.'

Mary turns to turn towards Lauren. She is forlorn. Lauren gets out of the car and goes to help her mother. Mary is shaking, but manages to climb out herself. She all but falls into Lauren's arms. 'What's happened? I can't bear it.'

'We must.' She leads her mother across the car park and into the hospital reception. They go up to the desk. A nurse comes up to them.

'Can I help you?'

Lauren takes the initiative. 'Yes, we've come to see two patients...Frederick and Mark Wheatcroft.' Lauren glances at the clock. It's 01.10. The nurse consults the register.

'Yes. You'll need to see Dr. Moorcock. I'll call him. Take a seat, please.' She nods in the direction of a row of chairs against the opposite wall. She picks up a phone and dials, waiting. 'They're here, Sir. Will you come down?' She replaces the receiver. 'He'll be here in a few minutes. Can I get you a cup of tea?'

Mary shakes her head and Lauren answers for them both. 'No thank you.' She sits down next to her mother. They wait as patiently as they are able. Mary wrings her hands together, not knowing where to look. Lauren puts her hand over her mother's to try and calm her. They wait for another five minutes or so before Dr. Moorcock arrives. He pulls up a chair and joins them.

'Your son is fine. His injuries are minor and he'll be able to leave hospital tomorrow. His face is grazed so he looks a lot worse than he is.'

Mary sighs and slumps. She looks like a little girl - scared and lost. Lauren's heart goes out to her.

'However I am not able to say the same for your husband Mrs Wheatcroft. He is seriously injured and... he may not survive the night. I'm sorry. He has lost an eye and his right foot.'

Mary flinches, clutching Lauren's hand. She is shaking.

'If you'd like to follow me I'll take you to see your husband.' He attempts a smile and falters, turning away. Mary and Lauren follow him. Lauren is reminded of the first time she visited her grandmother. Then she remembers that she hasn't called the college to speak to Dominic.

'Excuse me, Dr. Moorcock.'

He stops and turns back to her. 'Yes?'

'Would it be possible for me or someone to call St Andrew's College to get a message to my brother Dominic to tell him what's happened.'

'Certainly. Yes. I will have a member of staff make the call. D'you want your brother to meet you here?'

'Yes. I'll wait at least until he gets here.'

Moorcock nods and leads off again.

At the end of a long corridor they climb two flights of stairs and the doctor leads them to a door marked Intensive Care. Before he opens the door he turns to Mary and Lauren. 'Please prepare yourselves. Professor Wheatcroft is unconscious, but I think you should see him so I can outline the extent of his injuries and our current prognosis.' He opens the door and they follow him into a brightly lit reception area and then through to a door, which already has Freddy's name pinned to it. He goes in and they follow. Freddy is lying on a bed. He is wearing a green robe. His head and leg are bandaged.

Mary and Lauren stand dumbly beside the bed. 'Your husband...father has a fractured skull. He has lost his right eye, but the other is undamaged. His spine is broken in two places and his right foot was severed at the ankle. We have not been able to save it.'

Mary lurches forward. She takes Freddy's limp hand. Her body is wracked with sobs. Lauren goes to her, putting an arm around her mother's shoulder. Dr Moorcock waits for the initial shock to wear off a little.

'Until he regains consciousness we won't know the extent of the damage to his brain and his cognitive functions. He'll almost certainly lose motor control of his body from his waist down. In due course I can explain the implications of

241

this.'

Mary looks at him with dumb incomprehension as she struggles to take everything in.

'I feel I must make you aware of the fact that there was a very high, and I stress very, high level of alcohol in his body. I would hazard a guess - an informed guess - that this was the cause of the accident. I'm sure that you'll appreciate this.'

Mary does not respond and Lauren steps in. 'Thank you doctor. You have made it…this all very clear. You'll understand that we need time to absorb these facts.'

'Certainly. I think you have seen enough and that I've told you enough for now.' He gestures towards the door and they follow him meekly into reception.

'Please take a seat.' He walks over to the desk and talks to a nurse. He comes back to them. 'Your son, Dominic, is on his way here now. Mark is asleep. I suggest that you wait until he wakes before you see him.'

Lauren turns to Mary. 'Why don't you go home, Mummy? We should ring Dobbo and ask her to come here to collect you.'

Mary nods her assent without uttering a word.

'We'll phone your home and ask D…'

'Dobbo Dobbo Finding. She's our housekeeper, cook. She can look after Mummy. She'll cope.

She's a strong lady.'

Dr Moorcock goes back to the desk and issues instructions. He returns to Mary and Lauren. 'We'll arrange for a taxi to go to your home to pick up your housekeeper and bring her here. I suggest that we go back to the main reception to wait for her and Dominic.'

The two women nod their assent and follow him out.

Dobbo takes Mary back to Adams Road and half an hour later Dominic arrives at the hospital. He is disheveled and unshaven. He sees Lauren stand to greet him and runs over to her. They hug.

'How is he…how are they?'

'Mark's OK. The worse for wear and tear, but he'll be fine. Things don't look so good for Daddy. He's badly injured. He drove the Bentley off the road. Mark was thrown clear but Daddy went through the windscreen. His skull is fractured and his back is broken. They won't know how serious things are until he comes round.'

Dominic is shaken and can barely believe his ears. 'But wasn't Jack driving?'

'It appears not.'

'I don't get it.'

We won't know the full story until Mark wakes and can explain what happened. I can tell you, though, that Dad was very drunk.'

'Oh, no!'

'I don't know what's happened to him. He used to be so…in control.'

Dominic sighs. 'Can we get a coffee? I need something to…'

Lauren stands and goes to the reception desk. The nurse points up a corridor. Dominic joins Lauren and they walk hand in hand in the indicated direction. They go into the canteen and order coffees. Dominic drums his fingers on the counter. 'How's Mum?'

'I don't know if she's going to get through this. She looks…broken.'

'Dobbo's a big help and she's a strong woman. She'll do and say the right things.'

'Yes, but…in the future.'

'The future? It's very uncertain, Dom.'

'You could say.'

Their coffees arrive. Dominic pays. They take them to a table and sit next to each other. Dominic takes Lauren's hand. 'You know I asked Swami Ji why there was so much suffering in the world.'

'And?'

'Amongst other things he quoted a Sufi mystic, who said more or less that God created the universe in order that he could know himself. He had to allow for anything to happen - the good and the bad - so that he could know *everything* there is to know about himself. Joseph

244

Stalin, Adolph Hitler...the whole damned shooting-match.'

Lauren shakes her head in wonderment. 'Too much for me.'

'Me too.'

She thinks for a minute or two. 'If Daddy's paralyzed will he be able to live at home?'

'I imagine so. I mean, does it matter where he is?'

'I don't know. Will we know how to...look after him?'

'If we don't, I guess we can learn.'

'But will Mummy be able to cope?'

'I don't know. Maybe she's stronger than we give her credit for.'

'But without Daddy...'

'She'll have to learn to make decisions on her own...not lean on him, rely on him to make the moves.'

'What about if his brain is injured?'

'You mean mentally impaired?'

'That's what I mean.'

Dominic is lost for words. 'I...what...we'll just have to see...nothing else we can do.'

They finish their coffees in silence. Lauren stands. 'Let's go and see if Mark's awake.' They leave the canteen, walk back down the corridor and up one flight of stairs. They find the Mark's ward and go to the nurses' station.

'Can I help you?'

'We've come to see our brother. Mark Wheatcroft. Is he awake?'

'Yes, sir, he is. But strictly speaking these are not visiting hours.'

'I'm sure you can make an exception, can't you? We haven't seen him since the accident and we do really need to talk to him.'

'I'll ask Matron.' She leaves the station, walks down the ward and goes through a door at the far end.

Dominic shrugs, doing his utmost to control his frustration, which threatens to get the better of him. Lauren looks round the ward, but in the dim light it's impossible to tell one patient from another. She leans her head on Dominic's shoulder. He squeezes her hand.

The nurse comes back to the ward. 'Matron says that you can see Mr Wheatcroft, but has asked that you keep your voices down and that you don't stay too long.'

'We're not going to shout at him,' Lauren snaps back.

The nurse raises an eyebrow, but doesn't rise to the bait. She beckons for them to follow her down the ward and to a bed on the far left side. Mark sees them and waves. They reach his bed.

'Hello Lauren. Hello Dom.'

Lauren bends to kiss him on his cheek.

'Hi, Mark.' The two boys touch hands. Lauren and Dominic sit down on opposite sides of the bed. Mark's face is red and starting to scab. The abrasions are not deep. His arm is in a sling.

'What a cock-up!'

'What happened? I thought Jack was driving you.'

'He was until Dad sent him home on the train when we got back to the car.'

'Why'd he do that?'

'Said he wanted to drive, Dom. Insisted on it.'

'We've been told he was drunk. Couldn't you stop him?'

'He was drunk and we did - both of us - try to…dissuade him, but he wouldn't budge. You know what he's like.'

'I do. Thought he was number one…but he's not now, not anymore by the sound of it.'

'What d'you mean?'

'His back is broken and he has head injuries. They don't know how bad yet and won't until he comes round.'

'Fuck!'

'You could say.'

'What about you, Mark? How are you?'

'I'll be OK, Sis, once my arm mends and I get my youthful good looks back.' He smiles.

'What actually happened?'

'He was driving like a madman. Nearly had a pile-up just getting out of the West End. We were coming down the hill just before Broxbourne and the road takes a turn to the right, but he didn't.

247

We just kept on going straight doing about seventy.'

'Oh, my God. Must've been terrifying.'

'It was, Lauren, but honestly I didn't have much time to think or feel anything. We went through a hedge. The car turned over, throwing me out, then she ploughed into the ground. I was stunned but eventually found Dad. He was unconscious and I didn't want to move him. He looked all kind of twisted up. I remembered it's better not to move injured people 'less you have to. Then I heard someone calling from the road and saw a man there waving. He shouted that someone had gone to a phone box just down the road and that they were going to call 999. I shouted thanks and slumped down in the mud. My arm was hurting like hell and my face was bleeding. I didn't know how bad my injuries were. But I felt more or less OK. Just didn't like standing. I don't know how long I waited but the police and an ambulance seemed to get there pretty quickly. I gave up then and let myself be led to the ambulance while they tended to Dad.'

'Poor you.'

'Poor Dad, Lauren. How's Mum taking it?'

'With difficulty. Don't know how she's going to cope if...'

'If what?'

'If Daddy's paralyzed and…not OK in the head.'

'Why d'you think he might not be all right like

that...in that way?'

'Don't know what he might have done. His skull's badly fractured.'

Dominic holds up his hand. 'We must just hope for the best. Not be n...'

Lauren turns to him. 'I'm not being negative, Dom. Just realistic.'

'OK. Fair enough.'

Lauren stifles a yawn. She looks exhausted. Mark picks up on it. 'You're tired, Sis. You should go home. See how Mum is and get some rest.'

'OK. I will. I am tired.'

'You should go with her, Dom.'

'Are you sure you'll...'

'Yes. Yes. I'm fine. Well, could be better, but...'

Lauren stands. 'OK, Dom?'

He goes round the bed to join her. 'Bye, Mark. I'll come back soon.'

'Bye you two.' He lies back on his pillows and waves with his good hand.

In the cab on the way home they watch the sun rising up over the spires of Cambridge.

'Beautiful city, isn't it?'

'It certainly is, Dom. We're really lucky to live here.' They lapse back into silence. Then Dominic turns to her and says, 'I've met a girl I really like.'

'Oh? How exciting.'

'Yes, but it's early days. I've only just met her.'

'Well, if nothing else, I'm glad you like her.'

'Thanks, but there is a possible snag.'

'Which is?'

'I met her in Ranjit's rooms. I...I don't know if they're together.'

'You'll have to ask.' She smiles at him.

'I will.' He smiles.

Mary is asleep in her bedroom when they reach home. They go through to the kitchen. Dobbo is snoozing by the Aga. She stirs and turns to them.

'Sorry to disturb you. Just wondered how Mary is?'

'I was only dozing, Sir. Mrs. Wheatcroft is asleep.'

'How's she taking it?'

'It's not for me to say.'

Lauren walks over to her. 'It is, Dobbo. You're more like a friend than anything else.'

'Oh, I don't think so.'

'I know Mrs. W...Mary thinks so.'

'That's good enough for me. I gave her two of her sleeping pills. I thought she was that distraught she'd never get off without them.'

'That was the right thing to do, Dobbo.'

'Thank you, Mr Dominic.'

'I think we should all get some sleep and gather our strength for tomorrow.'

Chapter Twenty Six
A Rude Awakening
'Do what thou wilt shall be the whole of the law.'
Aleister Crowley

When Freddy comes round in the middle of the night he's totally confused - unable to work out where he is or how he got there. A nurse walks by and he groans, which is enough to catch her attention. She comes over to the bed, confirms that his drip is in place then looks down at him. 'Professor Wheatcroft?' She waits for a response. Freddy tries to make sense of her words and to speak. Nothing comes out - just a hoarse croak. She shines a torch into his eyes.

'I'll get a doctor.' She touches his hand then strides off purposefully down the ward. Freddy tries to turn his head to follow her. The bandages restrain him and he gives up. His head and face hurt when he tries to speak or move. He can't feel his legs.

Dr. Moorcock is standing at the window in his office. He looks out over the car park, lifting his hands on and off a radiator. There is a knock on his door.

'Come in.'

His secretary puts her head round the door.

'Mrs. Wheatcroft and two of her children have arrived.'

'Thank you. Send them in please.'

Mary, Dominic and Laura come into the room. They each shake hands with Moorcock then sit in the empty chairs opposite his desk.

'Professor Wheatcroft is making good progress and we're satisfied that he's well on the mend. He's still confused but we're happy that there won't be any lasting damage to his cognitive faculties.'

Mary sighs and leans towards Lauren. She puts her arm round her mother,

Moorcock looks down at the blotter on his desk. There is a pressurized silence. He lifts his head. 'Professor Wheatcroft's back was broken in three places. He will not walk again. We must wait to see what control of his functions he'll retain.'

All three are shocked. Dominic feels he is stumbling around in a dark room, seeking the light and some equilibrium. He cannot begin to consider what this news implies for the family, what effect it will have on them. He wants to talk about his father's mental state and how he'll cope when he finds out what the accident really means. He will not walk again. Dominic is not sure that his father will be able to rise to the challenge. He finally blurts out, 'Who will tell him? I...we can't. Can we, Lauren?'

She looks round at him. She is drained and lost. 'No.'

Mary shakes her head.

'The nursing staff here is very good. We'll make sure that he is supported.'

Mary sits up. 'Yes, but will he come home?'

'Yes, he'll go home. I assure you As soon as he's fit enough. Of course he'll mostly be on his back. He'll never sit up unaided. He'll be able to make use of an electric wheelchair, but will not be able to propel himself.' Moorcock pauses. 'You must be as prepared as you can. It's a big change that you'll need to come to terms with. His life will be very different and he'll need all the support you can give him. Patience will be essential. It's obvious, I know…' His voice trails away and he sits back into the desk chair and waits.

Chapter Twenty Seven
Solve et Coagulum
'He separates in order to unite.'
Paracelcus

Dominic and Rebecca are walking through King's College.

'When I went back last night he didn't say much, but he recognized me. They say it won't happen overnight but he'll recover from his head injury. I suppose we must just be grateful for that.'

'It's a hard thing...for him, your mother...all of you.'

Dominic shrugs. Rebecca puts her arm through his and pulls him close. They stop. He turns to her as she puts her face up to meet his. They kiss. They hold each other close until they are forced apart by the sheer quantity of students making their way to the refectory for lunch.

They stand apart to make way, their eyes locked. When the flood has passed they move close together again. 'I like you, Rebecca.'

She smiles, 'I like you too.' She takes his hand and they walk on down the side of the chapel.

'I feel bad though about...'

'About Ranjit?'

'Yes, Ranjit. He's my friend and he helped me get home from India. He's loyal too. He won't like this.'

'Don't tell him yet. We - him and me - are drifting apart. I'm not what he's looking for.'

'What's he looking for?'

'Fun, I think you'd say, Dominic. He doesn't want anything *serious*. He'll soon find someone to fill the gap.'

'Yes, maybe, but his pride will be hurt for sure. It'll be humiliating. Won't it?'

'It will. Other peoples' opinions of him are important. Maybe something to do with being Indian.'

'I think any man - most men - would find it hard to take. Loss of face.'

'It'll blow over.'

'I know it will in time. Problem is now.'

'We don't tell him yet. I will stop seeing him and you and I should keep in the shadows for a bit.'

Dominic laughs, 'In the shadows!'

'Yes. We won't rub his nose in it. Keep out of his way. I told you my room's in Jesus Lane. We should meet there. In fact we should go there now - right now.'

'OK. Yes.' He walks off, holding onto Rebecca's hand. 'It's just that...he's a good friend and I like him.'

'You mean you don't want to!'

'Of course I want to…nothing more. But…Ranjit…'

'You can't.'

'I think we should wait.'

'I don't want to wait.'

He throws up his hands. 'OK, you win. I surrender.'

She drags him off at a run. They cross the market place then head down to Petty Cury, past the Red Lion Hotel then out onto Sidney Street. They stop. Out of breath. Then walk off down Sidney Street.

Later when they are sitting in front of the gas fire Dominic asks, 'D'you know Richard Bannerman?'

Rebecca thinks about this. 'I've heard the name.'

'He's an artist. He lives up Hills Road.'

'Ah, yes I've got it now. I met him in El Patio. He's interesting looking.'

'How d'you mean?'

'He was tall and he had dark, far-away eyes. Like a romantic poet.'

'Did you fancy him?'

Rebecca laughs when she realizes that Dominic is jealous. She smiles sideways at him. 'Would it bother you if I did?'

'Well…' He is lost for words.

She takes pity on him. 'As a matter of fact I didn't.'

Dominic looks away, embarrassed.

'Anyway, why do you want to know?'

'Oh. My sister, Lauren, is seeing him. Well, she was seeing him. I don't know if she still is.'

'You don't seem too happy about it.'

'I'm not. I don't mean to be patronizing, but Lauren is easily impressed.'

'You are being patronizing. We can all be impressed, Dominic. I don't suppose she's any more impressionable than you are.'

'Probably not. It's just that he smokes a lot.'

'Smokes a lot! You mean pot?'

'That's what I mean.'

'And?'

'So...'

'And?'

'Maybe it's not doing her any good.'

'Maybe it's not doing her any harm either. I expect you've tried it, Dom.'

'Uh, huh. In India. Once'

'And?'

''Well, I liked it. Seemed harmless enough.'

'Stop worrying about her and this Richard. You've other more pressing things you should be thinking about.'

'Yes, I must go to the hospital tonight. See my brother...' He glances at his watch. 'I should go.' He leans over and kisses her. 'Can we meet for lunch tomorrow?'

'Not coming back tonight?'

'I should spend some time at home with my mother to discuss the future...my father.' He stands, grabs his coat and leaves. Rebecca doesn't move. She's thinking about him. She smiles.

Dominic drives Mary and Lauren to the hospital. Mary is sitting in the front of the Mini. 'Mark can come home this evening.'
'You told me that, Mummy.'
'Oh, did I? Sorry.'
'Will Dr. Moorcock be there, Mum?'
'I don't know.'
'Doubt it, Dom. It's a bit late. We should see Daddy anyway.'
'Of course. We should go there first.'
'Dr. Grayson came to see me today.'
'I rang him, Mummy. I thought you should talk to someone outside the family.'
'Well, he is like family. He saw you both born.'
'I know he's an old friend, but he's not related. Did he help you?'
'Yes. He did. It was good to hear him talk about Daddy in an optimistic way.'
'What'd he say?'
'He said that it'll be very hard for him to adjust to his paralysis. That it may take him years.'
'That maybe he never will.'
'Dominic! Don't talk like that. Please.'
'Sorry, Mum, but you know how proud he is with his physical fitness, his appearance. He'll feel his dignity's been stripped away. He may

not be able to cope with the humiliation.'

'It doesn't have to be humiliating.'

'Doesn't have to be, Lauren. I agree, but you know Dad. Humility's not his big thing.'

The Mini turns into the hospital car park. It's drizzling. They run into the main reception and go straight on up to the wards. They meet a nurse coming out of the intensive care unit.

'Good evening. Ah, Mrs. Wheatcroft. Your husband has just been moved into a private room. If you go up the next floor, turn left and it's the fifth door on the right. He's much better, but he's very distressed. He knows now that he won't walk again, but he refuses to accept it at the moment. It may take quite a while for him to come to terms with what he's…what's happened.'

'Thank you.'

'If you would like to go ahead I'll be up there in a few minutes. You can wait for me if you would prefer to.'

'No, we'll go ahead.'

The nurse turns and walks off down the corridor. The family climbs up to the next floor. They are dragging their feet, unwilling to face up to what they might find. They stand uneasily outside Freddy's door. Dominic finally turns the handle and opens the door. Freddy lies still, staring at the ceiling. The only movement is the rise and fall of his chest.

'Freddy. Hello, darling.' Reluctantly they go further into the room. Freddy continues to ignore them. They stand around the bed.

'Can't walk. Can't sit up. Can't feel my legs.'

'I know, darling.'

'What d'you know? You've no idea. Look at you *standing* there!' Freddy turns away to stare at the wall.

'You'll be all right.'

'How can I be *all right*. All right! My life is ruined, over, finished.'

'But it's not. We need you. We love you…whatever…however you are.'

'I did it though. It was my fault.'

'No, no, please don't say that…think that.'

'But it's true. Mark…'

'Mark is going to be fine. The worst thing was a broken arm. He's coming home tonight.'

'And me?'

'What, darling?'

'When will I be coming home?'

'Soon. As soon as you're stable and we have things ready for you at home.'

'What d'you mean ready?'

'Your bedroom. We have to…make some special arrangements.'

'Like what?'

'The right kind of bed for you.'

'That's me then - just a bed.'

'Dad, please!' Dominic turns away. It's almost

more than he can handle.

'We all want to help you, Daddy. We want you to be as comfortable as possible.'

'I'll never be comfortable, Lauren - ever again!'

'But, home...'

'I don't want to go home.'

'Stay here, Daddy?'

'Stay here! I hate it here. I don't want to be there or here. I don't want to be anywhere. Not now. Not ever. Finished. I want to have done with it.'

'You mustn't say that, darling. You can't...'

'I can and I will. I am me. I can...' Freddy breaks. He starts to sob. His shoulders sag and his chin falls to his chest. 'I'm finished with it. Can't go on.'

'You can, Dad. You must...for everyone.'

'But not for me. I can't even control my bladder! What kind of life..?'

'You can read. You can write, Freddy.'

'But not do my job.'

'Maybe you can once the transport is organized and we've got you used to a wheelchair. You could go into college, go to meetings.'

'I can't see it. Seems hopeless with all these...' He points down the bed. '...tubes and bags. Who could help me with these? Who would want to help me? It's disgusting, don't you think?' He looks at Lauren.

'We're all human, Daddy. We all have to do these things.'

'Yes, but we…you take care of yourselves. You don't need help. You don't need someone to clean up after you…clean you up. It's so humiliating. It's unbearable. Absolutely unbearable and I *can't* bear it. I've had enough - more than enough.'

'You have no choice, Daddy. You have to go on. We all have to go on. It's not what we would have chosen.' She shrugs, turning to Dominic. 'We don't always get what we want.'

Dominic is staring at the floor, looking for insight, understanding and strength. Trying to see the rightness of what has happened. He tries to think of Swami Ji, but he cannot conjure up his image in his mind. He tries to recall the sound of his voice, again without success. He wonders how it can all be for the best. He wants to ask his father how he could have been stupid enough to get so drunk and then insist on driving. He wants to accuse him, put him on the spot and make him admit the true import of his mistakes and face the fall-out. His compassion has drained out of him and he feels only anger. He turns from the bed and walks to the door. 'I'm going to see, Mark. I'll wait for you there.'

Dominic stands beside Mark's bed. 'He's not doing well. He can't take it…what's happened, what he's done.'

'I'm not surprised.' Mark is sitting on the side

of his bed. He's dressed. 'I want to go straight home. Don't want to see him.'

'I can understand that. Not surprised.' He looks up as Mary and Lauren come onto the ward. They both look drawn, but attempt to smile when they reach Mark's bed.

'Ready?'

'Yes, Mum.' He stands, picking up a small bag. 'Got my tooth brush. Let's go. I've had quite enough of this place.' He attempts a smile as he puts his good arm around his mother's shoulders and leads her off the ward. Lauren and Dominic follow them.

They discuss Freddy over dinner. They are not confident that they can handle him, find the patience and commitment to help him back into his life. There seem to be more pieces than they can pick up even as a family. After coffee Dominic and Lauren go out, leaving Mary, Mark and Dobbo going over practicalities in the drawing room. Mary is relying more and more on Dobbo's help and her fund of country wisdom. Both Dominic and Lauren are keen to get out, get away from the issue and the questions hanging over them. He drops Lauren at Richard's Hills Road house and drives round to Jesus Lane. Rebecca opens the door to her rooms, pulling Dominic in. She kisses him passionately.

'God, I've missed you.'

Dominic is grinning. 'What a welcome! Anytime you like.'

'Now.'

'Now?'

'Yes.'

'What?'

'Bed, silly!' She leads him across the room and sits on the bed.

Dominic takes her head in his hands. 'You're beautiful, Rebecca. I...it's amazing we met, to be with you...amazing.' They lie down together and slowly undress.

An hour later they are lying side by side in bed. On the wall shadows of bare winter branches sway, outlined by the orange streetlights.

'It's very difficult at home. My mother is so distressed and none of us know what to do to help her and to get ready for my father coming home. We've no experience.'

'I guess most people don't, Dom. It's not something that happens to everyone or very often.'

'You're right. But I'm left feeling frustrated and sad for us - particularly my mother. It's odd. I'm a mixture of elation and melancholia.'

'What are you elated about?' She knows the answer, but she wants to hear him say it.

'You know.' He feels awkward and frightened of expressing his feelings.

'I don't. Tell me.'

'You.'

'What about me?'

'Everything about you.'

'Which means?'

'Means...I...'

'Yes?'

Dominic takes a deep breath and, fearing rejection, he just says it straight, 'I love you.'

She looks at him then hugs him to her. 'I love you too, my darling, Dominic.'

'Yes?'

'Yes, of course. Can't you tell?' She laughs and he does too.

I can't tell anything anymore, Rebecca. My world's gone upside down. I flit between pleasure and pain. Between certainty and doubt.'

'That meditation and what you learnt in India must help.'

'Yes. Well...I hope so, though it all seems distant to me now. Like another life, something that happened to someone else. Some things are clearer, but some other things are very puzzling.'

'Well, I try not to think too much about the meaning of it all. If it even has a meaning. I just want to get on and live, have fun, enjoy things.'

'Things like my father can look forward to.' There is a note of sarcasm in his voice. He feels stung.

'Sorry, Dom. But it's not my fault he's hurt. I

can still live my life.'

'You can as long as things go along nicely for you.'

'Surely we've got to be optimistic.'

'Yes, of course. Optimistic, but realistic too.'

'If we can't understand it, does it matter?'

'Maybe not. Maybe we should just be as happy as possible and get on with it. But, you've got to wonder, Rebecca, what this universe is all about. In fact I often ponder on why there is a universe at all. What's the point when there's so much pain, suffering, disappointment in the world? Why didn't the creative force - whatever that is - make a decent job of it?'

'Make a decent job of it! What d'you mean?'

'Well, what d' you think is going on? Don't you ever wonder about this? Or do you take it at face value? What we see is what we get. It's not going anywhere. Honestly, Rebecca, you're a bright girl, so tell me, does it truly have any meaning for you or is it meaningless?'

'I've told you I don't think it matters if we don't understand anything. Your dogs don't understand and look how happy they are.'

'Good point.'

'OK. Thanks for that. Now give it your best shot. Come on, explain the world if you can.'

'You're on. Try this - the 14th Century Sufi mystic Kaygusuz Abdul wrote: "I was a hidden treasure and I desired to be known. Therefore I made the creation in order that I might know myself. Before creation the One Reality existed as undifferentiated unity. Because of the One Reality's wish to know itself, the world of differentiation and duality was created.'" He pauses. Waits. 'Get it?'

"Course I get it. If it helps you, then good. It's neither here nor there for me. Just philosophers philosophizing. Just words. Anyway how d'you know about this stuff?'

'I don't really *know* about these things, Rebecca. I just read books, remember and listen. Simple as that. Thing is in the end I believe that we can get in touch with the root energy, get back to the source of the whole damned thing. That's what Swami Ji told us and I believe him.'

Chapter Twenty Eight
A Painting You Might See the World Through

'One of the best things nature's given us is grass. Don't you think, Lauren?' Richard is painting broad brush strokes of radiant blue on a sheet of glass. It is two days later.

'Yeah, I'd agree with that. Grass and dogs too. Not to mention you and me, of course.'

'Of course. And trees too.'

'Broad beans.'

'Paper.'

'Ink.'

'Nail files.'

'Nail files?'

'Yes. Nail files. They come in handy - 'scuse the pun.'

Lauren walks round the easel to look at his painting. 'Glass, eh?' Well, I'll give you this, Richard, you do experiment, push at the boundaries. You're not afraid to…'

'What?'

'Oh, I dunno. Try different things.' She looks at the painting. 'What d'you call this?'

'A painting you might see the world through.'

'Clever! And you can.'

'What?'

'See the world through it.'

'I was just looking out the window - that window - the other morning and I felt I was looking at a painting. It occurred to me that the scene I was looking out at could in fact be painted on the glass and that if it was done very well, very real and you weren't too close you'd never know.'

"Cept if nothing's moving.'

"Cept if...true but if you just glance at it you might miss the fact that everything's frozen. It might be a still day with no traffic on the road or pedestrians walking by. In fact maybe you could just somehow project film onto the glass with the odd car passing and maybe a plane flying over.'

Richard steps back from the painting and dries his hands and his brush on a cloth. 'Talking of films, fancy going to the flicks?'

'T'see what?'

'They're showing *The Big Sleep* with Humphrey Bogart this afternoon up the Rex. What d'you think? Go?'

'Yup. That'd be good. Just what I need - a good thriller.'

'Right. Let's do it. I'll R a coupla Js. We can smoke one here and the other on the walk.' He looks out of the window. 'Not raining yet.'

They stroll into town and down Jesus Lane,

passing Rebecca's rooms without realizing that Dominic is there. They walk over Jesus Green, smoking the second joint, crossing the river by the footbridge over the lock. Richard pauses, looking down at the water.

'I'm sorry about our row at the hospital and that I never apologized to you.'

'That's OK, Richard. It was pretty ghastly for both of us. So...don't worry.' She puts her arm round him and they walk on.

'How's your dad?'

'Not good. He's all smashed up and he did it to himself. He feels like shit and I'm not surprised. Life doesn't hold much hope for him at the moment.'

'So what you gonna do?'

'How'd you mean?'

'When he gets home.'

'I'm not going to *do* anything. 'Cept maybe spend time with him, take him out for walks.'

'Well, in my book, that's doing something.'

'I thought you meant looking after him practically. Feeding him, washing him...that kind of thing.'

'Hadn't really thought too much about what he might need. But if he's paralyzed from the waist down he's gonna need a lot of care.'

'Look, Richard, I really don't want to talk about him. Let's not discuss it. OK?'

'OK, by me, princess.'

Lauren smiles at him and they head up Carlyle Road and onto Magrath Avenue.

A tall black man in a white raincoat steps out from the shadows and calls out with a booming voice, 'Hi, Richard.' He walks across the road to join them. 'How you doin', man?'

Richard and the black man shake hands.

'I'm good thanks, Scotty. How you?'

'OK, man. Good to be back in Cambridge.'

'Ah. Sorry. Lauren this is Scotty.' They shake hands. 'He's in the Air Force stationed out at Lakenheath.' He turns to Scotty, 'Where's Jackson?'

'Down in the town. Doin' some business. Meeting me up here then we're gonna to see the movie.'

'*The Big Sleep*?'

'Yup.'

'Same's us.'

'Hi there.' Richard turns to see another black man walking fast up the street towards them. 'Good to see you, Richard. You comin' to the movies?'

'Sure are, Jackson.' They shake. 'This is Lauren.'

'Pleased to meet you Lauren. You live in Cambridge?'

'Yes, I do.'

'Lucky girl. Great city.' He puts his arm round Richard and they walk across to the ticket office. 'Four for 3.30.' He gets out his wallet.

Richard steps up. 'Thanks, Scotty, but I'll pay for us.'

'No way, man. This is on me.'

'You sure?'

'Yeah, I'm sure. We just got paid and there's nothing to spend money on at the base.'

'You got your PX.'

'Yup. We got that. Reminds me, I'll bring your Levis next week. Got you a carton of Pall Malls right here in my sack though.'

'You're a pal, Scotty.'

'You too, Richard, man. You got no idea. Really value our friendship. Means a lot to me.'

'King Street Corner House?   Richard glances at Lauren. She looks puzzled and very stoned. He takes her hand and leads her into the cinema.

After the film they stroll back into Cambridge over Jesus Green. Scotty stops and, shielding one hand with the other, he lights a big joint. They sit on park bench. A low mist runs up from the stream and out across the green. Pedestrians sail through it seemingly without touching the ground. Richard and Scotty grin at each other.

'We gonna eat?'

'Good idea, Scotty. Where?' Richard stands and stretches his legs.

'

'Perfect, Lauren. Cheap and plenty of it. Let's go.' He takes Lauren's hand and heads off across

The Green. Scotty and Jackson follow, still grinning.

'Humphrey Bogart always makes me feel like Philip Marlowe. He's so...I think the word is cool.' Richard laughs self-consciously.

'Like Miles Davis and Chet Atkins.'

'Just so, my dear, Lauren.'

'I know what cool is and Bogart is that.' Richard responds.

'He doesn't – the character – he doesn't take any nonsense. He's smarter than anyone.'

'And fearless.'

'Positively heroic, Lauren.'

'Great hat too, Scotty.'

They cross Jesus Lane. They can see The Corner House on the corner of the lane leading through to King Street. Scotty catches up with Richard. 'You goin' to Millers this week?'

'Yup. 'Spect so. Who's featuring?'

'Art Theman and Dick Heckstall-Smith.'

'I'll be there.'

'Thought you would, man. That Art Themen is one cool horn player.'

'Second that.'

They reach The Corner House go in and down the stairs into the basement. It's busy but they easily find a table. They glance at the menu. A waiter comes to their table. Scotty holds up his hand, 'Four mousakas, if you please.' They all giggle as the waiter puts his head on one side, unsure if he has heard right. 'That's it, my man, four mousakas.'

'To drink?'

Jackson glances at Scotty, then at Lauren and Richard.

'Coke for me please.' He glances round the table. 'Make that four Cokes, my man.'

The waiter leaves and they break out in laughter. 'Pot-smokers' choice that! Never fails.' Richard nearly falls off his chair. Lauren glances around her, afraid they may be attracting too much attention, but in the event the other diners are lost in their own worlds, paying no attention to the giggling stoners.

Jackson plays with knife and fork. 'That Raymond Chandler is one cool writer. Reckon he must've done some grass.'

'No way, man. His thing was booze. Probably did for him in the end.'

'Wrote some good books along the way though. Wish I could write that well. Short pithy sentences. He keeps up a really hot pace.' Jackson shakes his head.

'How's your writing going, Richard?'

'Not as well as Chandler. Poetry's my thing and there's no money in that. Nobody's gonna base a Bogart film on one of my poems in a hurry either.'

'Didn't know you were a poet too, Richard.'

'Ah, well, Lauren, I hide my light under a

bushel or two.'

'Like to read some.'

'Any time, be my guest.' Richard puts his hand in his pocket and brings a crumpled sheet of note-paper. 'I wrote this…wanna hear it?'

'Sure thing, man.'

The other two nod their assent. 'OK, Jackson, you asked for it. Fortunately it's short. I don't know how sweet though.' Richard unfolds the paper and smoothes it on the table cloth. 'Ready?'

They wait. 'Here it is. It's called *Moribund.* He takes a deep breath and clears his throat. He's obviously nervous and Lauren is touched.

'The sad wakes leaving
Yes…only petals of
A yellow tulip – pickled in a
Rose bed grieving
The loss of morning.
The mortician's flower
Strewn room sees
Roses bloom
And petal gaily.
The river rides them
And the water dyes them
Black and
Sadly its eyes
Are grimly weeping
Into the bank
Waking
The bees to buzzing.'

Richard waits for a response in the ensuing silence. Scotty is the first to speak. 'Sounds great, man, but what's it mean?'

'What's it mean?'

'Yeah.'

'It means a whole lot of things, Scotty. You have to feel it…in the words, in the sentences.' He waits for a response again. There isn't one. 'OK, it's about mortality.'

'Mortality?'

'Yeah, Jackson. The fact that we're all gonna die sometime. It's the only thing we can be sure of in this life.'

'I picked up on *the mortician's flower-strewn room sees roses bloom*…very nice image.'

'Thank you, Lauren.'

The waiter arrives with their food. He puts the plates down in front of them. They are piled high. The four of them grin their appreciation.

'Can I have some o' that brown sauce, please?' The waiter nods and goes off for a bottle.

'Wow, Jackson that brown sauce is disgusting.'

'It's called A1, Richard.'

'Brown sauce for a brown man.' Scotty pumps Jackson on the shoulder.

The waiter comes back to them, placing the sauce bottle disdainfully in the centre of the table. Jackson picks it up, unscrews the cap, but loses his grip on the bottle, which springs from his hand, slurping the dark brown liquid across the cloth. Jackson looks down at the mess in horror. 'Oh, my God.' He's embarrassed and Lauren can see a blush on his cheeks and brow. Her heart goes out to him.

'It's no big deal, Jackson. It'll come out in the wash.' She waves to the waiter, pointing down at the cloth. He shrugs his annoyance, but fetches another, which he brings to their table. He takes off the plates, knives, forks, glasses and resets the table on a clean cloth. Jackson doesn't know where to look. He feels so goofy.

Richard picks up his knife and fork. He nods to Lauren. 'Let's get stuck in then.' They start to eat.

'D'you come into Cambridge much?'

'Yup, Lauren. Whenever we can.'

'I thought you could get anything you want out on your base.'

'Yeah, well…material things. But not good company.'

'I thought you boys all hang together. Brothers in arms and all that.'

Scotty laughs. 'Not like that. No. There's black airmen and there's white officers.'

'What d'you mean?'

'I mean segregation. I mean being black, being second class citizens.'

'But…'

'No buts. Like I said, there's black airmen and then there's white officers.'

'You mean if you're black you don't get promotion.'

Jackson laughs. 'You could say, Lauren.'

'I'm shocked. I thought that had all changed.'

'It's changing, but very, very slowly.'

'May never get there, Jackson.'

'Well, true enough, Scotty, but I live in hope.' He turns to Lauren. 'See, in Cambridge, we don't feel that racism. I mean you guys accept us for what we are. You don't *seem* to have any colour prejudice.'

'Jeez, Jackson *seem*. 'Course we don't. Never think of that shit. I mean you've given us Thelonius Monk, Charlie Parker, Oscar Peterson, Billie Holiday. Need I go on?'

'Indeed you need not.' Scotty laughs. 'The white folks like the music, but not the people who make it. Like Billie sings:

Southern trees bear a strange fruit,
Blood on the leaves and blood at the root,
Black bodies swinging in the summer breeze,
Strange fruit hanging from the poplar trees.'

'Get it, Richard?'

'Well, I get it Scotty, but it's hard to believe in…this day and age.'

'Hard to believe, but even harder to live with, my friend.'

Jackson comes in with, 'My guess is that not all English cities are like liberal Cambridge.'

'Yeah, Cambridge is…uhm…enlightened. Lot

of intelligent people live here obviously Might be like this in Oxford too I'd guess.'

'Yes, Oxford for sure. Maybe London too and Liverpool,' Richard adds.

'Not too sure about London. Get the feeling when we go down there that we're not that welcome.'

'You surprise me Scotty. I must admit that racism has never been big in my mind.'

He laughs. 'That's because you're white, Lauren. You'd never notice this kinda thing. Ever been to the US of A?'

'Nope. Never have.'

'Well you go down to those southern states and you'd soon see what I mean. Segregation. We're despised down there. We're used. Cheap labour and no laws to protect us from exploitation. And, boy, we are exploited.'

'But, Sidney Poitier, Harry Belafonte, Scotty.'

'They like our music, our voices and our piano playing, but they sure as hell don't like us.'

'Why? Do they feel threatened?'

'We ain't no threat, but they don't know this.'

Richard has been silent for a while. 'Seems to me it's human nature.'

'What is?'

'Wanting to look down on others, feel superior in some way.'

Jackson jumps back into the conversation. 'Well, they sure can't do it with brain-power.

Some of them southern rednecks are as dumb as shit. 'Scuse my French, Lauren.'

Lauren laughs. 'I've heard worse.'

'Bet you have. But let's call a spade a spade.' They all laugh.

They finish eating. Scotty turns to find their waiter. 'How's about I get the bill and we head on down to the Kenya for some fine African coffee?' He signals to the waiter.

'Sounds good.'

Richard brings out his wallet. Scotty holds up his hand. 'This one's on us, my man. Like I said, nothin' to spend our money on out there on the base.

The waiter arrives at their table and writes out a bill. Scotty takes it and pays. 'Keep the change.'

The waiter beams when he sees the size of the tip. 'Thank you, Sir. My pleasure.'

As he walks away Jackson comments. 'I like that 'sir'. Ain't no one calls us that in the Air Force. Just nigger, come here. Nigger do this. Nigger do that.' He gets up, puts on his coat. The other three follow him to the door. He meets them outside. 'Got me a coupla more pre-rolls. Let's smoke one on the way. What say?'

'Say, yeah.'

'Good girl, Lauren. You clearly know what's best for you.'

'How d'you get hold of this stuff?'

'Like I said, Lauren, everything's available on

the base. 'Cept good company.' He smiles at her. 'Comes in on the transport flights. Everyone gets a cut and everyone's happy - 'specially us!' He lights up as they cross Christ's Pieces. He takes a deep drag and slips the joint to Lauren. 'We got guns, grass and gold out there at Lakenheath. But we ain't got pretty, smart girls like you.'

'Thank you, Jackson. You are just too kind.' She takes a deep drag, holds it and passes the joint to Scotty. Lauren stops dead in her tracks. Richard turns to her.

'What's the matter?'

'That's my brother Mark just crossing the road.'

'Which one?'

'The one with his arm in a sling. I don't want to...oh, my God. He's seen me.'

Mark waves.

'I guess he don't smoke grass.'

'I guess you're right there, Scotty,'

He hands the joint to Richard, who does his best to finish it before they draw level with Mark.

'Hello, Lauren.'

'Hello, Mark. We've just been to the cinema.'

Mark is puzzled. He eyes up the two black men, who smile kindly in a stoned kind of way.

'Uh...Mark, this is Richard, Jackson and Scotty.'

Mark shakes their hands. 'Pleased to meet you.'

Scotty is the first to pull himself together. 'Likewise.'

'How's your arm?'

'It's OK. Thanks Lauren.'

'Did you see Daddy today?'

'No. Last night. Doesn't say much. He seems to be locked inside himself.' Richard shuffles his feet, He wants to be moving.

'I'll go in tomorrow.'

'OK.'

'We've got to get on too, Mark.'

'Give my love to Mum.'

'I will.' She gives Mark a kiss on the cheek, takes Richard's hand and sets off with Scotty and Jackson in tow.

'D'you think he realized?'

'Realized what, Lauren?'

She giggles. 'How very, very stoned we are.'

'I doubt it.'

'Good. I don't want *him* on my back. I want you.'

Dominic goes up the stairs to Ranjit's room with leaden feet. The door is ajar. He knocks, pushing it open at the same time. 'You there, Ranjit?'

'Sure, Dom. Come on in.'

They shake hands and Dominic sits in the proffered armchair.

'So, how are you?'

'OK. Thanks, Ranjit. How 'bout you?'

'Not so bad.'

'There's something I want to talk to you about.'

Ranjit holds up his hand. 'I saw you and Rebecca on The Backs the other day.'

'Ah, yes.'

'You were walking hand in hand.'

'Uhmm.' Dominic is decidedly uncomfortable.

'And not like brother and sister.'

'No, well, my sister would never hold my hand like that in public.' He tries to lift the tension.

'So?'

'Err...'

'Yes?'

'I'm feeling bad, Ranjit. You're my friend.'

'I thought you were mine.'

'I am.'

'But a disloyal one.'

'Look, I'm here to come clean.'

'Oh, yes, Dom?'

'Yes.'

'Bit late in the day, don't you think?'

'It is. I agree.'

'So?'

'So, I'm sorry, Ranjit.'

'D'you like her?'

'Yes, very much.'

'She's very beautiful.'

'Yes, very.'

Ranjit stands and Dominic thinks he's going to hit him, but Ranjit smiles broadly. 'I forgive you, Dom. Our friendship is bigger than this difficulty. We can, we will put it behind us. And anyway, I'm spoken for.'

'Spoken for?'

'Yes, I have an arranged marriage.'

'Arranged marriage!' Dominic is taken aback.

'Yes. It's very common in India.'

'I thought all that was a thing of the past.'

'Oh, no, it's how things work over there. It's very much of the present.'

'I had no idea. Sounds crazy to me.'

'It isn't, Dominic. It works, I would say. Very often better than a marriage based on romantic love.'

Dominic shakes his head in disbelief.

'Well, believe it or not, it lets you off the hook.'

'That's something to be grateful for.'

'It is.

'So, still friends?'

'For sure.'

Chapter Twenty Nine
Canoeing Down the Danube

The phone rings. Putting down her pen on her writing desk, Mary picks up the receiver. 'Good afternoon. Cambridge 55795. Mary Wheatcroft here.'

There is no answering voice just faint, somewhat crackly organ music. She holds the phone away from her face as if waiting for some explanation then puts it back to her ear. 'Hello. Is there anybody there?' She waits. 'You really must stop doing this. We don't like it.' She hears the phone line close at the other end and puts the receiver back on the cradle. She sits back in her chair, thinking, worrying. She gets up, leaves the room and crosses the hall to the kitchen. Dobbo is preparing dinner.

'I'm going to the hospital.'

'But you were there this morning, Ma'am. D'you…is it…?'

'I feel I should be with him, Dobbo. I can't bear to think of him all alone there trying to deal with…come to terms with what he's done.'

'I understand Ma'am. You should go.'

'I'll be back in a couple of hours.' She turns for

the door. 'Oh, did I tell you that Mark will be here for dinner too?'

'Yes Ma'am and Lauren and Dominic too.'

'That's right. They will.'

Mary leaves the kitchen, takes the Mini from the garage and drives across town to Addenbrookes Hospital.

Halfway down the corridor leading to Freddy's room she loses her nerve and leans against the wall, looking out over the rain-shiny car park, lost in thought. A passing nurse stops by her and asks, 'Are you all right? Can I help you?'

Mary comes back to the moment and does a double-take. 'Ah. No. Thank you. I am all right.'

'Good.' The nurse smiles and walks off and Mary carries on to Freddy's room. She steels herself at the door and goes in. Freddy is lying still, staring fixedly at the ceiling. Mary closes the door quietly behind her and walks to the bed. Freddy doesn't acknowledge her.

'Freddy.' Her voice is shaky. She cannot find the volume she would like. 'Freddy.'

He seemingly ignores her.

'Mark is feeling a lot better. The car's a write-off. Thankfully the police are not going to press charges.'

Freddy nods his acknowledgement.

'Aren't you pleased?'

He shrugs. 'I'm not pleased about anything.'

'But...?'

'But what?' He turns on her almost spitting out his words.

'You survived.'

'You call this survival?'

'Well…'

'You have no idea, Mary. Don't you get it? I can't walk. I can barely control my bladder…and not the other thing. It's disgusting. I'm disgusting. I disgust myself.'

Mary steps forward and touches his arm gently. Freddy shakes free of her hand. 'Don't touch me.'

'I'm sorry.'

'Don't be. I'm the one who should be sorry…and I am. But I can't turn the clock back, can't change the way things are.'

Mary sits back down. She looks at her hands. 'We have to make the best…'

'The best! Are you joking, woman?'

'I only meant…we still have each other, the children. You can still work.'

'Can I? How?

'From home…at College sometimes.'

'Shitting myself at meetings wouldn't do, Mary.'

She turns away, lost for words.

'The doctors say…'

'What do the doctors say?'

'That they'll start physiotherapy soon.'

Freddy's hands fly to either side of his head. He covers his ears. 'I don't want to hear.'

'Why?'

'Why, why, why! I don't want to hear or to talk...or to live. D'you understand?'

Mary finds some inner resolve. 'No, Freddy, I do not understand. What about me and the children?'

'What about you?'

'We need you. All of us.'

'Like this?'

'Any way you are, Freddy. You are us. You are the family.'

'I don't think so. Not anymore. You don't need me like this...crippled, broken. A mess.'

'We do. We love you.'

'Hah!'

'Yes. We love you.'

'You forgive me then?' He looks hard at Mary.

She doesn't respond. She looks away to the window.

'Well?'

Mary is struggling with herself and how she should respond. 'Honestly?'

'Yes, honestly.'

Mary sits up straight, pulling back her shoulders. 'No, Freddy I can't forgive you...not yet.'

Freddy turns his face to the wall. His shoulders shake and he starts to sob.

'Oh, Freddy, please...I...I'm sorry. Forgiveness will come to me in time. I'm sure it will.' She touches his shoulder. He shrugs off her hand. Mary recoils, drawing back.

'Mark?'

'He's doing well.'

'But...'

'I don't know Freddy. You'll have to ask him yourself.' There is a knock on the door then it opens a fraction and a nurse puts her head round the door before coming in. She pushes a trolley over to the bed.

'Time for medication.'

'Professor Wheatcroft', Freddy snaps back.

The nurse suppresses a shrug. 'Professor Wheatcroft.'

Mary stands and goes to the window, turning her back on Freddy and the nurse. She finds herself thinking about her wedding day in April 1939 at Great St Mary's church on King's Parade. It was a clear, bright day and her heart was full of hope. Her memory moves on to her honeymoon, canoeing on The Danube. She was deeply in love, but found herself disappointed by Freddy's lack of passion and his inability to express or share his emotions. War was brewing and Mary felt ill-at-ease. Freddy was enthusiastic about Adolf Hitler, his government and the ordered, efficient German society. He liked what he saw. Later, after war had broken out, he had to eat his words and humble pie. Not an easy thing for Freddy.

Mary shakes herself back into the present and goes to the bed. She touches Freddy's arm and, without saying anything, she picks up her head scarf and handbag and leaves the room, closing the door quietly behind her.

Chapter Thirty
A Stitch in Time

*'Yet, Karellen knew, they would hold fast until the
end: they would await without despair whatever
destiny was theirs. They would serve the Overmind
because they had no choice, but even in that service
they would not lose their souls.'*
Arthur C Clarke. Childhood's End

The sun slants through the leaded windows of
Dominic's bedroom, across the bare wood floor
and over his desk. He is lying in bed, watching
the dust motes floating in the light, remembering
his first day at prep school and his nerves. He
had been scheduled to have a minor operation
on his face to remove a strawberry birthmark
from his left cheek before the start of term, but
the family had been delayed in New Haven
where Freddy was a visiting professor at Yale.
The presentation of an award had to be
rescheduled to accommodate a change to the
American Vice President's diary. They were a
week late returning home and Dominic had
missed his surgical appointment. There was no
other slot available before the start of term even
though Mary had put on as much pressure as
she possibly could, but with no positive result.
So Dominic had started his new school with his
facial blemish and he was ashamed. He felt ugly,

stupid and humiliated when he saw other boys staring at him and smirking behind his back. Their cruelty surprised and hurt him. He said nothing to his parents just got on and lived with it. As the days passed it became less of an issue and he made some friends.

A poem - maybe a song - is taking shape in his mind. He jumps out of bed and crosses the room to his desk. He opens a note-book and writes:
When I was young
I had a face like a clown
And I stumbled around
Pounding the ground...

Rebecca climbs the stairs to Dominic's door and knocks gently.

'Who's there?'

'It's me, Rebecca.'

'Come in.' Dominic pulls on his dressing gown and goes to the door to meet her. They kiss and she steps back and looks around the room. 'You're late getting up. What're you doing?'

'Oh, I don't know just day-dreaming.'

'About what?'

'This and that.' He leads her to the bed. 'I was remembering my first day at prep school and how frightening it was.'

Rebecca shivers. 'Horrible. Very frightening. Well, it was for me too.'

Dominic smiles. 'I was writing a poem.'

'About that time?'

'Yeah, I guess it is.'

'Can I read it?'

'Not finished yet. To be honest hardly started.'

'OK.'

She undresses and climbs into bed pulling the covers over her. She watches Dominic take off his gown and pyjamas. He climbs in next to her and takes her in his arms.

Richard is in the back garden of his parents' house. He is playing with a bouncing, handsome Labrador. Lauren comes out of the house, picks up a ball and throws it for the dog. Richard walks to her. 'I've had an idea.'

Lauren nods and waits.

'I want to set up some poetry readings.'

'Really?'

'Yup. Give it a try. When I was up at the Edinburgh Festival last year I met some young British poets. They were holding readings every night at a small venue. I went along. I took some of my work - poetry - with me just in case. Well, they knew I wanted to read because we'd discussed it but I was unknown to them. They were all received as poets in artistic circles. In London, Cambridge, Oxford, Liverpool and a few other places. I know I could get some of these people to come here if I paid their travel and a little extra. So I plan to charge for tickets, hire a cheap room - large, but not a hall. We couldn't fill a hall. Above a pub or something.'

'I'm impressed.'

'Thanks.'

'So, what first?'

'Ring round the poets and see what their schedules are. If I could get two to Cambridge on the same day that would be fine.'

Lauren picks up the ball that the dog has dropped at her feet and throws it down the garden.

'I'm having coffee at the Cambridge Union this morning with Johnny Jenner.'

'Who's he?'

'President of the Union.'

'How d'you know him?'

'Same taste in music. 'I met him at the 2i's in London. We were there to see Vince Taylor.'

'Brand New Cadillac.'

'The very same.'

'What was he like?'

'Who?'

'Vince Taylor.'

'Tight black leather suit and gold bicycle chain. Very sleek. You know what he looks like?'

'Not really.'

'He's like England's answer to Elvis Presley and Gene Vincent. Not as good it might as well be said, but he's got bravado. The band's called The Playboys. He's quite something. Georgie Fame and The Blue Flames played that night too. Very good band. We should go…tonight, tomorrow. I'll call and see who's playing.'

'OK. So what about the President of the Union?'

'He was there too. I was standing next to him and we got talking at the end of Vince Taylor's set. He told me about things he was trying to do at the Union.'

'Such as?'

'More live music, short plays - innovative stuff. He's quite a revolutionary. Very left wing. He wants to break new ground.'

'Sounds positively subversive.'

'He is, Lauren.'

'So, what are you hatching with him?'

'This. We want to put on a two-hour show of poetry mixed with dance, live painting and music. A blend.'

Lauren considers what he's said. 'It's what they call a *happening* in the States.'

'My God! Yes, you're right - a happening. I thought it was more a Dadaist thing, breaking down the accepted view of art. Deconstructing.'

Later Lauren is sitting on the couch in Richard's room. She's reading *Childhood's End* by Arthur C Clarke. Richard pokes his noise round the open door. 'Well, we're in luck. Joe Brown and Jet Harris are on tomorrow night. Show starts at eight. Want to go?'

'Yes. Love to.' She starts to pin her hair up.

Richard watches her. 'Let's go down early afternoon, go to The Tate and eat before the show.'

'Sounds good to me.'

'I've never seen your hair like that before. It's looks so...' He bends down and kisses the nape of her neck. 'Beautiful. Your neck is...I love the way these few fine locks are uncovered - so soft like silk.' The silver sunlight shines through the fine gossamer. Richard is mesmerized. He breathes in deeply. His head is spinning.

Lauren turns to him and they kiss. She pulls him down onto the couch beside her. They kiss again. She pulls back to look at him. She studies his face, his mouth, his eyes. He smiles at her. She looks down at his hands, turning them over. 'You have beautiful hands. Delicate fingers and they're soft for a man's.'

'Is that a bad thing?'

'Oh, no. Sensitive. An artist's hands.' She laughs. 'You're a handsome boy, Richard.'

'Well, thank you, Ma'am. You're pretty good yourself.'

'Pretty?'

'Well, yes...*very* pretty.'

'Thank you kind, Sir.'

'My pleasure.' Richard gets up and crosses the room to look at the painting on his easel. He twists it round to catch the light. He stands back. Lauren walks over to stand next to him.

'So how'd it go at the Union with Johnny Jenner?'

'Good. Thanks. Good. We got on well. We've sorta got the same ideas. Well, at least we're not running on completely different tracks.'

Chapter Thirty One
LIFE IS JUST...
One Damned Thing after Another

The day is fine and bright. White clouds race across a deep blue sky. Freddy is traveling home alone in a hospital bus. He stares out of the window, looking lonely and confused. He didn't want Mary or any other member of the family to meet him or travel with him. He wanted to see Cambridge again alone. He wipes condensation from the window beside him with the cuff of his dressing gown. His mouth is drawn down at the corners and his eyes are dull. He looks and is miserable.

The bus turns into the Adams Road house and crunches over the gravel drive. Mary has been waiting patiently for this signal and goes to the front door. She pauses, gathering up her strength and resolve. Pulling the door open she steps out onto the drive. The bus draws up in front of her and the driver gets out and with a nod to Mary as he goes round to the back doors and opens them. The metal grinds as they swing open and Mary winces. It's not a sound she likes. It puts her teeth on edge. Her palms are wet and she wipes them on the back of her skirt. She goes round to the back of the bus where the driver has lowered a ramp. He gets into the bus and unhooks Freddy's chair.

'Hello, Freddy. Welcome home. I...'

Freddy doesn't acknowledge her. He stares down at his feet as the driver wheels him down the ramp and onto the drive.

Mary points out across the garden. 'Spring is coming. Look.'

Again Freddy doesn't respond. The driver looks questioningly at Mary.

'Oh, in here, please.' She leads the way into the house. The driver follows. Freddy closes his eyes. The dogs bound out of the house to greet him but he takes no interest in them however how hard they try to attract his attention. He is irritated. Mary takes the dogs aside to allow the driver space to push the wheelchair into the hall. She follows them in.

The phone rings. Mary glances at it, pauses then picks it up. 'Hello.' She waits. 'Hello.'

Freddy glances at her with fear in his eyes.

'Hello.' Again she waits. 'Argh.' She places the phone back on its cradle.

Freddy speaks for the first time. There is a tremor in his voice. 'Who was that?'

'I don't know. No one there.'

'No one?'

'Just organ music.'

'Bach?'

'Yes, it was.'

Freddy looks shaken.

Mary sighs. 'Let me take you through to the study until Dobbo comes home and can help me get you upstairs to your bedroom.'

Freddy doesn't respond. Lauren comes down the stairs, doing her best to smile. 'Hello, Daddy. Welcome home.' She comes over to him, bends down and kisses him on the check. Freddy manages a crooked smile.

'Hello, Lauren.' He takes her hand and squeezes it.

'It's lovely to have you here again. We can…'

Freddy looks at her questioningly.

'We can…it's great to all be together again…now with the spring…'

Mary jumps in to fill the awkward gap. 'Mark and Dominic are coming for dinner. So, yes, all together again.' She wheels Freddy into his study. Lauren follows them.

Freddy sits at the head of the table with Mark on his right and with Dominic and Lauren to his left. Mary is at the other end of the table. Dominic is still a little tanned from his Indian trip. Mark in contrast is pale and drawn. Freddy stares at the plate in front of him.

'Aren't you hungry, dear?'

Freddy shakes his head.

300

'I'm not either.' Mark abruptly pushes his plate away to the centre of the table. It collides with Freddy's. Gravy spills across the white tablecloth. Mary looks up from her food, startled. 'Are you all right, Mark?

'No, I'm not.'

'Why are you ill?'

'No?'

'What then?' Lauren asks.

Mark stands abruptly. He is shaking. 'I was apprehended today in the public toilets on Midsummer Common.' All four look at him in shock.

'What for? Loitering?'

'No, Lauren.' Mark hangs his head. 'I was caught in the toilet with another man.'

Freddy shrieks, 'Jesus Christ!'

'Don't take the Lord's name in vain.'

'Shut up, Mary.'

She bursts into tears.

Lauren's jaw drops. 'What...what were you doing?

Mark squares up to her. 'What d'you think?'

'I don't know what to think.'

'We...masturbating...mutual masturbation it was called at school.'

Freddy shouts, 'I don't give a fuck what it was called.'

Mary gets up from the table and heads for the door. Dominic follows her, putting his arm round her shoulders. Lauren sticks it out.

'Are you going to be charged?'

'I have been."

Freddy pushes his wheelchair away from the table, crashing into the wall behind him. 'Holy shit! I…I thought…?

'What did you think, Dad?'

'Don't call me Dad. I'm not your father.'

'Daddy, really!' Lauren gets up and goes towards her father.

'Keep away from me all of you.'

'Of course you're his father.'

'Not any more, I'm not.'

'You are and you always will be. You can't turn your back on him. He needs your support *now*.'

'I will turn my back on him and I will not support him. He can go to hell.'

Mark breaks down in tears. 'I…'

'You fucking wimp!'

'You're a two-faced bastard, Daddy. We stuck by you after you messed up. Look at you. Look what you've done to yourself.' Lauren immediately regrets what's she's said, but it's too late. She runs from the room, leaving Freddy and Mark alone.

'You realize what you've done I presume?'

'What have I done?'

'Ruined your chances, wrecked your life.'

'And you haven't?

Freddy doesn't respond.

'Look at you. You couldn't fuck a donkey if you wanted to.'

Freddy doesn't respond.

'You're a cripple and you brought it on yourself.'

Freddy starts to wheel himself out of the room. Mark follows him. 'D'you really think you're a good example of what a father should be? You're a drunkard and a bully and it's finally caught up with you. You're finished. You're on the scrapheap.'

Freddy stops by the door. 'And you're not?'

'I may go to prison. I may get a criminal record. But I will stay true to myself…to my nature.'

'Your nature! You're disgusting.' He kicks the door open and wheel himself across the hall and into his study.

Chapter Thirty Two
Man Killed Dead by Spider

'There, by the starlit fences,
The wanderer halts and hears
My soul that lingers sighing
About the glimmering weirs.'
A. E. Housman. A Shropshire Lad

The River Cam rolls on regardless through The Meadows then down by The Mill, out past The Backs, through the historic colleges and into the black-soiled, windswept fens that run their flat, endless way up to Kings Lynn and The Wash. King's College Chapel stands out majestically watching over the sacred and the profane. Richard had a part-time job the previous summer as a tourist guide. He learned a great deal about English history, about intrigue, jealousy, the quest for power and the desire to build magnificent buildings to the glory of God. He enjoyed the job, being photographed in his beatnik clothes, entertaining the tourists. In the end he ignored the guide book, just making things up as he went along. It was a lot more fun and he was never exposed or caught out. He can think on his feet.

Richard is crossing St John's Street. Outside the

Blue Boar a newspaper vendor selling The Cambridge News and the London evening paper calls out his wares: 'Cambridge and London papers'. After innumerable repetitions this had become: 'Man killed dead by spider. Man killed dead by spider.' It never fails to amuse Richard and he feels a song bubbling up inside him. He goes up Rose Crescent, crosses the Market Square and into the Guildhall. A sign indicates that general enquiries are dealt with from The City Treasurer's Office. He climbs up to the first floor, rings the bell and waits. The door opens and he is taken aback by the sight of a very pretty girl.

'Can I help you?'

Richard is momentarily lost for words. 'Well, yes...I hope so.'

'How?'

'I want to hire a room for an evening in late April, just after the beginning of the Easter Term.'

'Come in, please.'

Richard follows her. She sits behind a desk and takes out a booking ledger, which she opens. She glances at Richard and smiles. His knees go weak and he steadies himself on the desk.

'Which hall are you interested in hiring?'

'Not sure.'

'How big will your audience be?'

'Hard to say, really. It's a bit of an experiment.'

Richard walks to the window and stares out

305

over the Market Square.

'It's poetry, you see. Modern poetry. Would you come?'

'I don't think so.'

'No. I expect you'd like something more immediate...like rock'n'roll, going to the cinema.'

'Romance and musicals. That's what I like.'

'Well...' Richard thinks. 'Let's say around a hundred people, maybe more.'

'Well, you won't want the big hall. The small hall would suit you.' She looks down at the ledger. 'A Saturday night?'

'If possible.'

'We've got Saturday 30th April free.'

Richard walks back to the desk. He has to make a decision. 'How much?'

'The hall is £35 for the evening. Then you'll need a barman, maybe two.'

'One'll do, thanks.' Richard is concerned. It's a lot of money for him to fork out on just a wing and a prayer.

'We can arrange to have the bar set up on a sale or return basis, if you like.'

'Good idea. Thanks. So how much for the hall and the barman?'

The girl takes out a price list. '£41.'

Richard exhales. 'Pheww. Not cheap.'

She doesn't respond.

'OK. I'll do it.'

'Please fill in this form. There's a pen over there

on that desk.'

'Thank you.' Richard takes the form and sits. He starts to fill in his details. He feels that the girl is watching him. He looks up. She is. '£41, did you say?'

'I did.' Their eyes meet. She smiles again. Richard feels his mouth go dry and his pulse race.

He completes the form and hands it over to the girl. She takes it and reads it through. She stamps it and puts it in a tray beside her. She puts her hands together and looks up at him.

'Anything else?'

'No. Er, yes…would you like…?' He thinks of Lauren, feels a wave of guilt and stops himself. He doesn't ask the question.

She waits.

'Nothing…not now…maybe later.'

She puts her head to one side and smiles.

Richard is charmed. 'Well, thank you very much for your help.'

'We'll put a bill in the post for you. You should settle it at least two weeks before your booking or you may lose it.'

'Got it. Thanks again.'

Richard goes out into the Market Square. He looks up at the sky, breathing deeply. He heads off to the Union to meet Johnny.

Rebecca is in El Patio to meet Dominic. He's late.

When he does arrive his greeting is cursory.

'Where's that sparkle, Dom?'

'Gone. Snuffed out for now I'm afraid.'

'Why? What's happened?'

'Things have gone right off the rails at home.'

'With your father?'

'Yes, in part. Now it's my brother who's the problem.'

'What's he done?'

'Can't really tell you, but he's certainly upset the apple cart.'

'OK, but if you want...'

'Thanks, Rebecca.'

'How's the poetry coming on?'

'I've written just one since I last saw you. It's hard to concentrate since the balloon went up.' He shrugs. 'Lauren's told me her boyfriend wants to start a band.'

'Richard?'

'That's the one. They're still together.'

'I saw them out the other day. They make a good-looking couple. Your sister's a very pretty girl.'

'She is, I know, but not as pretty as you.'

Rebecca laughs. 'You are too kind, my prince.'

It's Dominic's turn to laugh. 'It's the truth, though, my princess.' They lean across the table and kiss.

'Caught you at it then.'

They both look up. It's Richard. 'Can I join you

or would I be interrupting something?'

Dominic stands and shakes his hand. 'No, of course not. Sit down, please.'

Richard puts his coffee on the table and takes a seat.

'I've set up two poetry events. One at the Union and the other at the Guildhall.'

'I'm impressed.'

'No need, Dom. It was easy to book the slots. Problem is putting on a good show. Wanna read your poetry?'

'Very kind of you to ask...yes... I think I'd like to.'

'Think?'

'OK, OK. I will. Who else is reading?'

'Well, me obviously, and Ned Milton, John Horovitz and hopefully Bob Grey.'

'Don't know John and Bob.'

'They're from London. They work together a lot. Call themselves Breaking Ground. Eventually I want to get some American beat poets involved.'

'Ginsberg and Ferlinghetti?'

'That might be aiming a bit high, Dom. But possibly Piero Heliczer, George Andrews even Jonathan Williams.'

'Don't know them.'

'You will...I hope.'

'What about the Guildhall?'

'Hope to do something more adventurous

there, Rebecca. I've been talking to John Hart about working together with his band.'

'He plays at Millers, doesn't he?'

'Yes, double bass.'

'What d'you have in mind, Richard?'

'Reading poems to jazz.'

Rebecca ponders on this. 'Poetry and jazz? Why don't *you* form a band and actually sing?'

'Thinking about it.'

'Really?'

'Yup, Dom. Got a name for the band.'

'Already?'

Richard laughs. 'Well, you gotta start somewhere. In the beginning was the word. Right?'

'So it says.' Dominic glances at Richard and Rebecca. 'D'you want another coffee?'

They both nod. Dominic gets up and goes over to the coffee machine.

'So what's the band to be called?'

'Green Onions.'

Rebecca raises an eyebrow. 'Odd name if I may so say so.'

'You may.'

'Tell me about it.'

'After the single *Green Onions* by Booker T and MGs.'

'Ah, yeah. Of course. Great track.'

'Got some other local musicians interested.'

'Anyone I might know?'

'Dunno, Rebecca. You might.'

'Try me.'

'Logan de Wandlebury. He plays bass. The drummer's Flip Cox and we'll have Jonty Middlefinch on keyboards. Know any of 'em?'

'Yeah. I know Jonty. Dom was at school with him.'

'St. Faiths?'

'Umm.'

Dominic comes back to the table with three coffees on a tray. He puts them on the table, takes the tray back to the counter and joins the others.

'Richard's got Jonty Middlefinch interested in joining the band.'

'I remember him from prep school, but didn't know he was a musician.'

'He learnt piano at Harrow. He's going to play keyboards naturally. He's pretty damned good.'

'Who else?'

'Flip Cox and Logan de Wandlebury.'

'Logan de what?'

'Wandlebury, Dom.'

'Like the ring up on the Gog Magog Hills?'

'The same. He's the son of the Earl.'

That makes him a Viscount then?'

'It does indeed.'

'So you're mixing with the nobility now.'

'Can't be helped.' Richard laughs. 'You gotta take what you can get...*and* he's a brilliant bass player!'

'Who's the lead singer?'

'Afraid it's me, Rebecca.'

Chapter Thirty Three
Mother Suck Your Universe

It is early evening and Lauren, Rebecca and Dominic are with Richard at his parents' house. They have a couple of hours before the event at The Union. They are smoking a joint and putting the final touches to their plans.

'Are the mikes being set up for us?'

'So they tell me. I've also asked for an easel and some blank white paper sheets.'

Rebecca takes the proffered joint. 'What're they for?'

'Dom wants to write poems on 'em.'

Rebecca takes a big pull, holds the smoke in and passes the joint to Lauren. She does the same then glances at Richard. 'Why've you called the event Northwards?'

Richard and Dominic laugh. 'Because it doesn't mean anything.'

'Except what it says,' adds Dominic.

Both girls look puzzled.

'It's Dadaist.'

'Dadaist? What's that when it's at home?'

Dominic rises to the challenge. 'Well, Lauren, it was a movement begun by a group of artists and poets connected to the Cabaret Voltaire in Zurich. Dada rejected reason and logic, prizing nonsense, irrationality…and intuition.'

'Cool, but what's the word actually mean? Where's it come from?'

'Don't mean nuthin' as they say, Lauren. The origin's unclear. It's a nonsensical word.'

'So what you're going to do tonight is nonsensical then?'

Dominic takes the joint, takes a puff then replies, 'Of course.'

'Why, of course?'

'Well, sister dear, can I ask you what makes sense in this world?'

'What makes sense?'

'Yes, what makes sense?'

'Dunno. Don't think about it all that much.'

'Well, the Dadaists did think about it and concluded that nothing makes sense.'

Richard watches them with amusement then chips in, 'Does life make sense?'

'Is it supposed to?'

'Probably not, Lauren.'

Rebecca picks up the baton. 'Doesn't love make sense?'

'Love?'

'Yup.'

'Great as it is, Rebecca, I don't think it makes sense.'

'It is what it is.'

'Well said, Dom.'

'And so what's your take, brother dear?'

'My take is…'

'Yes?'

'D'you really want it?'

'Of course.'

'OK. This my current view. Mathematics.'

'Mathematics?'

Dominic takes another pull on the joint and hands it to Richard. 'The thing that's come clear to me recently is that the universe appears to have been created using mathematical principles.'

'What's that mean?'

'It means that God is a mathematician.'

'And that means?'

'It means that when God, the creative force, higher intelligence - call it what you will - made the universe it was made so it would work according to a mathematical description. Maths describes the how things work and not, I grant you, why things work.'

'Getting deep here, Dom.'

'I am, my boy. And that's exactly where I like to be…in the deep end.'

'When you say that maths describes how things work give me an example.'

'Sure, Rebecca. Easy. Get this: the only way to describe activity at the sub-atomic level is by using mathematics.'

'Well, I wouldn't know about that.'

'No, well, I guess not, Lauren.'

'Why d'you guess not?

'I just meant…'

'Don't be patronizing, Dom. It's a tendency you have.'

'That right?'

'Yes 'tis too.'

Dominic is irritated. He doesn't take criticism in his stride.

'I didn't mean anything by that, Lauren.'

'Yes, you did. You implied that I was too stupid…'

'I did not…I only meant if you hadn't looked into that area you couldn't be expected to know.'

'You're not a mathematician, are you?'

'By no means.'

'So how do you claim to know so much?'

'I was talking about it to Ranjit.'

'What the hell's he know about it, rich Indian boy?'

'Well, he is reading maths.'

'Never told me that.'

'Probably never came up with what you were doing, Rebecca.'

'Now, now, Dom. No jealousy, please. If anyone should be jealous it's him not me.'

Richard glances at his watch. 'Let's have another spliff and then we'd better get going. We're gonna need at least half an hour to set up.'

The house lights dim and the spots come on. Dominic and Richard are standing on either side of the stage with heads bowed. They are both nervous as hell, but it doesn't show. Lauren and Rebecca are sitting off to the side of the stage. They are equally nervous. It's all a bit experimental and they know it and it's pretty much a full house. The advertising has worked. The Union organizers are pleased. They're going to show a profit on the night. The bar's been busy.

Dominic steps up to the mike centre stage. Richard picks his electric guitar and hits several hard chords. Dominic reads:

'Feet Pounding
Metal Door-Knobs
Slip away
Piling at the corridor's end.'

He steps back from the mike and walks slowly and purposefully across the stage to stand beside Richard, who plays out some single notes on the edge of melody. He goes to the mike. Dominic takes his seat.

'Over and over doors sweep open
And faces blossom like tulips opening
Everything closes.
The gas chamber is
Mobile again
And makes good speed –
God speed.

The yawning awning
Collapses sideways
On the massing crowds.'
Richard hits a big chord, then steps back as
Dominic walks into the spotlight and reads:
'Time struck in the intervals of space the atom-
lover makes his way,
More weary in a weightless sense than Atlas
overspent and out of reach
Soft feet upon a fallen leaf.
I sit astride the sun and speak with God.
He burns and spreads my flesh to show blood's
wisdom.
Meaning is in the making.'
Richard joins him in the spotlight and they read
in duet, almost singing the words.
'We take our passage through the ceiling of
books' doors.
We fly through woods, green lanes, loaded
hedges, fields, dust and our wings cloud the
rain.
We stop and hide to see Death watch my coffin
burn.
The laughing wood explores my Flesh. I touch
the eyes of love. A smile.
Conclusions concluded the feelings follow me.
Beside my eyes I see your dreams have walked
away, sweet tears.
My ears eat air. I read my distance in the clouds,
old winds, Blue skies turn to trees so quiet, soft

feet upon a fallen leaf.

Look - stand - be off!'

Richard walks out of the spotlight and Dominic continues on his own.

'He weeps the songs of rivers burning.'

Dominic points at Richard.

'I wait for breath to celebrate the page.

Our joy in alleys dark and beautiful.

Dangerous as speech.

Spare me!

Voices from within my straining thighs inspire the moaning little things to answer me.

This building's girders dream.

His agents trap the falling words

And stop.'

Dominic walks out of the spot to join Richard at the back of the stage. Richard is taking some newspapers out of a canvas bag. He hands half of them to Dominic.

'House lights, please.'

The lights come on and the audience is bathed in light. Richard and Dominic walk out into the audience and pass out newspapers at random.

Richard goes back onto the stage. 'Right, everyone, this is what we're going to do. Open your papers, please, and hold them so I can see you.' Those with papers do as he's asked. 'OK. That's great.'

Dominic steps up to the mike.

'So now when one of us points at you please

read out a sentence or a phrase from your paper. This way we'll get a random poem in the style of William Burrough's cut-up method of writing. OK, here we go.' Dominic points to a girl in the front row.

'School teacher throws himself under train...' The two men take it in turns to point and the poem gets under way.

'...a small amount of fertilizer has contaminated several tons of wheat...'

'... the tour ended in disaster when the stage collapsed...

'...as the shop-keeper opened for business...

'American forces made significant advances in the Mekong Delta.'

'...at the same time he apologized for anything he might have implied in his statement...'

'...while four children had a narrow escape when the car they were in plunged into the River Ouse...'

The audience is starting to get the feel for it and the laughter starts to build

'Slowly but surely did the trick this time," the Prime Minister responded angrily...'

'When the two men were sentenced to 10 years in prison...'

'She claimed that she did not open the door as the milkman implied...'

'Fourteen is a suitable age to introduce...'

'Steam baths on the Isle of Wight...'

Dominic and Richard fall about laughing, but continue pointing to different members of the audience.

'The local vicar opened the bazaar with a bang...'
'They hoped that the outcome would not be as bad as was first anticipated...'
'...while stocks last...'
'...and the peanut harvest was far better than was expected given the appallingly bad weather.'

Richard holds up his hands and draws the sequence to a close and Dominic walks over to a flip-chart and writes in large black letters: MOTHER SUCK...He pauses as a gasp of surprise and embarrassment ripples through the audience. He continues to write: YOUR, He pauses, then writes: UNIVERSE to a collective sigh of relief from the audience. He steps to the front of the stage and bows.

The event goes on for another hour of poetry, interaction and music. Once the auditorium has emptied Dominic, Richard, Lauren, Rebecca and Johnny head round to Rebecca's rooms in Jesus Lane and get very stoned.

Chapter Thirty Four
Coming To Terms

*'I entered even into my inward self...and beheld
with eye of my soul, above my mind, the light
unchangeable.'*
Saint Augustine.

Mary is reading the post to Freddy. He is lying
back on his bed, eyes closed. His face drawn and
grey. The curtains are closed. Mary sits by a
bedside lamp.

She opens a brown envelope, takes a letter out
and reads it. Her hand flies to her mouth and
covers it. A small groan escapes her.

'What is it?'

Mary doesn't respond.

'Mary?'

'It's regarding, Mark. It's for him. Shouldn't
have opened it. Didn't notice. Sorry.'

'What's it say?'

'Doesn't matter.'

'Tell me.'

'No.'

'Tell me.' Freddy makes a grab for the letter.
Mary jumps up from her chair, holding the letter
out of his reach. She starts to go towards the
door, stops and makes up her mind.

'It's a summons for Mark to attend the

Magistrates Court on 16th at 10.00am.'

Freddy groans. Mary looks like she would gladly rip up the letter. She screws it in a ball.

'Oh, fuck, shit...whatever next?'

'Freddy!'

'Don't *Freddy* me, woman!

'I only meant...'

'I don't care what you meant. I've had enough of this.'

'What d'you mean?'

'I mean, I've had enough. More than enough. I wish someone would come in right now and put a bullet through my brains.'

'Don't say that.'

'Fuck off. Leave me alone. Go and talk to your son.'

'Our son.'

'*Your* son!'

Mary turns away from him and leaves the room, slamming the door behind her. Freddy sobs. She goes down the stairs, across the hall and into the garage. She gets into the Mini and hurtles out onto the main road, just avoiding a collision with a baker's van. She drives into Cambridge and parks in King Street. She strides purposefully into St Andrew's College to Mark's door. She knocks. Mark comes to the door, opens it and she goes in without a word of hello. She goes across to the fireplace, turns round and hands Mark the letter, which he takes, reads and stares at uncomprehendingly. He can barely look at this mother. She waits for a response.

'That's it, then.'

'What's it?'

'It's all over for me. I've had it. It'll be prison…'

'Maybe not, Mark, if you make a good impression in court, stand up for yourself and apologize.'

'Apologize? What good'll that do?'

'You might be able to call on the magistrate's compassion and understanding.'

Mark slumps into a chair. He throws the letter on the fire. 'I doubt it, Mum.'

'You have to try. Your father's all but given up on you. *You* have to try. You have to weather this storm and show us what you're made of. Show your father that you're made of sterner stuff and give *him* something to live for.'

'I have no strength. What strength I did have has just drained away. I'm empty. Lost and empty.'

They sit in silence for a minute. 'I want to see Dad…talk to him.'

'No, no, no! You can't do that…mustn't do that.'

'Why not?'

'He can't help you.'

'He could if he would forgive me.'

'He can't. He won't.' She pauses, then adds, 'Talk to Dom.'

'Dom?'

'Yes.'

'Why?'

'Because he loves you and...he has some insight.'

'And Dad doesn't?'

'He loves you, of course, but he's consumed by his own pain and suffering. And he's intolerant of things...of things he cannot understand. His love for you is lost in his anger and disappointment.'

'Disappointment?'

'Yes. With you and what you...are and with what's happened to his life and what he's done to himself. I don't know if he'll ever really pull through.'

'I don't really understand Dom anymore with his mysticism and his...'

'Faith?'

'Yes. His faith.' Mark shrugs. He's angry. 'Faith is just faith. It has nothing to do with reality!'

'I beg to differ.'

'Well, you would.'

They sit in a silent impasse. Mary stands. 'Please talk to Dominic. I'll talk to our solicitor.'

'What! Old Berry?'

'Yes.'

'Isn't he a bit past it?'

'No, he isn't, Mark. He's very experienced. He's a family friend too and he *will* defend you to the best of his ability.'

'All right, Mum. All right. Thank you.'

'OK, darling. I'll make an appointment with Berry and we'll go and see him together. In the meantime please talk to Dom.'

'I will.'

'Good boy.'

Chapter Thirty Five
Boys Will Be Boys

Mark stands at the door of Dominic's college rooms. He hesitates then lets himself in. 'Hello, Dom.'

'Hi, Mark. I'll just finish shaving then I'll be out.' Dominic runs the tap. 'How are you?'

Mark slumps in a chair, throwing his head back. 'I'm all right I suppose. Hanging on.'

Dominic comes through from his bathroom 'Any developments?'

'How d'you mean?'

'I wondered if you've seen any more of Berry…if he has any new ideas.'

'No hope of that, Dom, I'm afraid.'

'No. I suppose not.' Dominic sits in the armchair on the opposite side of the fireplace.

'D'you sleep OK?'

'Sometimes. I often wake in the night and then can't get back to sleep. Stuff going round and round in my head. Horrible, really.'

'Must be.'

'Look, Dom. Mum said I should talk to you about…the homosexual thing. She said you'd understand.'

'I hope I'll understand…I think I will.'

'So, let me ask you, at Stowe did you do

anything?

'Like hugging, kissing?

'And more, Dom.'

Dominic puts his shoes on and ties the laces. 'We played with each other. Sometimes in the dorm across the gap between the beds. Sometimes out in the fields. I remember once being masturbated by another boy in the house library. Bit dangerous. Part of the attraction I suppose.'

'At Oundle it was more or less the accepted thing - having crushes on younger boys…crushes…and then the physical thing. So exciting! It thrills me to think about it now, Dom. Often we did it in the loo. Many times…maybe that's how I got a taste - sorry! - for what I was caught doing in those bogs on Midsummer Common. You know…and we did screw each other too. It was OK then. There was so much freedom and so many opportunities.' He pauses. 'Here it's different. It's very different. I haven't met anyone yet to share with. That's why I went on the common. For the thrill, yes, but for those few moments of intimacy. With someone, anyone. He stops and looks at Dominic without speaking, then, 'D'you understand? Does it mean anything to…?'

'Me?'

'Of course.'

'I can accept that you find men and not women

attractive. I've found men attractive too.'

'It's not that I don't like women. I like to see a beautiful woman, a pretty girl. I find women easy to get along with.'

'What I don't understand, I'll admit, is why people are homosexual. How it starts? What it means…what the point is?'

'What the point is?'

'Yes.'

'It doesn't have a *point*. It just is what it is.'

'All right. Mark. Let's go back. I'd like to ask how it started. I mean, were you born like that or did it start later?'

'You mean like nature or nurture?'

'Yes.'

'I'd say nature.'

'So when did you know you felt like this? How old were you?'

'It's hard to say exactly. Maybe when I was about twelve…you know, the first stirrings and all that.'

'So what did you…?

'I felt confused. I just wasn't interested in girls like the others at school. They were all fascinated by the female body and it did nothing for me. I preferred to look at boys in books, in the showers…you know.'

'I have another question.'

'Go on then.'

'You often talk about evolution and the

survival of the fittest. So wouldn't fitness here mean the ability to reproduce?'

'Why?'

'Well, obviously if we were all homosexual we wouldn't reproduce and that would be that.'

'Uhh, yeah...I...'

'So what's it mean?'

'*Mean*?'

'Yes, in terms of evolution...survival of the fittest. I mean, why would human genes choose to make beings who wouldn't reproduce?'

'Genes don't chose. Not really.'

'What do they do then?'

'Just carry information.'

'And where does that information they carry come from, Mark?'

'Ah, now you're asking.'

'Well?'

'I guess the information just came along with the universe.'

'*Just came along*!'

'Yes.'

'Doesn't that strike any sense of wonder in you, Mark? The mystery is what set it up, set it going, don't you think?'

'Never really thought...never wanted to dwell on something that mysterious. Makes me feel uncomfortable.'

'Yeah, but it is mysterious though isn't it? That big question.'

'Well, we can't answer it.'

'True. We can't answer it, but we can ponder upon it. Just be struck by the mystery. And you know that explains to me the mystery of homosexuality…the mystery of your homosexuality.'

'What d'you mean?'

'Look, Bro, this is getting intense. I want to go on with it, but I want to go out. How about taking a punt?' Dominic waits as Mark adjusts to this new direction and takes on the suggestion.

'Great idea. It's ages since we went on the river together.' They pick up their jackets, race across the room, then jostle and bump down the stairs like two teenagers.

They take it in turns punting out to Granchester. They've had a lot of practice and they glide along at a steady lick. The sunlight that filters through the leaves falls on the greenness of the river and on them. Other boats pass by going in the opposite direction. There is a holiday atmosphere and the boaters exchange friendly greetings. Mark is punting and Dominic is lying in the boat as they glide into the bank. Dominic gets up, jumps into the bows and swings up and onto the towpath, tying the boat off on a weeping willow. He waits for Mark to join him, wondering how to pick up the threads of their conversation, but Mark steps up to the plate as they sit down on the grass.

'I remember being down here one afternoon with everyone when I was about fourteen. We'd had a picnic and were lazing when I saw a boy swimming upstream towards us. He swam to the bank and climbed out. He stretched his limbs and sat with his legs dangling in the water. I thought he was the most beautiful thing I'd ever seen and I knew then for sure.'

Dominic listens. He picks a stem of grass and chews it, enjoying the cool, green sap and the strength of the fibres.

'I watched him. I thought he would feel my eyes on his back, somehow the strength of the attraction, but he never turned to look at us - not even a glance. After about ten minutes another boy swam up the river to join him. I was intensely jealous and had to walk away, turn my back on them. It was more than I could take. I walked up the riverbank away from them and lay down in the orchard. When I came back they were gone. I felt relieved and bereft at the same time.'

'That's quite a story, Mark. Very evocative. I can see the strength behind this attraction and I don't hold it against you. It is what it is. But it still puzzles me.'

'It puzzles you, but it causes me distress and guilt...real deep guilt.'

'Why guilt if you think it's natural, which I take it you do?'

'Guilt because…I'm not what my father wants me to be. I haven't lived up to his dream.'

'Yes, but it is only *his* dream.'

'True but in a way I'd like to be…normal.' Mark picks up a small branch and spins it into the river. He watches it fall and splash in. 'But that I'll never be.'

'Whatever normal is.'

'Don't you feel normal, Dom?'

'No, not really. I feel something of an outsider.'

'What?'

'Well, how many people d'you know who've been to India to find a guru?'

'Only *you* could do that.' They laugh and fall back on the grass.

Chapter Thirty Six
Richard and Sally

'.........yet
Stands the Church clock at ten to three.
And is there honey still for tea?'

Rupert Brooke

Richard is cycling across Grantchester Meadows. He looks up at the fleecy clouds sailing across the sky. His gaze is held.

'Hey! Watch out.'

He looks down and swerves off the path to avoid the girl from the Guild Hall, who's riding her bike in the opposite direction. She comes to a graceful stop, but Richard loses control, spins off his bike and into the long grass. She comes over to him and offers her hand to help him up. He takes it and gets back on his feet. He doesn't let it go. They look at one another. Richard makes a decision and guides her towards a small copse. She does not resist and he leads her into the darkness of the trees. She turns to him, looks up at him. He bends and kisses her. She responds with an immediate passion.

'I've been waiting for this ever since you came in to book the hall. I've even dreamt of this.' She kisses him breathlessly and they sink onto the grass. Without a pause she pulls up her printed cotton dress and his hand goes down between her legs. She squirms in ecstasy, pulling at the button on his trousers. He helps her and she pulls off her dress. She isn't wearing a bra. He cups her breasts and kisses them as he slides into her. She gasps and they roll into an awe-inspiring climax.

They lie still for a while locked together. Richard breaks the silence. 'We should get dressed. Someone might come along.' She smiles and starts to put on her dress. She stands. Richard looks up her. 'What's your name?'

'Sally.' She looks down at him and waits.

He finds it hard to focus. He's enchanted. 'Ah, yes. Richard.'

She puts on her knickers as he pulls up his trousers and buttons them. 'That was...quite something, wasn't it?'

'Certainly was, Richard.'

He attempts to pull himself together as a wave of guilt sweeps over him.

'What's the matter?'

'I...nothing.' He pulls her to him and they kiss. He steps back to look at her. His head is spinning. 'I must go now. Got to...'

'That's all right, Richard. Come on.' She laughs, takes his hand and leads him out onto the meadows. 'Let's get our bikes.'

They pick up the bicycles and stand facing each other. Richard climbs onto his bike and goes to set off.

Sally stops him. 'Can I see you again?'

'I hope so, but I dunno. It's not so easy.'

'You have a girl-friend?'

'Sort of. You?'

'No one at the moment.'

'Let's just see, Sally. I...'

'OK. We'll leave it like that. If I see you in the street don't worry I won't throw myself at you.' She comes up to him and they kiss again. She rides off towards Cambridge and Richard heads on across the meadows.

Chapter Thirty Seven
Moments of Truth
Honour the warrior, not the war.

Six months later the gang of four are in El Patio. Richard sets down a tray, sits and hands round the coffees.

'When I was at Skippy's scoring grass I met a New Zealander guy called John Mase. He told me about this new wonder drug he calls LSD. He gets it from Timothy Leary, who gets it direct from the Sandoz Laboratory in Switzerland. He said it's like mescaline and very powerful and not to be messed with. He's offered to come up to Cambridge and take us on what he calls a trip. You up for it?'

'I am,' Lauren replies immediately.

'How 'bout you?' he asks Dominic and Rebecca.

'Me too.' Rebecca sips her coffee.

'What about you, Dom?'

'I'm not sure. Swami Ji advised me against taking mind-altering drugs.'

'Yeah, but this is *different*. John says it's a truly spiritual - mystical experience. Like in Huxley's *Doors of Perception.'* He takes it very seriously and says it's not something you fuck about with. Says you must take it somewhere where you won't be disturbed and with people you trust.'

Dominic ponders the proposal.

'Well, Dom?'

'I heard about this in India from a guy called Marco at the Meher Baba ashram. So...don't know Might be dangerous.'

'Dangerous?'

'We know nothing about this...drug, Richard.'

'What's LSD stand for - apart from our currency?'

'Well, Rebecca, it stands for Lysergic Acid Diethylamide 25.'

'Wow! Knowledgeable.'

'Nah, Rebecca. John told me.'

They drink their coffees in silence while they wait for Dominic to make up his mind.

'It's not illegal, Dom.'

'No?'

'No.'

'Maybe not...but that's not the point, Richard.'

'What is the point?'

'Point is I made a promise to Swami Ji.'

'But he's not gonna know.'

'Again that's not the point, Richard.'

'You're starting to repeat yourself.'

Dominic stands abruptly, spilling his coffee across the table top. 'Fuck you, Richard!' He turns his back on them and walks straight out of the coffee bar without looking back.

They are left speechless. Rebecca gets up and goes after Dominic. Richard shrugs. Lauren looks dismayed.

'He'll be alright.'

'Maybe…but.'

'Really. He will. He's strong. Got a lot of inner strength. But even the strong can get rattled now and again.'

Lauren does her best to put on a brave face.

'I've something I must tell you that's really been bothering me and I don't know how you'll take it. I don't really have to tell you this, but honesty is…' He dries up.

Lauren looks at him intently. 'So?'

Richard takes a deep breath, 'I was riding my bike over the meadows and somehow I collided with another cyclist. A girl. A girl I met when I went to the Guildhall to book a room.'

'Yes…and?'

'And we went into the woods and…did it.'

'You made love to her?'

'Yes, that's it, 'cept it was more of a fuck really. Just a fuck.'

'You…you're telling me it didn't *mean* anything?'

'Exactly, Lauren.'

'Well, let me tell you something, Richard. It did mean something. It was something. And how d'you think she feels? She gave herself to you.'

'I didn't ask.'

'That's not the point. How d'you think *she* feels?'

'I don't know. Haven't seen her again. Haven't

asked.'

'Well, I'm glad about that!'

'But you. What about you? Can you...?'

'Forgive you?'

'Yes. Maybe.'

'Maybe?'

'Well, you're not going to get off that lightly. You have dues to pay, Richard.'

'You're not angry?'

'I didn't say that. I am hurt. You've disappointed me.'

'It won't happen again.'

'It had better not or it's curtains for us, my son.'

'I promise.'

'But what will you do when you see her again?'

'If I see her again.'

'Come on, Richard. Cambridge is a small place. You'll see her.'

'Well...'

'So what'll you do?'

'Say I'm sorry and that was that.'

'You won't be tempted?'

'No...I...'

'You will.'

'I won't.'

'Don't lie to me, Richard. You're hopeless at it. I can see it in your eyes. I can read you like a book.'

'Female intuition.'

'Something like that, yes. You've certainly lost

some points. Not that you had many to start with!'

'Look, I'm really sorry, Lauren. I didn't mean...I didn't plan to cheat on you. It was impulsive.'

'I know that. That's why I forgive you...almost. This time, OK. But just this time.'

Richard nods his assent. They get up and leave El Patio.

Rebecca catches up with Dominic as he turns down Peas Hill, heading for Kings Parade. 'Dom! Wait. Please wait. Are you all right?'

He stops and turns.

'You all right?'

'Thanks. I am now. It's just that Richard was starting to annoy me. He didn't respect or even try to get any understanding of what I was saying about the promise.'

'I guess it's hard when you've never experienced that thing with a guru. I don't think he's the kind of man who takes easily to commitment - making promises he might not be able to keep.'

'Where're you going?'

'I've got a lecture in Mill Lane.' He glances at his watch. 'In ten minutes.'

'I'll walk with you.' She takes his hand and squeezes it.

He smiles. 'I'll go and see Richard and apologize

for storming off. It was good of him to offer.'

'Will you take it, join us on the trip?'

'Of course I will. Swami Ji has a loving heart. He can take it.'

'He's not going to take it. You are.'

Dominic laughs and kisses Rebecca goodbye.

Chapter Thirty Eight
Amazing Grace
'Be still and know that I am God.'
Psalm 46 Verse 10

Lauren is sitting in Bohm's secretary's office. She is nervous. His secretary is blissfully ignorant of her distress. Lauren stares down at the patterned carpet doing her best not to fidget. Eventually Bohm comes out of his office and walks over to her. Lauren stands. They shake hands.

'This really is quite a coincidence though not a happy one.'

'Why's that?'

'Come through to my office, please.'

Lauren follows him. He closes the door behind her and points to a chair. She sits.

'I spoke to your mother this morning, Miss Wheatcroft...Lauren. I asked her to come to the hospital, but she couldn't. She explained that there are some problems at home and that she couldn't get here.'

'I don't understand. I mean you don't call to ask her to come here usually...do you?'

'No you're right. I never have before but...'

'Yes?'

Bohm plays with the pen on his desk and glances up at the window as if seeking inspiration or comfort.

'Around dawn this morning we thought your grandmother was going to die.'

'Lauren gasps and jerks forwards.

'We don't think she'll live through this night. She has a heart condition and there's little strength left in her.'

'Can I...'

'Yes, of course. D'you want to go now?'

Lauren nods and Bohm stands. He comes around his desk and takes Lauren's arm, leading her out of the room.

They climb the stairs slowly. Bohm is allowing her time to compose herself and gather her strength. They walk to Grace's door and go in. She is lying on the bed, quite still. Her chest barely rises and falls. Her face is calm and there's almost a smile on her face. Lauren breathes a sigh of relief. She hadn't known what to expect and is reassured. Bohm picks up a chair and sets it next to the bed. He goes to stand by the window as Lauren takes Grace's hand and sits quietly beside her.

'Can I stay with her?'

'Of course.'

'I mean until...all night.'

'That'll be OK, Lauren.'

'Thank you.'

'I have to go now. I've a meeting. Will you be all right?'

'Yes. I'll be fine. She looks so peaceful.'

'She does, doesn't she? It's a rare sight...a rare thing.' He leaves the room.

Lauren sits back in her chair, still holding Grace's hand. She feels calm and filled with a strange but comforting lightness. She's never been this close to death before. She isn't frightened, which surprises and even empowers her. Grace barely breathes. The room is silent in the warm glow of the setting sun.

As evening moves into night and the sky darkens Grace's breathing becomes more and more shallow. Lauren senses her grandmother's consciousness leaving her body and she is filled with a feeling of awe and wonder to be present with her at this unique time. She is deeply moved. She stands and leans over Grace, watching her intently, waiting. At around midnight Grace sighs and takes her final breath in this world. Lauren continues to hold her hand as it grows colder and colder.

An hour later a nurse comes into the room and confirms that Grace has died. She offers to fetch Lauren a cup of tea, which she accepts gratefully. She is at once exhausted and elated by what she's experienced and shared with her grandmother. She feels a deep inner calm and sense of meaning. She sees that everything is ultimately for the best in this life even if at first it doesn't seem so. She knows she's been blessed with insight and she's grateful for this.

The nurse returns with the tea, which she sets down on the bedside table. 'We have a room set aside for families if you'd you like to lie down and rest.'

'Thank you, no. I'll stay here with my grandmother, if that's OK.'

'Of course it is. If you would like to talk you can find me in the nurses' station at the end of the corridor.'

'You're very kind. Thank you.'

The nurse leaves again and Lauren drinks the hot tea gratefully. She goes to the window, opens it and looks out over the moonlit park. The night is clear and she can see the stars. Once again she is filled with awe. She thinks of Richard and her heart goes out to him. She thinks too of her mother, father and her two brothers. She resolves to do whatever she can to help them all through their current troubles and difficulties. She realizes how much her father and Mark need her love and affection and resolves to do more for them. She understands that it would be better for her own well-being and peace of mind if she could learn to put other peoples' needs before her own. She recalls Dominic telling her that this was one of the points that Swami Ji had made to him in India. He had been insistent on this.

At around four Lauren dozes. She is woken by Bohm at seven fifteen. She turns to him as he crosses to the bed. He smiles and she smiles back. He draws the sheet over Grace's head then holds his hand out to Lauren and helps her up. He leads her down to his office.

'I think we should telephone your mother and let her know.'

Lauren ponders this, then says, 'No. I'll go home now and tell her myself.'

'As you wish. It's probably the best way.'

'I think so.'

Bohm looks into her eyes. 'You're very calm, Lauren. I've never seen you quite like this.'

'I had a moving experience up there watching Grandma die. It was very powerful. I've never witnessed anyone's passing before. It was uplifting. That's all I can say.'

'You're fortunate.'

'That's how I feel. That's why I want to go home now and tell Mummy myself.'

Lauren arrives home just after nine and she finds Mary in the garden. She is pruning roses. Lauren watches her in silence. It's an idyllic scene - touching and romantic. Mary turns and catches sight of her. She stands.

'Hello, darling. Where've you been?'

'I stayed the night at Marchman House with Grandma.'

Mary looks puzzled.

'She died last night.'

'You were there…with her?'

'Yes, right through it.'

'Oh, my poor darling.'

'It's all right, Mummy. I'm glad I was there. It was very moving.'

'How was she?'

'She was happy. Well, she *looked* relaxed and she died peacefully. I can assure you of that.'

'How...wonderful you could be with her. I should've been, I know. But it's for the best. Her life...'

'It was right. It felt right that I was there.'

'Did she ask for me?'

'No, Mummy. She didn't say *anything*.'

Mary looks content with this. 'I'll just tidy up here then go in and talk to the hospital about the funeral arrangements.'

Chapter Thirty Nine
I Am the Breeze that Blows Through Me

"There is neither knower nor known. Only he who has discarded his ego, who has come out of his attachments and bondages, can attain this state."
Swami Sat Chit Ananda

It is Sunday. John Mase sits in a chair by the window, watching. Rebecca is sitting on a sofa while Richard and Lauren are stretched out on the carpeted floor. They are in Rebecca's rooms in Jesus Lane. There is a sign on her door that reads: *Not to be disturbed under any circumstances.* John had pinned this up on his way in that morning.

They are waiting for Dominic. There is a knock on the door. Rebecca opens it. Dominic comes in, his hair wild from the wind. Bella-Blue and Tiger-Lily, follow him and look round the room with interest.

Richard sits up. 'Dogs!'

'Thought they'd be good companions.'

John smiles. "You're right. Good idea.'

Dominic smiles and sits down next to Rebecca. The dogs greet John and Richard. Lauren sits up and hugs them both. They are very happy, wagging their tails, showing their affection.

Dominic waves them over and they come and sit at his feet.

John dispenses the LSD from an eye-dropper, taking great care to administer the precise dose. He doesn't take any himself.

An hour passes where very little is said while they wait for the experience to begin. And it does in surging waves of power, driving through their bodies, as it starts to take effect. Sound and light become unified and everything appears to be dancing to the same tune and in perfect harmony. Dominic knows that they're all sharing the same state of consciousness, can feel the same things. He looks around the room. He can feel his face smiling wide and clear. His eyes glow and gleam.

Rebecca looks down at the dogs. They lie still, but their fur trembles and ripples as they breathe in cascading waves of colour. Each hair looks alive and almost unbearably beautiful. She stretches out her hand.

'I feel...I'm filling up.' Richard's voice crackles across the space between them. Dominic laughs and it's infectious. 'I feel!' They all crack up, a lightning, pulsing explosion of pleasure. John watches, smiling.

Rebecca glances at Dominic and their eyes meet. She feels the light flowing into her. He looks godlike. Everything about him is perfect - harmonious, balanced and beautiful. There is no self-consciousness between them. Just a seeing - without judgment.

Richard looks around him. His smile fades into fear. His face becomes grey and stony. He attempts to stand. John goes to him and helps him up. He leads Richard to the window. They stand side by side looking out on the street. Richard looks puzzled and confused. John puts his arm around his shoulders and guides him over to the full-length mirror on the far wall. He places Richard in front of the mirror and waits. He stares aghast at what he sees and attempts to turn away, but John holds him fast, gently but firmly.

'That's you, Richard, but it's more than you. It's everything. You are everything. You are light and sound and life - the whole universe. Just let go and it will reveal itself to you in all its splendour. Look hard at what you see and let yourself flow into it. Become one with it.'

John waits patiently. The other three watch with rapt attention, almost willing him to let go. Richard starts to relax and to stare hard at his reflection.

'It's all love. You are love - infinite, eternal love. That is all there is. It is the be all and end all. Some people call this God, which is what you are. You are it. You are everything and always.'

Lauren comes and stands beside them. She takes Richard's hand. John steps away and goes back to his seat by the window. Richard turns to Lauren and his face creases into a smile. They look intently at each other. Dominic picks up an orange from a bowl of fruit on the table. He holds it out to Rebecca. They both stare at it, full of wonder. He turns it slowly in his hands and starts to peel it, slowly and with enormous care. Rebecca watches in silence, her gaze held fast by the orange. Richard opens the window and the curtains shift.

Dominic looks up. 'I am the breeze that blows through me.' He throws back his head and laughs.

Almost three hours pass without movement or a word passing between them. John glances at his watch. 'We'll go out soon.' He stands. 'It's nearly time for evensong at King's.'

Richard looks puzzled. 'Time?'

John laughs. 'It's just a name. Something to help us out.'

'How?' Lauren asks.

'It's a measure of this planet's rotation and movement round the sun...and other things.'

'What is it, though?'

'No one knows, Lauren.'

They lapse into silence. Gentle traffic sounds ripple through the room.

'It may be something we move through or something we carry along with us.'

'I don't understand.'

'No one does, Lauren. It's a mystery.'

Dominic looks up. 'What's the point of it?'

'The point is that it's a useful measure...a tool to help us from day-to-day. The idea has a practical use.' He walks across the room to the door.

Dominic ponders this then asks, 'How?'

'With clocks - watches - we can synchronize ourselves in space. For example I can tell you that evensong will begin in thirty minutes...probably. So, follow me. And keep the faith!'

'Dogs?' Lauren asks.

'Dogs?'

'Yes, the dogs.'

'Dogs can stay here.' Dominic waits for Lauren to pass him. He looks back at the dogs. They watch him attentively but they don't stir from their place on the rug. He shuts the door gently.

As they walk out onto the street Rebecca asks, 'What's space?'

John stops and opens his arms. 'This is space. This and that.' He points at the sky. 'It has no end. It's not *inside* anything. It just is what it is.'

Rebecca shivers and John puts his arm round her shoulders. 'There's nothing to be afraid of. We are in it and we are it. There's nowhere to go to. It is just what is.'

He leads them on and they walk out onto King's Parade and into King's College. They stop and stand, overwhelmed by the grandeur and beauty of the chapel. John walks on and they follow him in. Bach's Prelude & Fugue rolls out from the organ through the nave and up into the vaulted roof. Dominic and Lauren freeze. An electric and almost tangible shudder passes between them. They are overwhelmed and horrified. Their paranoia and fear are palpable. John stops and turns back to them. He goes and stands between them, taking their hands. They both turn to leave the building but John holds them fast. Eventually they succumb to the pressure of his will and follow him into the depths of the candlelit building.

They are seated in time for the procession of the choir through the chapel singing the Gregorian Chant *Deus in Adjutorium*. Gradually a warm confidence settles on Dominic and Lauren and they are swept up by the beauty of the service. The setting sun sends shafts of rainbow light through the stained glass windows in waves across the walls and the congregation. Dominic is transported to a state approaching divine revelation. He wants to laugh and cry and sing. He turns to Rebecca and sees the angel in her. He's filled with love for her and for the world. He sees and he knows that there is just one and it always will be so thanks to the LSD, of course.

Chapter Forty
A Brief Courtroom Drama

Inspector Grayson is reading his statement to the magistrates. 'The accused was taken into custody in the men's lavatories at four pm on Thursday 6th April. He did not resist arrest, which is in his favour.'

The magistrates are nervous. They are out of their depth and comfort zone, aware at one and the same time of who Mark's father is and the crime of which Mark is accused.

'Two of my officers observed the defendant enter the toilet with another man. They waited for a minute then followed the two men in. The stalls were empty, but they could hear movement in one of the cubicles. Constable Perkins entered an adjacent cubicle, climbed up on the toilet seat and saw through the space between the cubicles the two men - one of them the accused - engaged in a sexual act.'

Mark raises his head and looks across the courtroom towards his mother, Dominic and Lauren. Mary is ashen. She stares down at the floor in dumb disbelief. Dominic looks straight ahead, but Lauren manages a weak smile of encouragement. Mark is strengthened by their presence and support. He looks across at

Grayson, ignoring the other members of the public in the room, two of whom are clearly reporters. He glances at John Berry, the family solicitor, who nods to Mark in an exaggerated way. Mark doesn't respond, but stares blankly back at him.

The chief magistrate asks with great embarrassment, 'And...' He clears his throat. 'What was that...er...act?'

Grayson squirms and Mark shrinks back into himself. Mary wishes she were dead or anywhere else but in this courtroom at this time.

'The two defendants were masturbating each other, Sir.' Grayson flushes red from his temples to his neck.

'Were there any other witnesses?'

'No, Sir.'

The chief magistrate turns to Mark. 'Have you anything to say in response to this statement?'

John Berry holds up his hand to still Mark, but he's not to be stopped.

'No,' Mark responds with a low, rasping voice. 'What the inspector says is true. I don't deny it.' Mark shakes his head. 'I can't deny it.'

The three magistrates confer and the chief turns to Mark. 'Very well. Mr. Marcus Wheatcroft, you shall be bound over until the Quarter Sessions. In the meantime you'll be free to leave as and when someone stands your bail, which we now set at one thousand pounds.'

Mark is led away and the three magistrates rise in unison and leave the room. Dominic stands and helps Mary to her feet. He leads her out of the court and Lauren follows them.

They stand outside in the light, drizzling rain and Mark opens an umbrella. 'I could see that there were at least two reporters in the court so we can safely assume the story'll appear in the *Cambridge Evening News* and probably...eventually in the nationals and there's nothing whatever we can do about that. It's what you might say is juicy news...sensational...and it'll sell papers for sure.'

Mary shakes herself. She is suddenly alert. 'We must try to keep the papers away from Daddy at least for the next week or so.'

'Hopefully he won't ask me to read the news to him for a few days. Sometimes he forgets.' Lauren is doing her best to be optimistic and hold herself together. Her acid trip still echoes through her mind in fragmented memories, cascading colours and shards of sound. 'If he does, I'll make some excuse...a date or work or something.'

Berry comes down the steps to join them. 'As you instructed me, Mary, I've arranged with the clerk for you to stand bail. I'll wait here and bring Mark home to Adams Road as soon as the formalities are completed.' He shakes their hands and goes back into the building.

Dominic takes his mother's arm. 'Let's go home, Mum. There's nothing we can do here now.' He leads Mary gently off down the street. Lauren takes her other arm.

Chapter Forty One

James

'The feeling which we call love is, in fact, a form of hatred. In making love we make another our means for happiness; and hatred begins. In making love we live for our own self; to serve our own selfish end. We do something for another only when we have some hope of getting something from him otherwise we do nothing. That is why our love may turn into hatred at any moment.'
Osho.

Lauren is reading in the lounge when the phone rings. Apart from her father she is alone in the house so she answers the call. 'Hello. Cambridge 55795.' Silence, except for the faint sound of the Toccata and Fugue. 'Hello.' She waits. 'Please say something.' She waits.

'Hello.' A voice at last!

'Yes. Can I help you?'

'Who's there?'

'Lauren Wheatcroft.'

'Lauren?'

'Freddy Wheatcroft's daughter.'

'It's Freddy I want to speak to.'

'Uh…'

'Yes?'

'Who shall I say is calling?'

'Just say an old friend.'

'Is that all?'

'Yes. It'll do.'

'Hold on. I'll just go and tell him. I have to go to his room.'

'Can't he come to the phone?'

'No.'

'Why not?'

'He's paralysed. Motoring accident.'

'That's ironic.'

'Why?'

'It just is. Now, please put him on the line. I'm calling long distance and it's expensive.'

'OK.'

'Thanks.'

'Hold on.'

'I will.'

Lauren goes upstairs and knocks on Freddy's door.

'Yes.'

'It's me. Lauren.'

'What is it?'

'There's a call for you, Daddy.'

'Who is it?'

'He won't say. Just an old friend is all he would say. It's long distance.'

'Long distance?'

'Yes.'

There's a pause. Lauren waits. 'Can you reach the phone?'

'Yes, I can.'

'OK.'

'And please put that phone back on the hook when you get downstairs. I'm connected now.'

'OK, Daddy.'

'Thank you.'

Lauren returns to the lounge. She picks up the phone and is very tempted to listen, but true to her word she resists the urge and puts the phone back on the hook.

In the dimly lit bedroom Freddy listens in shocked silence then answers, 'Yes, it's me, Freddy.'

'James...but...' Freddy's hand is shaking, but he holds the phone close to his ear and listens to the distant voice of his brother. 'Where are you?'

'Bogota, Colombia.'

'Why?'

'Why not?'

'We thought you were dead. We've thought that ever since...'

'I didn't die in that car crash. Only my lover William died and I killed him. That's why I'm here.'

'What! You did what?'

'I killed William.'

Freddy gasps for air. His head is spinning. He feels he's falling into a deep, dark hole. 'But...' Is all he manages to croak.

'I'm homosexual. Got it, Freddy?'

Freddy groans again.

'Got it? Got it?

'Yes, I've got it, James.'

'I could never tell you I was a homosexual. You wouldn't have been able to accept it. I knew that. For all your intelligence and education you were very narrow-minded. Probably still are by the sound of it. So I had to hide it from you.'

'I...'

'Don't say anything, Freddy. Just listen for once. My relationship with William was falling apart. He'd found someone else. He wanted to break up. It was awful. I couldn't tell anyone, or turn anywhere for support. I was broken. I wanted to end it all, but I just hadn't the courage. William came down to stay for one night on his way to the West Country. I took all my savings out of my bank account and packed the cash, my passport and a few clothes in an overnight bag. I found the keys for father's Bugatti and put a mallet from the work bench under the driver's seat.

I invited William to come for a drive so we could be alone and part in some sort of an adult, civilized way. After lunch I drove him down towards Ampthill. We had dinner at the Prince of Wales and, while I drank very little, I made sure that William drank a lot. He was nervous and only too keen to get blotto. As we left the town I swung the car off the main road. I drove a down a narrow lane and eventually pulled the car onto a rough track through the woods. I drove a quarter of a mile then stopped the Bugatti under some over-hanging oaks. I told him I had to pee and got out of the car. I turned away from William and heard him climb out on the other side and walk to the edge of the track. While his back was towards me I stepped over to the car and slid the mallet from under the driver's seat. I strode silently up behind him and with all my strength I swung the mallet down on the back of his head. William crumpled like a sack of potatoes and I laid into him, striking his head again and again until I heard his skull crack. I tossed the mallet into the trees and opened the Bugatti's surprisingly big boot. I dragged William's body round to the back of the car and lifted him in. His heart had stopped beating and his head was a mess. I vomited then folded him up into a neat bundle, closed the boot and drove off.

I motored across country and through the night to North Wales. I half filled the tank of the Bugatti and a can at a remote petrol station in Snowdonia. Ten miles or so further on I pulled up at the top of a steep hill I knew from previous visits. I swung the car off the road, opened a five-bar gate and drove onto the field. The hill ran straight down to a solid stone wall at its base.

I heaved William out of the boot, dragged him down the side of the car and rammed him into the driver's seat. I took the petrol can out of the boot and let the handbrake off. I stepped round to the back and gave it a shove with my foot. It rolled forward then slipped away from me slowly gathering speed as it hurtled towards the wall at the bottom of the hill. I ran after it. It seemed to take forever but eventually it hit the thick stone barrier at a helluva lick, pushing the engine and the body-frame into the front seats. The back end of the Bugatti looked as if it was going to flip right over, but it didn't. Just bucked up with a scream of tearing metal and fell back to the ground shaking it.

I unscrewed the cap of the petrol can, lifted it and emptied it through a gash in the roof over the seats and William. I lit a match, dropped it in his lap and jumped back, moving rapidly away up the hill. I closed the gate behind me. The car exploded as the heat hit the tank. I moved off across the fields at a good pace. I glanced back once or twice to make sure it was still burning. I could see the glow from miles off. I caught a train at Llanfrothen, changed at Machynlith for Aberystwyth. I took a boat from there to Dublin and flew to New York. I made it in fits and starts down to Bogota and I've stayed here ever since. Suits me to a tee.' He lapses into silence.

Freddy struggles to take it all in and straighten it out in his mind. He's bewildered and shocked speechless.

'I needed to tell you this story. I needed you to know that I was still alive. I don't ever want to see you or talk to you again. I am someone else, but you are my brother and always will be. I had to unburden myself as much…'

'Stop. Enough!'

James waits.

'How could you do this to me…and, and the family? How could you…?'

'Had to. No choice.'

'Don't be…of course you could choose…and save us all that pain and…and why the tormenting phone calls and the Bach?'

'Knew you'd recognize it. I was kind of warming you up, softening you up.'

'Didn't work like that on us. Nasty.'

'I did what I had to do - then - and don't worry, I've paid the price.'

'So did we, you bastard. You fucking, fucking bastard,'

'Say what you like, Freddy. You can't hurt me. Not anymore. I'm queer and I like it.'

'Like it? How can you *like* it? Mark…'

'Mark?'

'My twin son. Yes. And he's…like you.'

'Like me?

'Yes. He's like you, he's…'

'You can't even say it, can you?'

'He's bent. He's a homosexual. He's queer. Yes,

that's it.'

James laughs. 'What goes around comes around.'

Freddy is tiring rapidly and can't go on. He mutters weekly, 'Yes it does.'

'Cheer up, Freddy, you might have something of it in you too.'

'Never. No. Never!' He throws the phone across the room. The connection is broken.

Chapter Forty Two
Payback

'As ye sow so shall ye reap.'
Galatians VI

Following this phone call Freddy finally reads the facts of the court case and it's the bitter end for him. He wheels himself across the study to his desk. He takes a small key from a drawer at the back. He unlocks a panel, which he opens. He slides out a shallow shelf. On it is a 45-calibre revolver. He slides the panel further out and picks up a box of ammunition. He takes out one round and slides it into a chamber in the cylinder, which he turns until the round is next into the breech. He cocks the revolver and pushes the barrel into his mouth. An image of Mark in the toilet flashes across his mind. A wave of disgust and fear crawls across his face and he pulls the trigger.

Jack hears the explosion from the bottom of the garden. He's startled and looks up at the house. He drops his fork and runs. He goes straight to Freddy's study and throws himself at the door. After Jack's second attack the door crashes open to the sound of tearing wood. Even though he half expects it the sight that meets his eyes is terrible. It all but knocks him off his feet.

Bedford prison is not overwhelming or austere. On his previous visit to see Mark, Dominic was struck by the relaxed atmosphere. That's not to say it's been easy for Mark. It hasn't. He came under a lot of pressure to have sex with other inmates and he'd been beaten-up on several occasions by prisoners and the guards during his four years in prison. But his sentence was reduced for good behavior and he has survived.

On the day of his release Dom is there to pick him up and take him back to his flat in Cambridge.

Dominic and Rebecca have married and opened a small book shop in Petty Cury, specializing in popular science, modern poetry and mysticism. Rebecca is pregnant with their first child. Dominic and Mark become closer, finding more and more common ground in their originally irreconcilable beliefs. They start to read the same books and enjoy the same films. They spend a week in the summer with the ageing dogs staying at the Victoria Hotel in Holkham. They take long walks and swim every day in the icy waters of the North Sea. They discuss Mark's sexuality and they laugh a lot. Mark is frequently given to dark moods, which Dominic tries and mostly fails to help him through. Without Dominic's affection and support Mark could never have reclaimed any of his old confidence and feeling of self worth.

The Adams Road house has been sold and Mary has moved with Lauren to southern France. Mary found Cambridge intolerable after Freddy's suicide. She was too ashamed to show her face in public and unable to cope with the averted glances and the false sympathy of her old friends. The warmth of the south beckoned and she chose France so that she would not be too far distant from Dominic and Rebecca and the grandchildren she longed for. She had prayed they would have children and bring new love and meaning into her shattered life. Her joy on hearing of Rebecca's pregnancy was almost tangible. She ran barefoot through the wild flower garden whooping for joy. She struggled to forgive Freddy for what he had done to them all and over the years she achieved this, finally finding a place of love for him in her heart. Her faith never left her, never let her down.

Lauren had split up with Richard and, inspired by his art, started to paint herself. She gradually made new friends in the flourishing art community around the village where they lived. Her painting slowly but surely improved and she began to have her work featured in exhibitions. Appreciation of her talent grew and she started to make some sales. The future looked bright and promising especially when she met and fell in love with another local artist. Richard had become something of a rock star and *Green Onions* have completed one successful tour in the USA. The big-time beckoned.

Dobbo had gone back home to her family at the Post Office in Lolworth. Jack never got over Freddy's suicide, but had manages to hold down a menial job at the Botanical Gardens and to pay his way. He never ceased to hanker after his previous life with the Wheatcrofts - a family closer to him than his own - his flower-beds and his beloved kitchen garden.

Like Jack, Mark didn't recover from Freddy's suicide or from the shame and humiliation of his arrest and imprisonment. He managed to survive a year in Cambridge staying with Rebecca and Dominic. Then one summer morning he announced that he was going to leave England and move to the USA. They received one letter from him six months later and then never heard from him again. To all intents and purposes, just like his Uncle James, he disappeared off the face of the earth. Mary waits for the phone call but it never comes.

Chapter Forty Three
The Father and the Son

'It is defeat that turns bone to flint; it is defeat that turns gristle
to muscle; it is defeat that makes men invincible.'
Henry Ward Beecher

The morning is very still with not the slightest breeze and a mist hangs over the meadows. The sun struggles to break through to the dew soaked trees. The sound of bird song overwhelms Dominic as he walks down to the river bank. Even in the misty dark he can see fish glide in the green gloom of the water. He sits under a weeping willow and takes out a blue aerogram letter from his jacket pocket. He studies the address on the front. It is his. He looks at the Indian stamp for a few seconds then turns the letter over. He reads the sender's name and address: Satchit Ananda, The Sat Nam Centre, Jaipur, Rajasthan 6, India. He unfolds the letter carefully and reads:

Dear Dominic,

Thank you for your letter and your good wishes for my health. I am well and hope that you are too.

With regard to your question about your father and what has happened to him, we must realize that we are all weak struggling souls. You write that your father was not a good man, that he was not loving, caring or understanding. Does nature give everyone an ideal father, or simply a father, Dominic? When it comes to your fundamental duty as a son, whatever your father's character was, whatever his personality or habits were is secondary. The divine order does not design people or circumstances according to their tastes. Whether you found him to be agreeable or not, this man, when all is said and done, was your father and you must respect that. We owe everything to our parents. You are not an isolated entity, but a unique, irreplaceable part of the cosmos. Please never forget this. You are an essential piece of the puzzle. Each one of us is a part of a vast, intricate, and perfectly ordered community. That is all that can be said. I hope it is helpful to you.

I am always by your side.

Affectionately,

Satchit Ananda.

Fugue

'Gonna write me a song
'Bout what's right and what's wrong
About god and my girl and all that
Quiet while I make like a cat
'Cause I'm a poet
Don't you know it
And the wind, you can blow it
'Cause I'm Mr. Dylan the king
And I'm free as a bird on the wing'

Syd Barrett

6th January 1946 - 7th July 2006
Founder member, lead vocalist and
guitarist with *Pink Floyd* (1965- 1968)

Here is Nigel Lesmoir-Gordon's earlier novel:

Nothing and Everywhere

John Smith, an unpublished and regrettably named novelist, has his computer stolen and with it the only copy of his latest novel. Despite fear of his guru's disapproval, John mysteriously acquires two handguns, a load of cash and a crack team to reclaim his work. Together with Susie Bellavista, a beautiful and enigmatic maths genius, Biro, a Hungarian ex-RAF Regiment sergeant and March Klossowski, one-time activist and fellow-failed writer, John explores the power and wonder of mathematics in an attempt to solve an imponderable, real life mystery. Where will this whirlwind adventure lead? Back up your files and enjoy the ride!

Nigel Lesmoir-Gordon

NIGEL LESMOIR-GORDON's long directing career in film and television ranges from pop videos, commercials and corporate promotions to TV broadcast. He followed the production of the award-winning documentary The Colours of Infinity with Is God a Number? then Clouds are not Spheres. Colours has already been transmitted in over 50 territories worldwide and is currently available in four languages. Nigel recently completed his firstf eature film, Remember a Day, which is now out on DVD. He has published two books: Introducing Fractals in 2009 and The Colours of Infinity in 2010.
Nothing and Everywhere is his first novel.

'Nothing and Everywhere is a lively entertaining read. I sped through it in a single sitting, which is the highest compliment I can bestow on a writer.' Randy Smith. Author.

'You've heard of books you can't put down, well I couldn't close this book. Compulsive reading, thoroughly enjoyable.' David Russell Smith. Film Producer.

'Nothing and Everywhere is innovative, imaginative, and thoroughly gripping reading, taking the reader on a wild journey through the British Isles.' Carol A Weiss. Mathematician.

Gordon Books

REVIEWS of Nothing and Everywhere

'Nigel Lesmoir-Gordon is a very funny writer.'
Kathy Harty. TV Producer.

'Nothing is as it seems and nothing is subject to the usual laws of reality in this book, peppered by snippets of advanced mathematics, deep spiritual truth and cosmic science, as well as a whole belly-full of hilarious action and real laughter.'
Alastair McNeilage. Author.

'Nothing and Everywhere is thoroughly entertaining - humorous and tough by turns.'
Will Shutes. Writer and Art Historian.

'Exquisite, enlightening prose!'
Pasquale Falbo. US National Guard Fighter Pilot.

'I really enjoyed this book. It's quirky and it captured my attention.'
Samantha Mills. Yoga Teacher.

'Nothing and Everywhere is certainly an original work and I can well see it being picked out and celebrated as such.'
Damien Enright. Author.

376

45489127R00213

Made in the USA
Charleston, SC
25 August 2015